USA Today Bestselling Author

CHEYENNE McCRAY

TABOO

What the critics are saying...

ꟈ

TAKING INSTRUCTION

4 Hearts "Cheyenne McCray brings readers a sexy fantasy come to life in Taking Instruction." ~ *The Romance Studio*

TAKING ON THE LAW

4 Hearts "Taking on the Law is an extremely erotic story about two old friends who meet again in a difficult situation. […] The story has interesting twists and an ending that is not to be believed! Another fun and sexy story by Ms. McCray." ~ *The Romance Studio*

"This book is pure fantasy from its opening until the final scene. Hot and steamy probably best describe just about each and every scene in this novella. […] The perfect little story to stir both your senses and your longing for a real love connection between the characters." ~ *A Romance Review*

TAKING THE JOB

5 Hearts "I highly recommend Taking the Job to everyone. No matter what genre you usually prefer, you are going to love this book." ~ *The Romance Studio*

Taking It Personal

4 Hearts "Ms. McCray didn't disappoint with TAKING IT PERSONAL. Although it is part of a series it can be read as a standalone. But why deny yourself the enjoyment of all these delicious Bennett brothers!" ~ *Love Romances*

An Ellora's Cave Romantica Publication

www.ellorascave.com

Taboo

ISBN 9781419956829

Edited by Sue-Ellen Gower.
Cover art by Syneca.

This book printed in the U.S.A. by Jasmine–Jade Enterprises, LLC.

Trade paperback Publication December 2007

Also by Cheyenne McCray

Blackstar: Future Knight
Castaways
Ellora's Cavemen: Seasons of Seduction II (*anthology*)
Ellora's Cavemen: Tales from the Temple III (*anthology*)
Erotic Invitation
Erotic Stranger
Erotic Weekend
Hearts Are Wild (*anthology*)
Kalina's Discovery
Lord Kir of Oz *with Mackenzie McKade*
Stranger in My Stocking
The Seraphine Chronicles 1: Forbidden
The Seraphine Chronicles 2: Bewitched
The Seraphine Chronicles 3: Spellbound
The Seraphine Chronicles 4: Untamed
Things That Go Bump in the Night III (*anthology*)
Vampire Dreams *with Annie Windsor*
Wild 1: Wildfire
Wild 2: Wildcat
Wild 3: Wildcard
Wild 4: Wild Borders
Wonderland 1: King of Hearts
Wonderland 2: King of Spades
Wonderland 3: King of Diamonds
Wonderland 4: King of Clubs

About the Author

ℰ𝒪

USA Today Bestselling Author Cheyenne McCray has a passion for sensual romance and a happily-ever-after, but always with a twist. Among other accolades, Chey has been presented with the prestigious Romantic Times BOOKreviews Reviewers' Choice Award for "Best Erotic Romance of the Year". Chey is the award-winning novelist of eighteen books and nine novellas.

Chey has been writing ever since she can remember, back to her kindergarten days when she penned her first poem. She always knew one day she would write novels, hoping her readers would get lost in the worlds she created, as she did when she was lost in a good book. Cheyenne enjoys spending time with her husband and three sons, traveling, and of course writing, writing, writing.

Cheyenne welcomes comments from readers. You can find her website and email address on her author bio page at www.ellorascave.com.

Tell Us What You Think

We appreciate hearing reader opinions about our books. You can email us at Comments@EllorasCave.com.

TABOO

TAKING INSTRUCTION

Author's Note

ꟹ

Taking Instruction incorporates only elements of Domination/submission and BDSM. It is not intended to accurately portray a true BDSM or Dom/sub relationship.

Chapter One

ℌ

Jessica Grayson looked up from her term paper to stare at Professor Bennett. Her mouth watered and she squirmed in her seat from the ache between her thighs.

Professor, yeah right. The man was so damn gorgeous and *built* like he'd just come out of a fitness magazine—he didn't look like any professor or teacher she'd ever had.

Dark hair framed his chiseled features. He had an angular jaw, high cheekbones and eyes as beautifully blue as the clear Arizona sky.

She had a thing for men with tight asses, and his slacks fit him just right. Sometimes when he'd move away from the podium she'd get a good look at his package. Definitely worth unwrapping like the rest of his delectable body. Broad shoulders, biceps that flexed beneath the snug-fitting sleeves of his shirts. She'd bet her last pair of panties that he had rippled abs and a smooth chest that she could slide her hands over to feel his muscles bunch beneath her palms. And she'd dig her nails into that taut ass as he rode her hard.

Jessica wriggled in her seat and smiled to herself as she caught Professor Bennett checking her out again. She leaned forward a little more so that her breasts looked like they'd spill out of her bra. His throat worked before he turned his gaze back to the podium.

Jessica grinned.

It was the end of the second semester of her freshman year at the University of Arizona. She'd be a sophomore in the fall.

She'd found a man she wanted more than anything.

And she intended to get him.

All semester she'd worn shirts or blouses with necklines that showed off her cleavage and emphasized her breasts. She wore tiny shorts or skirts that hardly covered anything.

And he'd noticed her. Oh yeah, he'd definitely check her out when he thought she wouldn't notice. When she was writing notes or working on a paper, she'd glance up through her lashes and see him looking at her. He tried to appear casual, but she knew there was a connection between them that went beyond pure lust.

Sometimes their eyes would meet and hold before he broke away and went back to doing whatever it was he'd been dealing with at the time.

Jessica dropped her gaze back to her term paper and tried to concentrate on finishing her essay. She'd ace it since English was her best subject, but with Craig Bennett standing behind that podium, hiding what she most wanted to see, she had to force herself to get her mind off him and write.

It was the last day before summer break, and she didn't plan on spending it alone.

She was going to give Professor Bennett a time he'd never forget.

Craig Bennett's gaze kept straying to Jessica Grayson's breasts. Damn, his student was stacked.

It was a good thing he stood behind a podium when he gave his lectures or his students would see his constant hard-on whenever he was around Jessica.

At this moment his class had their heads down while they pored over their term papers. It gave Craig time to indulge in a few fantasies about Jessica. If she weren't his student, he'd ask her out and fuck her until there was no tomorrow. He'd have to paddle her for being a bad girl, turning her ass a nice shade of pink.

At that moment Jessica glanced up at him and gave him the sexy little smile she slipped him whenever she had the opportunity .She shifted in her seat to reach up and twirl one of her fingers in her long black hair and gazed at him with eyes so green and sultry that he could barely think, much less get his hard-on under control.

"Professor Bennett," came a female voice just to the left of the podium. "Where do you want us to leave the essays?"

Craig jerked his attention to—what was her name? "I'll take it," he said as the petite blonde looked at Jessica and back to Craig. By her expression, he knew she'd caught him staring at Jessica.

He cleared his throat and glanced down at her English term paper. Gloria—that was her name.

"Thanks, Gloria." He focused his attention on her even as he felt the burn of Jessica's gaze. "Have a good semester break."

Gloria glanced at Jessica again. "Yeah. You too," she said with a smirk in her tone.

Craig dismissed her by studying her paper. As always, her work was excellent.

Christ, though, he had to get his mind off Jessica Grayson. She was his student for God's sake. He'd seen that she'd signed up for a fall semester with him, English 210, Intro to Writing Fiction.

He knew what he'd rather introduce her to.

It was going to be fucking hell to have her in his class again and not fantasize about her breasts, and how her full lips would feel wrapped around his cock.

He glanced at Jessica, which was a mistake. She was looking at him, her nipples pushing against the fabric of her low-cut T-shirt and her lips moist with a slight shine to them.

He turned away and ground his teeth. He was going to have to lock the door to his office and deal with his hard-on by taking his cock in hand as soon as class was over.

More students came up to him, turning in their papers and thankfully helping him to focus on class and keep from looking at Jessica.

When the tone for class dismissal came over the loudspeakers, he breathed a sigh of relief. End of semester, reprieve from fantasizing about Jessica. Shit, what was she, twenty, twenty-one? And he was thirty. A little old for anything between them, even if he didn't have to worry about teacher-student ethics. Hell, he'd just gotten his tenure. Didn't want to screw that up.

The remaining students brought their essays to him and he arranged them neatly to keep from looking at the black-haired beauty who was taking her time getting up to the podium. He wasn't sure he was going to be able to get out a coherent word when she finally turned in her paper.

She was the last, of course. He knew she loved to torture him, and she did a damned good job of it.

He re-stacked the papers studiously, trying to keep his calm. All semester she'd been teasing him by flirting and hinting that she'd like to be more than the teacher's pet.

And he'd sure as hell like to make her just that—leash, collar and all.

He knew the instant she reached him. No other woman smelled the way she did. Hot, sensual and of warm vanilla.

He raised his head to see she was, indeed, the last student in the room. Shit, his hand trembled a little as he took her essay from her. The podium was still between them, thank God. His slacks were no doubt tented where his cock pressed against the material.

"What are your plans this summer break, Professor Bennett?" Jessica asked in her low fuck-me voice.

If she didn't leave, his cock was going to explode. He cleared his throat again. "Nothing special."

"Really." The word was a purr from her lips that almost made him groan aloud. "My family is going to Europe for the summer, so I'm going to be all alone."

Craig forced a smile. "Looks like we're in the same boat."

Ah hell. Why did he go and admit that? Like the girl needed any encouragement.

As he expected, she gave another one of her smiles that made his cock harden. "Maybe we could get together for coffee...or perhaps dinner."

"Listen." He steeled himself and forced himself to say what he didn't want to. "You're my student. It wouldn't be ethical for me to date you."

She raised her eyebrows, an innocent look to her expression. "Who said anything about dating...just two lonely people having coffee together. Or dinner."

"Sorry, Jess—Ms. Grayson." Goddamn, it was all he could do to get his mind off his cock—in her body, in any number of positions—and force out the words he had to. "I can't."

"But you want to," she whispered and winked before she turned away and walked toward the door.

She wore a tiny red skirt that showed off her incredibly toned, long legs. Her matching red T-shirt molded her frame, tapering down to her small waist.

He watched until she disappeared out the door then he sucked in a deep breath.

It took him a while to get his erection under control. He had to think of the piles of essays he had to grade. His grandmother. The faculty meeting this afternoon. Anything but Jessica.

When he had things under control—which meant getting his cock to cooperate—he stuffed the papers into his briefcase, snapped it shut and headed out of the classroom. The slam of the door echoed in the hallway as he entered the almost empty corridor. Students were more than ready for the summer break and it didn't look like anyone was interested in hanging around. Not that he intended to be around here longer than he had to either. He'd told Jessica the truth, he didn't have a damn interesting thing planned, and more than anything he'd love to take that girl to his bed and keep her there all break. A girl like her would probably enjoy his toys and a little bondage. Maybe a lot of bondage.

Shit. This was going to be a long three months before classes started again.

Craig made his way to his office, trying to turn his mind to other things and not succeeding.

He definitely needed to jack off to get the pain in his groin under control. He opened the door to his office, stepped inside, and immediately locked the door. He turned around—

And promptly dropped his briefcase.

Jessica Grayson was sitting on his desk.

Naked.

Chapter Two

ฐ

Oh God.

Jessica's body was even more beautiful than Craig had imagined, than it had been in so many of his fantasies. Her long black hair fell past her delicate shoulders to her tiny waist. Her breasts were large, her nipples high and pert. Every bit of her body was firm and toned from her shoulders to her ankles. And if he could see it, he'd bet she'd have a nice ass too.

"Hi, Professor." Jessica braced her hands to either side of her on the desk. "I need some help with an assignment," she added in a purr.

No words would come to Craig. He couldn't move. Maybe he should try picking his jaw up off the floor, but at that moment it felt like it would take a monumental effort to do so.

Jessica slipped off the desk and his heart raced as she slowly walked toward him. Her hips had a natural sway to them and the closer she got, the more he could tell her nipples were taut and begging to be sucked.

His cock was so hard it was a wonder he didn't come in his slacks.

When Jessica stood maybe an inch from him, she reached up and slid her hands into his hair. The feeling was so erotic he almost groaned out loud.

"Do you know how sexy you are?" she whispered as she brought his head down so that his lips were close to hers.

"Jessica. No. We can't—" he started when she pulled him down so that their lips met.

He was a goner.

There was no going back now.

Jessica nibbled at his lower lip and he groaned. She immediately slipped her tongue into his mouth. Almost without realizing it, he brought his hands to her ass and pressed their bodies so close he felt her nipples through his shirt. He ground his cock against her belly and she moaned into his mouth and kissed him with even more passion.

Craig couldn't help the feeling of satisfaction it gave him to turn Jessica on the way she was. She made small whimpering sounds as he clenched her ass cheeks with his palms and kissed her with dominance and control.

If Jessica Grayson wanted to play, he'd damn sure show her exactly how *he* played.

Jessica couldn't believe the intensity Professor Bennett was putting into his kiss. She hadn't been positive how he'd react to finding her in his office, naked, but now she knew.

God, he was an incredible kisser. The way he held her, the way his mouth took control of hers—it was completely dominant and totally turned her on more—if that was even possible.

He shook his head, like he was coming out of a dream. "How old are you, Jessica?"

Her heart beat a little faster. "Does it matter?"

He frowned. "You know it does. If you want to play with me, you play by my rules."

The steel in his voice stoked the fires inside her. She felt naughty. Delighted and abashed. And compelled to answer.

"I just turned twenty," she said as she reached for the button of his slacks. "Old enough to know what I want when I see it."

"Not old enough to drink," he said as he reached up and caught a handful of her hair, the look on his expression intense. "But old enough to fuck."

Her thighs grew damper and thrills rolled through her belly. "Damn straight."

"You need to understand something, Jessica." His fist gripped her hair tighter. "I don't stop being the professor when I leave the podium. When it comes to sex, it's *my* classroom too. I'm the boss. What I say goes. If you can't live with that, leave now."

She shivered and it wasn't because she was naked. It was the thrills caused in her by his words. The way he spoke to her was so *hot.* "I'll do whatever you want."

He released her hair and brought his hand between the two of them to slip his fingers into her pussy.

Jessica gasped at such an immediate, bold move and tilted her head back, breaking the kiss. He trailed his mouth along her chin to her neck. Slow, erotic kisses that made her wetter than ever.

And his scent—spicy and male.

She rode his hand hard as she rubbed her palms over his shoulders and arms. She couldn't get enough of touching him.

"Good," he murmured as his mouth neared her breast. "Wild. I like wild."

Jessica squeezed his biceps and moaned. Everything he said was turning her on, exceeding every wet dream she'd had about him.

He pinched her clit and she gave a little cry of surprise and excitement. "Tell me what you really want, Jessica."

Wasn't it obvious? She wanted his cock inside her so badly she could hardly stand the wait. "I—I want you to fuck me."

"Minus two points—and that's the only time I'll be nice," he said as his lips rubbed over her nipple. "I'm not all you want. You had fantasies before you met me. Tell me those fantasies."

She felt a little heat rise up her neck at the same time she gripped his shoulders tighter. "I've fantasized about you fucking me in the classroom." She cried out when he bit her nipple. "Bending me right over the podium."

He gave what sounded like a grunt of approval as he continued to drive her crazy with his mouth and hands. "What else?"

"Um..."

"Jessica..." His tone held a warning note to it as he pinched her clit again.

"I've thought about having sex with you somewhere public." She cried out as he hit just the right spot with his fingers. "And in your home." No one had ever made her act like this. "Oh God, Professor Bennett. Yes, right there," she squirmed against his hand, "right there."

He gave a soft laugh as he traced her nipple with his tongue. "Ms. Grayson, you've been a very bad girl." He moved his fingers from her clit and slipped them inside her core. "You're not allowed to climax until I give you permission." He lightly bit her nipple. "Do you understand, Ms. Grayson?"

Jessica squirmed even more. "Yes, Professor." Her words came out in a heavy pant, "I'll do whatever you want."

He bit her other nipple and she cried out, louder this time. "You'll have to be quiet," he said as he licked the spot he'd just bitten. "Or I'll have to give you another punishment."

The way he said *punishment* sent a thrill through her that went straight to her pussy.

"Damn, you're wet," he said as moved his head up from her breasts and buried his face in her hair. He pulled his fingers out of her core and she made a sound of disappointment.

"On your knees. Now," he said in a tone of complete authority.

A jolt of surprise and excitement shot through Jessica. If she'd thought she had any control over what was happening between them, she was getting a wake-up call. This man didn't mess around.

She eased to her knees on the thin industrial carpeting of his office. She looked up at him as he pushed down on her shoulders, guiding her the way he wanted her. His eyes were like blue fire, his features intense, his jaw hard. The look of barely leashed power on his face caused her to shiver and the thrill ran from her belly to between her thighs again.

She forced herself to look from him to the button of his slacks. God, his erection was huge. She couldn't wait to see what it felt like to have a real man—real *big* man—inside her.

She gripped his cock through his slacks, feeling the length and girth of him. Her mouth watered and he made a hissing sound through his teeth.

"Unbutton my slacks. Now, Ms. Grayson."

She shivered with excitement, loving the way he continued to role play with her. He was the teacher and she was his student.

Jessica unbuttoned his pants easily and unzipped his slacks. He wasn't wearing any underwear and his cock released from its confines and was right in front of her lips in an instant.

"Suck my cock, Ms. Grayson." He fisted his hands in her hair tight enough she felt it at her roots. "And look up at me."

Her whole body was one electrical charge as she obeyed. When she grasped his cock with one hand she felt the soft skin over the hardness of his erection.

It was to her immense satisfaction that he groaned when she took his cock into her mouth. She tasted the pre-come on the head of his erection before the salty flavor of his skin.

She moved her hand in time with her mouth as she looked up at him. The intensity of his gaze as he watched his cock slide in and out of her mouth was almost more than she could bear.

He fisted his hands tighter in her hair and began to fuck her mouth by thrusting his hips forward. She took him as deep as she could. He was so big though.

Jessica was so freaking aroused that she had to come. She slipped the fingers of her free hand into her folds and began stroking her clit.

He stopped moving his hips and drew his cock out of her mouth. "I didn't give you permission to masturbate, Ms. Grayson. Do not touch yourself without permission. Understand?"

"Okay." Jessica withdrew her hand, somehow feeling the need to obey anything he told her to do.

"When you answer me, say 'Yes, Professor'." He looked so powerful and dominating that Jessica shivered—not from fear but from lust. "Is that clear?"

"Yes," she said.

He cocked an eyebrow. "Yes, what?"

She took a deep breath. "Yes, Professor Bennett."

He gifted her with a smile so sensual she felt it through her entire body. He glanced at his watch, then back to her. "Get dressed, Ms. Grayson."

"What?" The shock in her voice was obvious.

He tucked his erection back into his slacks, zipped them up and buttoned them. "You didn't address me properly. Punishment comes with disobedience."

Oh jeez, what did she get herself into? But she had to admit this was the hottest she'd ever been in her life.

Jessica swallowed hard. "Uh, yes, Professor Bennett. Why do you want me to put on my clothes?"

He folded his arms across his chest and gave her a stern look. "Ms. Grayson, you're to obey me without question if you wish to continue this, is that clear?"

God, she did *not* want this to end. "Yes, Professor Bennett."

He smiled again and caressed the top of her head. "Good. I'm going to give you directions to my home. If you want to continue where we left off, be waiting for me. Naked." While she was still on her knees, her heart thumping like crazy, he moved around to his desk. He pulled open his center drawer and scooted some things around. "I have a faculty meeting now." He brought out a silver key and took it to where she was kneeling and handed it to her. "Do you know how to cook?"

Damn straight. That was another thing she was very good at. "Yes, Professor."

He began scribbling on a piece of notepaper. "Fix us something to eat—whatever you want."

She took the paper when he handed it to her. "Yes, Professor."

He grabbed her by the shoulders and drew her up so that she was standing. Her body tingled like crazy as he brushed his lips over hers. His eyes were still dark, almost smoky. "I'll see you when I get home, Ms. Grayson."

"Yes, Professor," she whispered as he picked up his briefcase. He unlocked the door, slipped out and shut it tight behind him.

Jessica dropped into a chair in front of his desk.

"Wow," was all she could think of to say as she sat there, stunned for a moment. What the hell just happened? If she went to his house would she be getting in deeper than she should be?

Damn.

She jumped up from the chair and hurried to get her clothes on and get out of the office as fast as she could.

* * * * *

Craig grinned as he drove home. He'd turned the tables on Jessica Grayson. He wondered if she'd be waiting for him when he got there or if she'd taken off.

He was willing to bet money she was waiting for him, exactly as he'd ordered her to. The way she'd obeyed him without question in his office told him a lot of things, including the fact that little Ms. Grayson might be aggressive on the outside, but inside she was a born submissive, through and through.

His home was on an acre lot on the outskirts of Tucson. He'd bought the property before housing prices and the population had exploded in the area and was glad to have his semi-custom home built with some breathing room. And enough distance from his neighbors that they wouldn't hear Jessica's cries.

Cries of ecstasy. He was going to teach that girl about true pleasure.

When he drove into his driveway, he wasn't surprised to see the little red sports car waiting in front of his walkway. Fiery and sporty, just like its owner.

The moment he entered his home, his stomach growled. Smells of grilled beef and vegetables came from the kitchen, along with what smelled like fresh flour tortillas.

He set his briefcase down and deposited his keys on the entryway table.

Craig strode past the formal living and dining rooms to the open kitchen, nook and living area. He stopped in the doorway to the kitchen. He hitched one shoulder up against the wall, crossed his arms over his chest and smiled when he saw Jessica setting the table. She was wearing an apron, but she had her backside to him and he had a clear shot of her ass and shapely thighs. God, he couldn't wait to fuck that ass.

Her black hair swung as she turned to face him and she gasped. "I-I didn't hear you come in, Professor."

He pushed himself away from the wall and strode toward her. The apron she wore covered her breasts and her pussy.

"I just didn't want grease to splatter on my skin," she said when he reached her, looking a little nervous.

"That's good, baby." He leaned down and brushed his lips over hers and she sighed. "I wouldn't want you to get hurt." He reached around her and untied the apron. "But now that I'm home I want to see your beautiful body."

She shivered beneath his touch as he removed the apron and tossed it on a countertop. Shit. Her body was so gorgeous it just about took his breath away.

"Everything's on the table." She sounded like she was having a hard time talking as he squeezed both of her nipples. "I—uh, I made fajitas with homemade flour tortillas."

He kissed her softly again. "Smells wonderful." Craig released her and looked down at her reddened, hard nipples. "I have something I'd like you to wear." He gestured to the table. "Have a seat. I'll be right back."

It didn't take long for him to return with a pair of green crystal nipple rings that matched the color of her eyes.

She widened her gaze as he sat down and squeezed one of her nipples so that it was even harder, then slipped the loop of the nipple ring on. He tightened it with the slide beads and she gasped.

"Does that hurt, baby?" he asked.

She bit her lower lip and nodded before saying, "Yes, Professor."

"Good." He took her other nipple and squeezed it just as hard then slipped the ring on the nipple and tightened the ring. "Now, is it starting to feel good in a pleasure-pain way?"

She looked down at her breasts and returned her gaze to him. "Yes, Professor."

"You're going to feed me now." He loved the contrast of her naked with the nipple rings on while he was fully clothed. God, his cock was going to fucking fall off.

"Yes, Professor," she said.

She reached for a flour tortilla and began filling it with sizzling strips of beef, onion and bell peppers. When she finished she raised it up and he leaned toward it and bit into it. He kept his gaze focused on hers as he devoured it down to the last bite. She moaned as he held her wrist in his hand and licked each of her fingers.

"I'm going to feed you." He was having a real hard time talking. Goddamnit but he needed to get her into his toy room.

After he fed her a fajita, he brought a glass of iced tea to her lips. The moment she swallowed her tea, he slipped his free hand into her folds and started stroking her clit. She groaned and moved her hips against his hand.

He plunged two fingers into her core and rubbed his thumb against her clit. "Are you close, baby?"

"Yes." She squirmed and tilted her head back. "God, yes."

"That's another punishment." He withdrew his hand and she looked at him with surprise on her features.

"What did I do?" she asked.

"That's twice." He stood, took her by the hand and brought her up so that their bodies were flush. He could feel the heat of her body through his clothing. "You didn't address me correctly."

He gripped her ass and rubbed his cock against her belly, wishing he didn't have anything on.

"I'm sorry, Professor Bennett." She sounded breathless. "I won't do it again."

"But you still need to be punished." He took her mouth in a fast, hungry kiss, bringing her so close he felt her nipple rings through his shirt. He raised his head and looked into her green eyes that were glazed with passion.

"But we need to talk about one thing before we take this any further." He brushed her hair from her face. "You need a safe word. The minute you say that word this all ends and I'll send you home in that little red sports car."

Her brow furrowed. "I don't get it. Um, Professor."

He cupped her face in his hands. "Know anything about bondage and domination, Ms. Grayson? Spanking, flogging and assorted other methods of sexual punishment?"

Jessica's eyes widened and she parted her lips. "You'd flog me?"

"Uh-huh," he said as he brushed his lips over hers. "And I promise you'll like it."

She blinked. "Really?"

"Mmmmmm..." He nuzzled her neck, ignoring the fact she was forgetting to call him Professor. "The nipple rings—tell me, did they hurt, but now the pain has an intense feeling of pleasure to it?"

She groaned. "Yes. Okay, I'll try it. So I choose a safe word and you'll stop something if I don't like it?"

He raised his head. "Everything stops and you go home. So think carefully."

She paused for a moment then sucked in her breath. "Algebra."

He laughed. "Why'd you choose that?"

Jessica wrinkled her nose. "Because I hate algebra."

He shook his head and grinned. "Come on then. I have some toys I want to show you."

She raised her eyebrows. "Toys?"

"Yeah." He gripped her hand and brushed his lips over hers one more time. "I've given you some leniency, Ms. Grayson, but from here on out I'm your Professor and you're my student."

She gave him that sexy smile of hers that he loved and her eyes flashed with desire. "Yes, Professor Bennett."

Chapter Three

ℵ

Craig's hand felt large and warm around Jessica's fingers as he led her to the stairs that went down to what he called his "dungeon". Just the name of where he was taking her caused her to shiver. Cool air brushed her naked skin and her nipples ached. She was so wet between her thighs at being naked while her professor was still clothed.

The farther they walked down the stairs, the more nervous she became. *Dungeon? BDSM? Safe word? Punishments?*

She swallowed hard.

Craig crossed his chest with his free hand and tugged at the rings dangling from her nipples. She gave a soft gasp with each pull. It hurt—yet it felt good. A combination she would never have put together,

"I had this room custom built," he said as they reached the bottom of the stairs and she saw a pair of double doors in front of her.

Jessica's stomach twisted even more.

He pushed the doors open and she entered complete darkness until she heard a click and a light came on.

She caught her breath. It was a beautiful room—but filled with the strangest things she'd ever seen. The room had thick burgundy carpeting, cherry wood cabinets and accents, taupe walls and a white ceiling.

One wall had a cherry wood panel with an assortment of items that made her heart pound faster. Like whips, floggers, dildos and lots of things that she had no clue as to what they were used for.

A huge X-shaped cross took up one corner, a swing in another—and was that a stockade?

A pang of fear gripped her at the same time she felt both excitement and curiosity. It was an unusual combination of emotions that had her skin tingling. She looked up at her college professor, her eyes wide.

"Let me introduce you to my 'toys'," he said with a wicked smile.

He started with the stockade. "This completely immobilizes you so that I can spank you or fuck you from behind." Jessica gripped his hand tighter without really meaning to. The stockade was made so that the person in it would have to be on her hands and knees, her head, wrists and ankles restricted.

"Over here is a specially made saddle." He gestured to a leather saddle complete with stirrups—except that it had a big dildo sticking up from where the person would be riding it. Her cheeks heated at the sight of that rubber cock.

"This is a locking spreader." He gave her a look that burned with fire. "I can just see you in it now, your ass in the air, your ankles and wrists bound to the bar while I fuck you."

Jessica's knees almost gave out at the image. And her professor saying the word *fuck* to *her*.

Next he showed her something that looked like the strangest lounge chair she'd ever seen. "This has twenty-eight different fasteners for me to restrain you with," he said close to her ear. "You can kneel where this low part is, lean over the hump and I'll tie you down. Have you ever been fucked in the ass, Ms. Grayson?"

Jessica's attention snapped up to his face again. "Um, no, Professor."

"We'll take care of that."

Uh-oh.

Yet the idea intrigued her too. *Really* intrigued her.

He led her to the wall of toys she'd seen, that also had a rich cherry wood surface beneath it, with a cabinet that included several drawers.

"On your hands and knees, Ms. Grayson." Craig opened one of the drawers as she obeyed.

Her lips parted as he brought out a tube of lubricant and a thing with black straps and some kind of rubber object on it.

"A harnessed butt plug." He lubed the plug and she almost felt dizzy from all the strange sensations zinging through her body. He set the tube down before approaching. She automatically tensed as he kneeled behind her. "Relax, baby," he murmured. "It'll feel very good once you adjust to it."

Uh-huh. Sure. Relax.

"Trust me. You'll enjoy this. Once you get used to it." Slowly he pushed the plug past the tight ring of her anus and didn't stop at her cry of surprise. He just eased it in, keeping it slow until the plug was buried all the way inside her.

Oh. My. God. She'd never felt anything like it before. It hurt but it felt good. Then she noticed how full she felt with it inside her and how much wetter she was growing between her thighs.

He buckled the harness around her until the plug was firmly in place and there was no way that thing was going to come out. One strap ran through the folds of her pussy, against her clit, and she squirmed from the need to come.

"Stand, Ms. Grayson." He had moved in front of her and extended his hand.

She took it and found herself a breath away from him. His body heat radiated through his clothing and his eyes were dark with desire. She loved that the need in his gaze was because of *her*.

He placed his hand at the small of her back and continued guiding her around the large room. It felt odd walking around with a plug up her ass, but exciting too.

"A bondage bed," he said, pointing to a leather, padded surface big enough to be a twin bed but high off the floor on wooden legs that looked like they could be raised or lowered, and had restraints (surprise, surprise) fastened around it.

"And this is a suspension bar." He gestured to a device that looked like a giant clothes hanger, with chains forming a triangle from the suspension bar. It dangled from the ceiling from a long, thick-linked chain.

There was even a cage and a bondage chair. The cage made her raise her eyebrows.

She would never have guessed her college professor was *this* kinky.

He surprised her by bringing her around, hard against his chest, and taking her mouth in a rough and dominating kiss. He took command of her mouth, his tongue mastering hers, his lips hard and unyielding.

It was a *to die for* kiss.

When he raised his head, she felt the rise and fall of his chest against hers and her mind spun.

He took her hand and guided her to what he'd called a bondage bed. Butterflies tickled her belly as he helped her take a step up and had her sit on the edge.

"Lie on your back and spread your legs," he said in a tone that was definitely an order. "Arms over your head."

Jessica bit the inside of her cheek as she obeyed. She felt shivery, tingly and excited as he bound her ankles and wrists in leather cuffs so that she was spread-eagled. The butt plug felt even more snug inside her body and so deep, and one of the harness straps rubbed her clit. Cool air stirred in the room from the fans overhead and her nipples peaked harder within the nipple rings. The air brushed her pussy and the trimmed hair of her mound.

After she was bound, he knelt close and she smelled his spicy aftershave. He gently nibbled at her ear, then reached for one of her breasts and slipped the nipple ring off.

Instantly she felt another rush of pain followed by pleasure and she gasped. He repeated the act with the other nipple ring with the same results, and this time she moaned.

He murmured close to her, "You look so damn sexy, baby, that I want to fuck you now. But that'll have to wait." His smile turned into a stern look as he drew away from her. "Now for your first punishment for being such a bad girl at school, Ms. Grayson."

Jessica shivered in anticipation. In a million years she would never have believed she'd be in this position. Literally. But with Craig—something about him had attracted her from the first moment she saw him. Something more than the fact that he was the best-looking professor on campus. Something about the way he smiled, the way he spoke with authority but was down to earth. He was obviously always in full control of his classroom when teaching.

Now he had full control of her. And she more than a willing student.

Craig surprised her by bringing out a long ostrich feather from a drawer beneath the bondage bed. "Part of your punishment is anticipation and delayed gratification."

Oh, she was anticipating all right. It was the delayed gratification she wasn't so crazy about. She wanted him, and she wanted him *now*.

"Why don't you have your clothes off, Professor?" She wiggled against her bonds, testing them.

He frowned but she saw a glint in his eyes. "You're to stay quiet and not speak to me unless I say you can. Don't make any sounds. If you do, I'll add another punishment." He ran the feather down her belly, the soft, tickling sensation causing her to squirm, and she barely held back a gasp. "Do you understand, Ms. Grayson?"

Jessica started to say yes but clenched her jaw tight and nodded.

With a slight smile, Craig said, "Good."

And then he started stroking her with the feather.

Oh God! She wanted to cry out, to moan, to beg him to stop, to beg him to keep going. It was all she could do to clench her jaws tight and hold back every sound building within her.

He feathered her nipples, causing them to tighten and ache from the soreness from the nipple rings. He trailed the feather down to her bellybutton where it sent zinging sensations straight to her pussy.

Jessica thought her head was going to explode from holding back her cries. Not to mention the fact that her body wasn't going to be able to take much more without self-combusting.

When he reached her mound, she tossed her head from side to side and squeezed her eyes shut, trying to focus on not making a noise rather than on what he was doing to her.

"Look at me," he demanded and she forced her eyes open. His blue eyes were burning with passion. "I want you to watch everything."

Damn. She swallowed down another cry as he brushed the feather over her mound and moved to the inside of one of her thighs.

At least he didn't tell her she couldn't jerk against her bonds. She thrashed from the sensations of him stroking the feather down the inside of her thigh to her knee, and on to her calf all the way to her foot. He had a devilish gleam in his eyes when he ran the feather along the instep of her foot and tickled her.

Both a giggle and a scream fought their way up in her throat, but she clenched her teeth tighter.

What was more incredible was the fact that her pussy was growing wetter with every stroke of the feather, every whisper-soft touch. She ached so much to cry out and to come that it *was* painful while being pleasurable.

Sweat broke out on her forehead as he tickled her other instep and then moved the feather up the inside of her leg. It was sheer torture, and she thrashed against her bonds and tears leaked from the corners of her eyes. The need to climax was so great that she wasn't sure she could hold it back and a scream too. She had a feeling that would earn her two punishments, and she wasn't sure she could take another one like this.

He eased the feather up her side, and now she was biting the inside of her lip hard enough she tasted blood. She couldn't stop squirming and wanted to shut her eyes to fight the intense feelings he was raising within her, but she didn't dare.

"That's good, baby," he murmured as he teased her nipples with the feather. "You're doing great.

Great? She was freaking about to scream as loud as her lungs would allow her to.

With her spread-eagled, he was able to continue from her side to her underarms, and she thought she was going to die. Painful laughter from the tickling sensation lodged in her chest. He just smiled and went on, dragging the feather to her wrists, palm and fingertips. And then he went down the other side of her, repeating the same, torturous glide.

Tears continued to roll down the sides of her face. When he reached her waist he moved so that his face was close to hers. "Very good, Ms. Grayson." He kissed and licked the salt of her tears away. "Do you want me to fuck you now?"

Jessica almost screamed, *"Yes!"* but managed to hold it in and nod instead. Just the thought of his body pressed against hers and his cock inside her pussy was enough to make her climax.

Craig gave her a primal look of hunger and need and laid the feather beside her on the bondage bed before easing himself on the bed and settling himself between her thighs.

He pressed his body against hers and the cloth of his shirt and slacks set her body on fire because her skin was so sensitive. "Mmmmm," he murmured as he nuzzled the hair beside her face. She wanted to moan at the warmth of his breath and the feel of his solid body against hers. His erection pressed against her belly and she had to bite the inside of her cheek again to hold back yet another moan that wanted to escape.

With an intense look in his eyes, Craig eased himself up so that he was kneeling between her thighs and started to unfasten his slacks.

Chapter Four

ꕥ

Jessica held her breath as Craig pulled down his zipper and released his cock. It was just as hard and as big as she remembered and her mouth watered, imagining herself slipping her lips over his erection again.

But right now she wanted him inside her. She had to fight so hard not to beg him to hurry as he took his time. He took his cock in one hand while he braced his other palm beside her head.

"Do you want me inside you, Ms. Grayson?" His voice was low, seductive, promising her pleasure beyond her imagination.

Again, Jessica wanted to scream, *"Yes, yes, yes!"* but she only nodded.

He slowly fisted his cock while she watched and squirmed, her pussy growing wetter with every stroke of his hand. He moved his palm up and down its length and she saw a pearl of his come at the head of his erection. His cock was so close to her core and she was holding her breath, waiting for that moment when he would finally enter her.

Craig leaned back on his haunches and she let out her breath in disbelief. What was he doing to her? But when he reached into his back pocket and pulled out a condom, she breathed a sigh of relief. He was going to do it. He was *finally* going to take her.

The damn man took his time tearing open the packet and tossing it on the floor, then rolling the condom down over his erection. She tugged against her bonds in frustration.

Oh God, she needed him inside her so bad. So, so bad.

When he brought his cock to her pussy, he pulled the harness to the butt plug aside. He slid his erection into her core, just a fraction, and her whole body quivered. He braced both palms to either side of her head. "Are you ready for me to fuck you, Ms. Grayson?"

Yesssssssssssss!

Jessica nodded.

Craig rammed his thick cock inside her.

She couldn't help it. The cry tore from her throat before she could stop it. It felt so good. He was so thick, so deep, it felt like his erection touched her bellybutton.

The moment the shout escaped her, Craig stopped, his groin pressed tight against hers, his cock buried all the way.

He shook his head. "Bad girl, Ms. Grayson. That will earn you another punishment."

"Professor, *please*." She just wanted him to fuck her, right now she didn't care about any more punishments.

"You *cannot* come without my permission." He slid partway out of her. "Do you understand?"

"Yes, Professor." *Just fuck me!*

Since she was already in trouble, Jessica moaned with every thrust. The combination of the butt plug and his cock was out of this world. What would it be like to get fucked in the ass?

A climax built inside her so intensely she didn't know how she was going to hold back much longer.

"Jesus Christ, you feel good." Craig sounded hoarse as he continued his slow thrusts. "So. Fucking. Tight."

Another wave of perspiration coated Jessica's skin and heat burned at every nerve ending. Being spread wide open for Craig and unable to touch him somehow made everything feel even more intense.

She began to tremble as she fought her oncoming orgasm. Her body grew hotter and hotter. "I need to come, Professor, please. I'm so close!"

Craig stopped, withdrew his cock and knelt between her thighs. She stared in disbelief as he slipped off the condom, tucked his cock back into his slacks and fastened them again.

"What—"

"You haven't earned your orgasm yet." He strode away from her and tossed the condom into a wastebasket as her eyes widened and her jaw dropped.

One touch of her clit and she'd come. Just one touch.

"No matter what," he said as he returned and started to unfasten her restraints, "you're not to touch yourself or have an orgasm without my permission. Do you understand?"

Jessica swallowed down a scream. "Yes, Professor."

He unfastened the last cuff. "Unfortunately, you added another punishment for crying out when I told you to be silent."

Craig helped her down off the bondage bed and held her up as her legs trembled. He caught her by the chin and tilted her face up. His touch sent shivers throughout her. "Are you sure you want to continue?" he asked softly. "Things are about to get a lot more intense."

"More intense than that, Professor?" she asked.

A smile curved the corner of his mouth. "Just how much do you think you can take? How far are you willing to go?"

"Anywhere with you." She reached up and put her hand over his. "I'm ready for anything. As long as you let me come."

He shook his head. "That'll have to wait, baby. If you want to play with me and my toys, you'll have to be open to anything and everything. If you're not, say your safe word and I'll send you home."

Safe word? Send home? No!

Craig placed his forehead to hers. "Do you trust me, Jessica?"

She didn't hesitate. "Yes, Professor. I trust you."

That earned her another smile as he drew away. "Then let's look at some more of my toys."

"Okay," she said.

"Let's try the stockades, Ms. Grayson." He took her hand again and her legs trembled as he started leading her to the contraption on the floor. "I can't wait to see that lovely ass of yours up in the air and ready for me to spank."

Jessica's heart raced into overdrive. Oh jeez. Could she really…?

She did. And the fact that it excited her and made her squirm was more than a surprise.

In no time, she was on her knees with her neck firmly restrained in the stockade. Her elbows were bent and her forearms against the carpeting. He locked her wrists in restraints fastened to the floor, and then her ankles.

She couldn't move except to look up and to wriggle her body a little from being so turned on. Her breasts and pussy were wide open for his examination—around the harness holding the butt plug in, that was. And that plug—it felt so deep and hard. She wondered again what something bigger would feel like in there.

A sound like a doorbell rang through the room.

"I'd better see who's here." Craig stood and smiled down at her.

Jessica's heart beat like crazy. "You're not going to leave me here like this, are you…Professor?"

He rubbed one of her ass cheeks then pinched it. "I'll be right back, Ms. Grayson." She watched him walk out the dungeon door, that tight ass flexing beneath his slacks.

If she could have moved her head enough, Jessica would have banged it against the carpeted floor. Again she asked herself what she was doing and if she was out of her mind, and again she had to admit how turned on she was.

But when she heard a pair of male voices coming closer, her heart pounded so hard she felt it against her breastbone.

He wouldn't bring another man in here!

He did.

Since she was facing the door, she saw him the minute he walked in with Craig.

A police officer.

Coming straight toward her.

"See you've captured the suspect," the man said with a grim look on his features.

Craig winked at her even as her jaw dropped.

She couldn't believe he'd just let another man into the dungeon while she was naked and restrained. And a cop!

He reached her, crouched down and took off his aviator glasses. He had gorgeous chocolate brown eyes, dark hair and what looked like a powerfully muscled body beneath that police officer's uniform.

"May I touch your slave?" the man said in a deep voice that caused her to shiver.

Slave?

"I don't mind," Craig said and smiled when she cut her gaze to his. "Do you, Jessica?"

"Uhhhhh..."

She gasped as the big man trailed his calloused fingers from her shoulders, all the way to her ass cheek, causing goose bumps to prickle her skin.

He gave a slow grin that caused an extra dose of butterflies to flutter in her belly. "Feel like sharing today, little brother?"

Little brother?

Sharing?

"Jessica, meet my big brother, Officer Dave Bennett. You'll refer to him as Officer."

"Hi, Officer." Jessica's voice trembled as she looked up at Dave.

"I have three brothers." Craig's mouth turned up into a grin. "All four of us are confirmed bachelors…and we like to share our toys."

Dave squeezed a handful of her ass and smiled. "I like what I see, Jessica." He said her name in a caress, then turned his gaze to Craig and raised his eyebrow.

"Sexy as hell, isn't she?" Craig knelt in front of her and ran one of his fingers over her lips in a slow, sensual movement. "Officer Bennett is going to join us unless you say your safe word, and then you can be off."

Jessica bit her lower lip. She was so confined, so at their mercy, that they could do anything to her. But Craig had given her a safe word and she trusted him.

But two men?

Two very, very gorgeous men.

Her teacher and a cop. God, that was *hot*.

"Yes, Professor," she said.

"Now it's time for your punishment for not being quiet when I instructed you to," he said.

Wasn't being put into stockades enough of a punishment? Guess not.

He approached the wall with the floggers and whips and other toys. Meanwhile, Dave trailed his fingers down her spine from her neck to her ass and back, causing her to shiver again.

Her belly tightened in anticipation—fear and excitement rolled all into one.

"I think while I punish Ms. Grayson," Craig said as he chose a flogger from the wall, "you can read her Miranda rights, Officer Bennett."

"Good idea." Dave moved near the cherry wood cabinet. He put his weapons belt inside one of the drawers and locked it.

Jessica's heart thundered as both men returned to her. Craig carried a leather flogger with soft, suede straps, and Dave unbuttoned his uniform pants.

Both men were incredibly gorgeous, and when Dave's cock and balls were freed from his pants, she saw that he was equally well-endowed to what she'd seen of Craig in the office—and tasted.

Craig stood behind her while Dave knelt in front of her, his cock inches from her lips. Her mouth watered and her pussy tingled.

"You have the right to remain silent," Officer Bennett said as he grabbed a handful of her hair and moved his cock to her lips. "Anything you say can and will be held against you..."

He slipped his cock into her mouth with a push of his hips and she sucked.

"Looks like she chooses to remain silent." Dave pumped his cock in and out of her mouth and she sucked and licked the shaft. He tasted as good as Craig did and smelled of fresh air and the outdoors.

Craig began trailing the suede leather straps of the flogger down her back to her ass in a caress that made her moan around Dave's cock. Craig slid the straps across each ass cheek and over the butt plug. Right now the plug felt so erotic, the harness rubbing her clit as she started to rock a little. He continued to trail the straps over her skin, relaxing her to the point that she forgot he was going to flog her.

Until he snapped the straps across her ass and she cried out around Dave's cock.

He continued to thrust his cock inside her mouth as she wiggled from the pain. Craig rubbed his fingers over the heated spot that he'd just flogged and she found the pain actually beginning to feel good.

Craig snapped the flogger on her ass repeatedly, each time rubbing the area he'd hit before flogging her again. Dave released her hair and reached down to tweak both of her sensitized nipples *hard*. Her eyes watered from that and the flogging, but what really got her was how much it made her ache for both of these men. How bad she wanted *both* of them to fuck her.

God! She'd never dreamed of being with two men. *At the same time!* Two very hot, hot, hot *men*.

And she was so close to coming. The harness strap rubbed hard against her clit and with Dave's cock in her mouth and Craig flogging her, she was squirming. So, so close.

Craig leaned over her back and trailed his lips over the curve of her ear. "Don't come, baby, or you'll get another punishment."

Jessica whimpered.

Dave pulled his cock out of Jessica's mouth and she looked up into his gorgeous eyes. "Did you say your slave has another punishment coming?"

"She didn't do as she was told." He began unfastening her ankle restraints and she sagged in relief. She was starting to get cramped. "So how should we punish her next?"

Dave stood, tucked his very erect cock and balls back into his uniform pants and looked around the room at the equipment.

In the meantime, Craig released her wrists then opened up the part of the stockade that had held her neck in place.

She rolled onto her hip and was surprised when both men knelt beside her. Craig massaged her ankles while Dave moved behind her, drawing her into his arms. She relaxed into him as he rubbed her neck then felt the hardness of his cock pressed up against her back.

Craig eased up so that he was straddling her, his knees to either side of her hips. She caught her breath as both men held her between them, their clothing rough against her bare skin.

Craig's eyes held hers as he took her wrists and massaged them. Her ass burned from the flogging, and the butt plug felt really deep since she was now sitting on it, and the strap of the harness against her clit was driving her out of her mind as they worked the slight bit of soreness away.

She was in sexual heaven.

And frustration.

Craig leaned close and brushed his lips over hers. "Ready for more, Ms. Grayson?"

Jessica gave a soft moan. "Yes, Professor Bennett."

Chapter Five

ꕥ

Jessica thought she was going to die if she didn't have an orgasm. If this wasn't punishment, she didn't know what was.

"What did you decide on, Dave?" Craig looked up from where he was straddling Jessica to meet his brother's gaze.

"She needs a little experience in the saddle." Dave got up from behind her at the same time Craig stood and they drew her up between them and pressed her close so that she was sandwiched by the men. "Don't you think so, Ms. Grayson?" Dave murmured in her ear.

Jessica caught her breath. "Yes, Officer Bennett."

Craig moved his mouth to hover over hers. "You've been a very bad girl, Ms. Grayson." His breath was warm over her lips. "Haven't you?"

"Yes, Professor," she murmured. "I have."

He took her hand and led her to the saddle that was on a very expensive-looking sawhorse of cherry wood and leather. Both men helped her onto the saddle so that her feet were in the stirrups, her hands holding the reins, the harness strap that had been over her clit pulled aside, and her pussy poised above the rubber cock.

"Ride it, Ms. Grayson," Craig said in a commanding voice, and both men pulled her down so that the cock thrust into her pussy, hard.

She cried out, gripping the reins tight in her fists. The pain of the entry of such a large device fled as the extreme pleasure took over. She was filled front and back with the butt plug and rubber cock.

Craig spanked one cheek of her already tender ass. "Lean forward and ride!"

Jessica obeyed, her breasts rubbing the saddle horn as she pushed herself up and down on the dildo, using the stirrups as leverage. Craig and Dave each spanked one side of her ass as she rode the cock.

She tossed her head back, her breasts thrust high. Each man pinched one of her nipples and she moaned. But when they both leaned forward and each sucked one of her nipples, she cried out. They didn't stop slapping her ass. *Hard.*

"I'm so close," Jessica gasped. "Can I come, Professor? Please?"

Her nipple slipped out of his warm mouth and he slapped her ass again. "No. Ride until I give you permission to stop."

Dave stopped sucking her other nipple and lightly bit it before setting it free, then gave her a hard swat on her ass.

She moaned. It was too much—how could she last?

Next thing she knew, both men were helping her off the saddle, and she felt an instant sense of loss with the dildo no longer in her. But then she decided she'd much rather have Craig's cock deep within while he fucked her. Damn, considering the outlines against their pants, he and his brother were big. They didn't have to worry about that dildo outshining them.

Now she had two male bodies pressed on either side of her, with two very erect cocks—one pushing at her belly, the other just above her ass. The men were so tall and big they made her feel small and delicate.

Craig kissed her and twisted her nipples as Dave squeezed her ass cheeks and ran his rough hands over her body from behind, as if trying to touch every part of her that he could reach.

Her mind was swimming from Craig's kiss and she wrapped her arms around his neck and pressed flush to him.

Dave's body was tight against her backside and he nibbled at her neck.

"Damn, your slave tastes good," Dave murmured. "Wonder how all of her would be."

"I'll find out and let you know," Craig said as he raised his head and looked into Jessica's eyes. Her knees wanted to give out just from the desire in his gaze.

Dave chuckled. "You do that, little brother."

Craig kissed his way down her body, pausing to suckle her sensitive nipples, and headed to her bellybutton where he darted his tongue inside, sending more wet heat between her thighs.

He buried his face against her folds and laved her clit.

"Oh my God," Jessica said as her knees gave out. Only Dave's hold on her from behind kept her from dropping to the floor.

He laughed softly and she moaned. Craig grasped her hips and his evening stubble abraded the soft flesh between her thighs. At the same time, Dave pushed her long hair aside and brushed kisses along her nape, causing her to shiver.

"I—I can't hold on much longer, Professor." Her breathing came in heavy pants as the exquisite sensations filled her, caused every part of her body to tingle and her thighs to tremble.

"No, Ms. Grayson," Craig said as he drew away and looked up at her.

She wanted to scream from the lack of contact of his tongue on her clit.

While he looked up at her he thrust two fingers into her pussy and she gasped. Her core spasmed a little from the movement, betraying how close she was to the edge.

Craig rose and nodded to his brother, who was still behind her. She tilted her head up and back, just enough that she was able to see Dave's grin. Her belly flip-flopped and she looked back at Craig but he'd turned and was walking toward the "toy" cabinets. Dave caught her arms at her sides, as if holding her prisoner as Craig withdrew a black silk scarf and a pair of leather cuffs.

Jessica caught her breath and her body trembled. What were they going to do to her now?

"I think Ms. Grayson needs to stop and have time to 'think' about things," Craig said as Dave guided her by her upper arms, following Craig.

Her entire body was going nuts from the need to have a freaking orgasm, and they wanted her to stop and think about "things"?

They reached the suspension bar that looked like a huge hanger, dangling from the ceiling on the chain. Dave steadied her while Craig took each one of her wrists and attached them to either side of the bar.

When she was cuffed to the bar, her toes barely touched the carpet. Would her heart ever stop racing?

Craig stood in front of her and smiled. He brushed his knuckles across one of her cheeks. Why wasn't he naked yet? Why wasn't Dave?

Why was she hanging like this?

But God, was it a turn-on. The plug was still harnessed in her ass and her arms were spread wide in front of her professor and a cop.

Craig pointed to a corner of the ceiling. She followed with her gaze and gasped when she saw a camera positioned to look right at her.

"I'm being taped?" Her voice rose as fear trickled through her. "Um, Professor?"

"No." Craig flicked each of her nipples. "That's so I can keep an eye on you from upstairs to make sure you're okay while you 'think' about your punishments and what's to come."

Her jaw dropped. "You're leaving me?"

He smiled. "There's audio, so you can shout your safe word if you want to end this, Ms. Grayson."

Craig reached up with the scarf and blindfolded her before she could think of a suitable response.

Everything went completely dark. He'd blindfolded her so well that no light came through at all.

"I'm scared, Professor," she whispered.

"Do you want to stop?" he asked. "Anytime, and you can go home. If you want to stay and play, I promise you'll be fine—and we'll fuck you so hard and so good you'll have the most incredible orgasm of your life."

Jessica caught her breath and then Craig took her mouth in a possessive kiss. His hands roved her body and his tongue explored her mouth. Her mind was spinning from the kiss and his touch, magnified by being unable to see, hanging from the suspension bar, and the butt plug up her ass. Dave pressed up against her from behind and palmed her breasts.

Then they stopped and stepped away from her. Tears leaked from Jessica's eyes that were absorbed by the scarf. She needed to come so badly she was ready to scream.

Craig lightly brushed his lips over hers. "I'll be back, Ms. Grayson. After you've had a chance to think about what a bad girl you've been. Do you remember your safe word?"

She nodded. "Yes, Professor."

"Good girl." He kissed her again and then his body heat was gone. "Say the word and I'll come and get you," he said, his voice sounding farther away. "And then I'll send you home."

A moment later she heard the dungeon doors close. She had been left alone, blindfolded, the most aroused she'd ever been in her life.

Jessica gave a soft moan. What had she gotten herself into?

Dave laughed as he and Craig walked up the stairs from the basement. "Where'd you find that babe?"

Craig shook his head, still unable to believe he'd taken Jessica up on her offer. "She's one of my students." He grinned and looked at his older brother. "She's been after me all semester. I walked into my office at the end of classes today and she was sitting on my desk without a damn thing on."

"No shit?" Dave raised his eyebrows as they reached the top of the stairs and stepped onto the foyer. "Never thought you'd go there, but hell, she gave you an offer you couldn't refuse."

"No kidding." Craig rubbed his hard-on through his slacks. "But I think my cock's gonna fall off if I don't fuck her soon."

"She's going to be one wild ride," Dave said when they were in the living room in front of the television.

Craig turned on the special volume control to the basement so that he could hear Jessica clearly if she did need him.

As he kicked back to watch an inning of baseball with his brother, he wondered at the alien feeling of possessiveness he felt with Jessica. If he was being honest with himself, he didn't want to share her at all. Once, that was it. Then she was *his*.

At the same time they watched the game, in a smaller window in the dual-screen TV, Craig kept an eye on Jessica to make sure she was all right. Just seeing her there with her beautiful naked body, the plug up her ass, her breasts jutting out, her head tilted back and blindfolded—he found himself staring at her and not at the game. He adjusted himself, shifting on the couch, trying to get his mind off fucking Jessica. Yeah, like that was going to happen.

After a good half hour had passed, Craig jerked his head toward the stairs to the dungeon and Dave grinned and got up from his seat.

They made it to the dungeon in record time. Craig could hardly restrain himself, to remain the calm, levelheaded, in-charge professor. Once they were in the dungeon they quietly slipped off their clothing then went to Jessica.

Jessica felt neither here nor there. She'd slipped into a place where reality didn't exist. Only the fire in her body and the headiness of the moment. She felt almost drunk.

When Craig spoke, it didn't even startle her. "Hi, baby." He brushed his lips over hers and she smelled his intoxicating scent. "Did you think about what a bad girl you've been?"

Jessica nodded. "I'll be good, I promise, Professor."

"Excellent, Ms. Grayson." His tongue darted out to touch the seam of her lips and her stomach flipped when he came close enough that his naked body rubbed against hers, his cock pressed into her belly. She wished she could see him, but she was still blindfolded. "One more exam and you're going to graduate with flying colors," he said.

She hoped to God that the "exam" included fucking her because she was going to die if she didn't have him inside her.

Strong hands worked at the harness around her, and in the next moment it was removed and the butt plug taken out. She felt an instant sense of emptiness but knew that it probably wouldn't last for long.

Another male body pressed up against her backside and she shivered between the warmth of their hard flesh. The feeling was erotic beyond words.

"Who do you want to fuck you in the ass, Ms. Grayson," Craig said, "and who do you want in your pussy?"

There was no doubt in her mind who she wanted in her pussy. "I-I want Officer Bennett to fuck my ass. I want you to fuck my pussy, Professor."

"Now, baby?" Craig said, a hard edge to his voice like he was having a difficult time restraining himself.

"Yes." She wasn't above begging. "Please fuck me, Professor. Please."

She wished she could see his gorgeous body and his beautiful eyes. She wished she could touch him. But being blindfolded made all her senses more acute. The slightest brush of their skin against hers set her off.

Craig grasped her beneath her thighs and lifted her legs. Dave grasped her around the waist and then positioned her so that his cock was at the entrance to her anus, and Craig's erection was poised right at her channel.

"Let's see if you pass your finals," Craig said at the same time he and Dave slammed into her.

Jessica screamed and tears spilled from her eyes behind the blindfold. The sensations of having both of them inside her at the same time was almost too much. She felt so full, so in need of an orgasm that she almost screamed again as they held themselves still inside of her. Dave was much bigger than the butt plug and his entrance into her ass had hurt, but now it felt so damn good.

"You're going to get the best fucking of your life, Ms. Grayson." Craig held himself tight to her, still not moving.

She nodded, tears still slipping from her eyes. "Yes, Professor and Officer."

Dave made a sound of satisfaction and then both men began driving in and out of her body.

She went wild in their arms. Even though she was cuffed to a bar, she squirmed and writhed and cried out with every thrust of their cocks.

"Oh God, Professor." Her words came out as a sob. "I need to come, I have to come."

"Not yet, Ms. Grayson," he said and she whimpered. "You've been such a bad girl all semester that we're making up for that now."

He latched onto her nipple with his warm mouth and Dave bit her shoulder from behind, both men continuing to fuck her, hard and fast.

Her body shook, every part of her started trembling. She fought against the oncoming orgasm with all she had. Her pussy, her ass, her nipples, Dave biting her, their hot, sweaty bodies, being blindfolded, all they'd put her through and all they had denied her.

It was too much!

"Not yet—" Craig started.

But she exploded. Her orgasm took her so powerfully that she screamed and cried and bucked. Her heart hammered and she felt like her skin was on fire, her entire body on fire. The sensations wouldn't stop as they continued thrusting in and out of her body. She felt like she was flying but grounded at the same time by the two men who were fucking her.

Orgasm after orgasm racked her body. "No more, Professor," she sobbed. "I can't take anymore."

"You failed your finals," Craig said in a voice husky with exertion. "You came without permission."

"I'm sorry, Professor." Jessica shuddered from the extreme pleasure as more spasms ripped through her. She felt her core clamping down on his cock with every contraction of her pussy. She felt the tightness of her ass as Dave drove in and out.

Dave gave a shout, pumped his hips a few more times and then held himself still inside her. Craig followed a few moments later, a loud cry tearing from him. Her core clamped down on his cock and she felt every pulse.

For a moment the three of them stood there. Sweaty, the men's bodies slick against hers, and the smell of sex and testosterone strong.

Dave pulled out and she felt partially empty without him inside her. He unfastened each of her leather cuffs, freeing her, and she collapsed against Craig. He held her tight and Dave pulled off her blindfold.

She blinked, the room slowly coming into focus as she looked up and into Craig's eyes. She continued to feel residual contractions and when he moved a little, it set off a whole set of more spasms.

He drew back and she looked at him. Damn, he was gorgeous. He caught her by surprise by giving her a hard, demanding, possessive kiss.

He finally let her slip down his body and withdrew his cock. Now she felt completely empty. She could barely stand as Dave and Craig disposed of their condoms.

"Looks like you'll need to take a re-test if you plan on passing this class, Ms. Grayson," Craig said with a serious expression. "Do you think you can pass the next one?"

She gave a weak, sated, exhausted nod, even though she wasn't sure at all. "Yes, Professor."

Chapter Six

ꟃ

Jessica slumped into a pool of exhaustion as Craig settled her on the odd-looking couch in the "dungeon". She felt so sore and well-used. She could almost feel both cocks inside her at one time and the thought made her wriggle, her pussy aching again. After what they'd put her through, making her wait so long for an orgasm, why was she so ready to go another round?

Dave watched her while he pulled on his uniform then unlocked the drawer where he'd left his weapons belt, and put his gear on. According to that big bulge in his uniform pants, he had an erection again as he looked at her. She almost smiled knowing she turned the big cop on enough that he wanted her again.

But Craig was who she wanted. It had been *amazing* taken by two men, but now she wanted Craig all to herself.

He slipped into his clothing and again she was the only one not dressed. She didn't care. She felt too damn good.

When Dave finished dressing he walked to her and knelt beside where she was curled up on the couch. He kissed her lightly on the lips and palmed her breast, and she caught her breath. "A pleasure meeting you, Jessica," he murmured before getting to his feet and turning to face his brother.

To Jessica's surprise, Craig didn't look happy—he looked almost *jealous.*

How cool was that?

Dave slapped Craig on the back. "See you in a couple of days, bro." Dave glanced at Jessica then gave Craig a wicked look. "If not sooner."

Craig looked so pissed, Jessica wanted to laugh. But he straightened his expression and slapped his brother on the back in return. "We'll talk about it later."

Dave winked at Jessica then strode through the dungeon doors, leaving Craig and Jessica alone.

Craig came straight to her and she couldn't help a smile. It turned into a gasp when he scooped her up in his arms and held her close. "You're so beautiful, baby," he murmured as he held her close. "From the first time I saw you, you knocked me on my ass."

Jessica grinned. "Took you long enough."

The corner of Craig's mouth quirked. "I had a little extra persuasion."

She gave a soft laugh and wrapped her arms around his neck and met his gaze, mesmerized by his beautiful sky-blue eyes. He kissed her hard before carrying her across the dungeon, out the doors and up the stairs.

His shirt felt warm against her naked flesh, and his smell of sex, sweat and man was an aphrodisiac—would she ever get enough of him? She wondered if he'd ever taken any other students to his dungeon, and the thought made her scowl.

"Hey." He touched her lips with his fingertip as he carried her into a huge bedroom. "What's the frown all about?"

She shook her hear. "Nothing."

Craig pulled back the thick comforter and settled her on the bed so that she was sitting up, her legs dangling over the edge. She braced herself with her hands to either side of her on the mattress as she looked up at him.

He had a stern expression on his features. "I don't accept lying. If you lie, you get punished. Understood, Ms. Grayson?"

Jessica bit her lower lip and nodded. "Yes, Professor."

"Now tell me what you were thinking."

Her cheeks heated a little. "I was wondering if you'd ever brought another student to your house and your dungeon."

"And you were jealous." His tone was matter-of-fact.

She looked away from him. "Yes."

He gave a soft laugh, surprising her. When she turned back to him, he smiled. "Jessica, not another student has been anywhere near this house. You're the first and only."

A weight of relief slipped off her shoulders that she hadn't even realized had been there and she smiled. She had no doubt he'd had other women here, but at least none of his students.

"That's better." He started stripping out of his clothes again and tossed them aside. Her hungry gaze took in his gorgeous physique and his golden skin. It looked like he managed to get in a little sun now and then. The way his body flexed as it moved made her mouth water and her pussy ache. She knew what it was like to have him inside her and wanted more.

When he was naked he moved closer to the bed. "Lie down and scoot over so there's enough room for me."

Jessica obeyed. She shivered with want and need as he climbed onto the bed and eased over to her. He pulled her to him roughly and pinned her legs with his thigh and she caught her breath.

"Goddamnit, Jessica." He fisted a handful of her hair and brought it to his nose and audibly inhaled. "You're so fucking hot."

"Do I have to call you Professor right now?" She placed her palms against his chest as her gaze met his.

"No." He released her hair and traced his thumb over her lips. "For now we're just Craig and Jessica, all right?"

She nodded and smiled and he replaced his thumb with his lips. He was gentle this time, lightly running his tongue along the seam of her lips before slipping it into her mouth for a gentle exploration. She tasted him, enjoyed his flavor, and even her own from when he'd licked her folds earlier. Soft moans rose up within her and she snuggled closer to him as one of his hands roved over her body from her neck down to her ass.

Craig's erection pressed into her belly and she rubbed herself against him and swore she felt him grow even harder. His kiss remained slow, as if he were savoring her. He lightly nipped at her lower lip and caught her sighs in his mouth. His free hand continued to stroke her flesh, roaming over her body, exploring her curves.

In turn Jessica slid one of her hands down his bare chest and back up again, loving the play of his muscles beneath her fingertips with every movement he made. His biceps were firm, hard, as if he worked out regularly. His breathing grew quicker as she dug her fingers into his ass cheek and his kiss became a little more urgent, as if he were having a harder and harder time controlling himself. When she released his tight ass cheek, she stroked his skin down to his thigh and cupped his balls, then grasped his hard cock.

As she stroked the length of him, he sucked in his breath against her lips. "I'm not going to last long if you keep that up."

"I don't want you to hold back, Craig." She let herself try out his name for the first time, and she liked the way it sounded coming from her.

He gave a strangled sound as he captured her hand in his. "Believe me, if you don't stop that, this will be over before it really starts."

Jessica couldn't help the soft laugh that escaped her, and he drew back, his gaze meeting hers. "You are so beautiful," he murmured, surprising her. "I've wanted you for so long."

"Same here." She kissed the corner of his mouth. "Too much to let you go away without getting your attention."

This time he laughed. "Baby, you got more than my attention."

"And more than I bargained for." She squirmed against him at the memory of the two men inside her and felt the sting of the flogging and spanking on her ass. Her nipples were still sore from the nipple rings. But she loved it.

"If you ever want to stop—"

"I know, say my safe word." She moved her face to the curve of his neck and inhaled his masculine scent as she spoke. "But that's not going to happen."

"Think you can take anything I give you?" he asked in a husky, very aroused voice.

Jessica licked a path from his neck to the stubble on his jaw. "Oooh yeah. Anything."

Craig drew away, grasped her shoulder and gazed into her eyes. "I can push pretty hard."

"And I can take it." She reached his mouth and bit his lower lip. "I want everything you have to offer."

A primal growl rose up in Craig that he couldn't hold back. "You said your family is gone for the summer?"

Jessica gave a strangled cry as he thrust his fingers inside her pussy. "In Europe until September." Her voice was completely breathless. "I don't have any plans."

"Now you do." He pumped his fingers harder inside her core. Damn, she was wet and slick. "I'll fuck you and spank you so many times you're going to be sore the entire summer."

She moaned and ground her hips against his hand. "That's what I want. To spend it with you."

Satisfaction flowed through Craig. "You'll be my fuck toy." He slipped his fingers out of her channel and brought them to her lips. "And I intend to play with you hard."

She whimpered when he removed his hand and then slipped his fingers between her lips, letting her taste herself. "Suck," he demanded, and she obeyed as if programmed to do whatever he wanted.

Hell yeah, this was going to be a summer that neither of them would ever forget. He wasn't about to worry about the start of next semester. For now he intended to enjoy her luscious body and everything she had to offer.

Which was more than he'd expected. She'd taken everything he'd done to her and was ready for more. And from this point on he planned to keep her to himself. Letting her have the experience of two cocks in her at once was a primer. He had no intentions of letting anyone else inside her. Not even his brother again. Dave could just kiss his ass.

"You still have a punishment coming." He sucked in his breath as she licked his fingers. "But right now, I'm going to fuck you, ride you hard. Is that what you want?"

He took his fingers out of her mouth and she nodded. "Please. Now."

"I should make you wait." He pinched her nipple, the nub hard between his thumb and forefinger. She gasped and he knew it was from not just the sensation, but from the soreness from the nipple rings. "You came without permission in the dungeon."

"Can you punish me later?" Her hand found his cock again and she rubbed her thumb over the slick bead of semen on its head. "You said we could be Craig and Jessica for now."

"I did, didn't I?" He took her mouth in another kiss, so hungry for her that he could hardly contain himself. She squirmed against him, growing wilder by the moment. Yeah, this was going to be one hell of a summer.

"Please don't make me wait anymore." She squeezed his cock. "I want you inside of me again."

Craig couldn't wait to be in her sweet pussy again. He had to stretch, but he reached over and pulled a condom out of a large box in his drawer. It didn't take him long to have his cock sheathed and to have his hips between Jessica's thighs. He placed the head of his erection at her core and braced his hands to either side of her head. She looked up at him with her beautiful green eyes. Her features were flushed, her eyelids shuttered as she waited for him to drive into her.

She writhed beneath him and dug her fingers into his ass. "Don't make me wait, please, Craig." He liked the way she said his name, as much as he enjoyed having her call him Professor when she played the naughty student.

Jessica was definitely a naughty student. And he enjoyed teaching her a lesson or two. More like, many.

"Do you want my cock, baby?" He lowered his head and bit lightly at her lower lip. "Do you want me inside you?"

"Yes!" Her expression looked almost like she was being tortured. She gripped his ass tighter, her fingernails causing pleasurable pain in his flesh.

Craig smiled and slammed his cock into Jessica's core and she cried out.

Jesus Christ, she was tight. He clenched his jaw and held still for a moment. Damned if he wasn't close to coming already. His cock ached and he already perched on the edge of a precipice.

He clenched his eyes shut, took a deep breath then looked down at Jessica. She arched her hips up and he started to slowly fuck her. He rocked their hips together, feeling the press of their flesh against one another. God, it felt even better than the first time he'd taken her with Dave.

Sweat had already broken out on his brow and he was damp from perspiration. She was flushed, her lips parted, her eyes fixed on him. Her warm vanilla scent filled him as he breathed deep, reveling in it and the scent of her musk.

He drew his cock in and out at a slow pace, drawing out her need to climax. They might not be role playing right now, but he still enjoyed making her want him until she was ready to scream.

"Oh God, Craig." She raised her hips and thrashed beneath him. Damn but he loved a wild woman. "Too slow. You're going too slow!"

He held himself back. He had plenty of training in self-restraint, although now was not one of those times that he was easily able to control it. "Baby, I'm going exactly as fast as you're going to get right now."

Jessica whimpered but continued writhing beneath him. She raked her nails down his back and he hissed from the pain and pleasure she was doling out to him.

A droplet of sweat rolled down the side of his face as he fought to hold himself back and to make her wait. But he was about to lose his self-control.

The man was driving her insane. Again. He felt so friggin' good inside her. So big—filling her, stretching her, reaching deep inside her.

But he was going too damn slow!

Sweat glistened on his forehead and he looked like he was struggling to hold himself back. Good, he was suffering too.

She looked down where they were joined, and her belly flipped again as she watched his cock slide in and out of her. She rocked and raised her hips up to meet his as far as possible, but still he took it slow.

Too. Fucking. Slow.

She was going to die.

For some reason this was even more intense than what had happened in the dungeon. Maybe because it was just the two of them and she'd wanted him to herself for so long.

She sucked in a breath and with it the scents of sex and spicy male. It filled her, spread throughout her. She dug her nails into his ass again, willing him to take her faster.

Finally he picked up the pace and she found herself making small cries as his long cock hit that special spot inside her. His erection stroked it, causing her to come closer and closer to orgasm. She tilted her head back and closed her eyes. Her thighs started trembling around his hips.

"Look at me, baby." His voice sounded like a growl. "Watch me fuck you."

Thrills rolled through Jessica's belly as she opened her eyes and saw his fierce expression. His jaw was clenched, his facial muscles tight.

His hips pistoned inside her harder, faster, deeper.

The room was beginning to spiral. "I'm going to come," she said as the world came closer to spinning out of control.

"Wait." His hips slammed against hers, his thrusts so hard she felt like her pussy would be bruised form the impact. "It'll be so much better if you hold on a little bit longer."

"I don't know if I can." Jessica grasped his biceps as she grew lightheaded and the room was beginning to fade.

"A little more, baby." His voice was rough, like sandpaper. She had no doubt he was on the edge and holding back too.

The whirling sensation in her head became more intense. She felt out of her body, like she was outside herself.

"Please." God, she was so close. "Please let me come."

He didn't reply as his hips slammed into her faster. She thrashed her head from side to side. She couldn't take any more. She couldn't!

"Now, Jessica!" he shouted.

Everything in her universe stopped spinning. All sensation rushed to her pussy, then expanded to her abdominal muscles, then to her chest, and throughout her entire body as her orgasm slammed into her. She screamed and cried and couldn't control the wildness she felt or the way she went crazy in his arms.

Craig shouted her name and she felt the pulse of his cock as he came. He thrust a few times more, then his arms gave out and he was pinning Jessica to the bed. His heavy weight felt good and she held onto him as her pussy continued to throb around his cock.

With a loud groan, Craig pulled out of her and tossed the condom by the nightstand, presumably into a wastebasket. Then he settled himself on his back and pulled her into his arms so that her head rested on his chest. She gave a shuddering sigh and her whole body went limp against his. It wasn't long until she fell into a deep, satisfied sleep.

Chapter Seven

ꟿ

Jessica woke, feeling slightly disoriented. She pushed herself up in bed and blinked at the sunshine streaming in through oak blinds. The sheet had fallen from her chest to her waist, revealing her bare breasts. Her heart started pounding as she slowly looked around the room.

Professor Bennett's room.

Craig's room.

Heat burned through her at the realization of what she'd just done the afternoon and night before—along with a bit of triumph at ending up in Professor Bennett's bed. She gave a slow, satisfied smile. She'd landed just where she wanted to be.

Although not exactly the way she imagined it.

More heat flushed over her skin when she thought about Craig and his brother, a police officer, fucking her. *Wow.* Not in her wildest dreams had she imagined herself naked in a stockade, or riding a rubber cock on a saddle, hanging from a ceiling or getting fucked in the pussy and in the ass at the same time.

Just the thoughts were making her folds wet again and her sore nipples hard. She felt bruised between her thighs, a good ache from being ridden hard. The slight pain in her ass was a little different, but she remembered how good it felt once she'd gotten beyond that initial blast of pain and had the cop thrusting in and out of her.

God, she was horny again.

"Good morning, Ms. Grayson," came Craig's voice from the doorway and her attention swerved to meet his gaze. He was carrying a bed tray and he wore his devastating smile. He was so gorgeous in tight blue jeans and a snug blue shirt that made his eyes seem even bluer and outlined all those yummy muscles. "It's already ten. I let you sleep in late—figured you were probably worn out."

She'd slept so late? "Good morning, Professor," she said, almost feeling embarrassed for some reason. Maybe it was because, like her, he was no doubt thinking of all the wicked things they'd done last night.

"Sit up a little more," he said when he reached her. The bed sank from his weight as he seated himself close to her. "Hungry, baby?"

Surprise filled her as she pushed up against the pillows and headboard and he settled the tray across her lap. She stared at the tray and her stomach growled at the smells of the scrambled eggs, sausage links, hashed browns and toast arranged on her plate. A white, pink-tipped rose arched above the plate and the goblet of orange juice.

Jessica looked up at him and smiled. "Thank you."

Craig lightly kissed her lips and tweaked one of her bare nipples. "I figured you'd have worked up a good appetite after last night."

Heat rushed over her again, and he grinned.

She started to pick up a fork but he shook his head. "Let me feed you."

He proceeded to bring a forkful of scrambled eggs to her mouth and she took it from him. "Tell me about your family," he said as he cut a sausage link then speared it with his fork.

The fact that Craig was interested in more than just her body made her feel warm inside. She swallowed the egg and smiled. "I have an older brother and an older sister. My brother is married and has twin boys, and my sister is dating a much younger man and says she never wants to get married."

Craig laughed and put the piece of sausage to her lips. She chewed—it was delicious. "What age difference between your sister and the man she's dating?" he asked.

Jessica gave him a sort of sheepish look. "Nine years. She's twenty-nine and he's my age."

That got a grin out of him. He sipped from her glass of orange juice then said, "And you're quite the opposite—dating a much older man."

Her belly fluttered and she looked up at him, not taking a sip of the orange juice he offered her. "Is that what we're doing?" she asked in almost a whisper. "Dating?"

He set the orange juice glass back on the bed tray and leaned so that his face was close to hers. "What do you want it to be, Jessica? A one-night stand or something more?"

"Dating." She swallowed down the thrill in her body. "Definitely dating."

"Good." He took her mouth in a sweet kiss and she tasted orange juice on his tongue. "I want more of you than just your body. I want to get to know the rest of you too."

Wow, was all she could think.

Craig picked up a triangle of buttered toast and she took a bite of it when he held it to her mouth. "I'm ten years older than you," he said while she ate her toast. "That doesn't bother you?"

She shook her head and he brought a napkin to her lips and brushed a crumb away. "What about you?"

He shrugged and speared another piece of sausage. "The fact that you're my student was the only thing keeping me from asking you out." She ate the piece of sausage while he spoke, her heart pounding. "Now you just need to drop that class you're signed up for in the fall, and you won't be my student anymore." He set the fork down on her plate and placed his forehead next to hers. "Sound like a plan?"

"Consider it dropped," she managed to get out before he kissed her again.

When he drew away, she could see desire sparking in his eyes, and when she glanced down she noticed the big bulge in his jeans. "You need to finish your breakfast, and we'd better get on another topic before I make you *my* brunch."

Jessica grinned then ate while he talked.

"You've met my older brother," he said as he fed her, and her face flushed with heat. "But that's the last time I'm going to let him get his hands on you." He let her drink some orange juice. "Because you're *mine,* Jessica Grayson, and I don't intend to share you again."

She almost melted into a pile of goo right then and there.

As he continued to feed her, he asked her questions about her parents who'd gone to Europe for the summer. Her brother lived in Sacramento and her sister in Washington. "She hates the rain though," Jessica said. "If it wasn't for her boyfriend and the fab job she has as a computer engineer, I think she'd move back in a heartbeat. She moved just to get out of the house, I think. She's always been kind of a rebel, I guess."

Craig raised an eyebrow as he set the fork on the bed tray. He reached up and brushed his palm over first one then the other nipple. "And you?" He gave her a mischievous smile. "I have a feeling you're one of those people that goes for whatever she wants until she gets it."

Jessica's body did crazy things as he touched her, and she felt more heat at his words. "I've always been driven, and I work hard. I've had straight A's since I was in elementary school. Failure isn't an option."

"I noticed." He pinched one of her sore nipples and she gasped. "So what made you go after me?"

She cleared her throat. "Um, well. You're not only good looking, but you seem like the kind of man I'd want to know better."

"And you wanted to fuck me." Craig grinned and pinched her other sensitive nipple. "How do you feel now?"

"Sore," she said, and Craig laughed.

He answered her questions in return. Not only did he have a cop for a brother, but he had two more brothers. One was a physical therapist and the other was a corporate executive.

"Do you all get into BDSM?" she asked

Craig shrugged. "Dave is, obviously. Drew and John got into it too. Dave told us all about it when we were sitting around watching football one night, and we all thought it sounded pretty damn hot."

"Have you done this all together?"

He shook his head. "Dave told us of some BDSM parties and conventions, and we checked them out. We liked what we saw."

Jessica took a deep breath. "Have you 'shared women' with all your brothers?"

"No." He took a napkin and dabbed her lips with it. "Just with Dave and only on a couple of occasions. They were his submissives both times. This was the first time I shared my woman with him."

Her stomach tripped. "Why me?"

Craig met her gaze. "Honestly...I didn't want to share you, I wanted to keep you to myself. But Dave happened to be over and I thought you might enjoy it. Did you?"

"I really did—it was an experience I'll never forget." She paused. "But I just want to be with you from now on."

That got another smile out of him. "I'm glad you feel the same way I do."

He took the bed tray with her mostly empty plate and walked over to a low vanity dresser where he set the tray down. She got a great look at his ass and how good he looked in his jeans. He turned back and he was holding the white, pink-tipped rose. "What do you think now that you've gotten to know how I like to play?"

"Honestly," she said with a flutter in her belly, "I've never done anything like it before, but I really got off on everything you did to me."

"You're so damn gorgeous." He sat on the edge of the bed and traced the curve of her neck with the rose bud. "Did my toys give you any fantasies beyond what we've already done, Jessica?"

She shivered as he skimmed the rose over her breastbone. "I'd like to try a little of everything."

That grin of his was so devastatingly sexy. "Believe me, there's plenty I'd like to do to you and with you." He brushed the soft skin between her breasts with the rose. "What do you want to do today?"

Her nipples were so hard and the ache between her thighs so great that her words came out in a husky whisper. "Whatever you want, Professor."

"Mmmmm..." Craig dipped his head and nuzzled her neck as he slid the rose down her belly to her abdomen. "I have a lot of things I'd like to do to you, Ms. Grayson. Which brings us back to one thing." He drew the rose along the fold in the sheet that hid her mound. "I still need to punish you for climaxing without permission."

He said *punish* in a way that made her squirm. Her ass still burned from last night, but still she was ready for anything he wanted to do with her. "I'll be good next time. I promise, Professor Bennett."

"Still need to punish you." He shook his head. "You were a very, very bad girl, Ms. Grayson."

He peeled away the sheet from her lap and tossed the sheet aside so that her body was completely bared. "You probably feel like taking a shower. You don't need to wear anything for what we're going to be doing," he said as he tickled her mound with the rose.

Her heart thumped. As he took her hand, she swung her legs over the side of the bed and he helped her to her feet. He lightly kissed her then pointed her in the direction of a door leading to what was obviously the master bathroom—she could see marble and brass through the doorway. She started to head to the bathroom when he swatted her ass, hard. She yelped and looked back at him.

"Don't make me wait too long," he said with his dominant look that meant they were role playing again.

"Yes, Professor," she said before she went into the bathroom.

The shower felt wonderful, the heat of the water easing the sweet aches in her body. When she was finished she dried her hair with a blow dryer and studied her features in the mirror. Her lips were swollen from Craig's kisses and when she turned and looked over her shoulder at her ass, she saw that it was still pink from the flogging and the spankings.

After her hair was dried she fluffed it around her shoulders, opened the door and walked out of the bathroom. It was such an erotic experience walking around naked, especially when she saw Craig still in his jeans, T-shirt and a pair of jogging shoes. And his huge erection was clearly outlined against the cotton of his jeans.

"You took a little too long, Ms. Grayson." He wore a stern expression. "That just earned you a second punishment."

Jessica caught her breath in both excitement and that sensual edge of fear. What would he do to her? "I'm sorry, Professor," she said.

"Come." He held out his hand and she took it. He strode fast enough that she had a difficult time keeping up with him.

Again he led her down to the dungeon and he opened the door and let her through before closing the door behind them. "This time the doorbell can be going non-stop, but we're not going to stop, Ms. Grayson," he said and she tried not to smile.

"Yes, Professor."

He took her to the strange-looking couch. The dimmed track lighting made the scene seem somewhat exotic. Air brushed over her skin as she moved, and the scent of musk was strong.

The couch was hard to describe. It had a huge hump on the left that rose up the length of a torso before curving over. The right side looked almost like a regular couch.

"Lie over the hump, Ms. Grayson."

She knelt on the lower end and draped herself over the high, rounded part. A soft fur material covered the surface that felt soft to her breasts and her mound.

Craig shackled her wrists and ankles, spreading her wide as he did, exposing her pussy. He rubbed his hand over her sore ass. "Perfect," he murmured. Everything he did and said turned her on, and she was so wet she could smell her own musk.

She turned her face so that her cheek was against the fur and watched him go to the wall of toys. He returned with a green ball with straps on either side of it and what looked like a whisk-type of handheld broom.

"Since you've been so bad, you're going to get a hard spanking," he said. "And you're not going to be able to scream. This is a ball gag, and you can bite down on it when you feel any pain."

Jessica opened her mouth in surprise and he immediately slipped the ball in as far as he could then tied the straps behind her head. With wide eyes, she looked up at him. Not only couldn't she move, she couldn't make a sound. A helpless, although exited feeling overtook her. She was totally vulnerable and couldn't even say her safe word.

Her gaze met Craig's and he looked serious. "If at any time you want me to stop, hold up two fingers. That'll be in place of your safe word. Understand, Ms. Grayson?"

Heart pounding, she nodded.

When he moved behind her, a shiver trailed her spine as he placed one of his hands on her lower back. He rubbed one ass cheek with his other palm in slow, sensuous circles.

Just when she started to relax, Craig's hand landed *hard* on the ass cheek he'd been stroking. Her eyes watered and she cried out behind the ball gag, but no sound came out. He slapped her again and this time she bit down on the ball. Her eyes watered from the pain as he spanked her. But it was so weird—the harder he spanked her, the wetter her pussy got, and the more she needed to come. She wanted to be fucked so bad she could just about scream—and would have if it weren't for the ball gag. Instead she bit down on the ball and felt the sting, burn and strange pleasure that came with the spanking.

"This is for being such a bad girl and coming without permission," Craig said in a stern voice. "Are you going to come again without my say-so?"

She moved her head side-to-side, the best she could with her face against the fur.

He stopped abruptly, and she gave a sigh of relief. God, her ass burned. "Very good, Ms. Grayson. You've taken your first punishment well. Now for your second."

Jessica almost whimpered. She was loving this, but at the same time she didn't know how much more she could handle. He was taking her to the limit.

The next thing she felt was what had to be the whisk broom thingee being run softly over her ass. It wasn't made of straw but of some soft, fiber-like strands.

It felt so good as he trailed the whisk over her ass, her back, her thighs and then down to her pussy. Again he whipped her when she started to relax. She gasped in surprise. The whisk didn't hurt as badly as the spanking had, but it heightened the sensations on her ass, causing more tears to flow down her cheeks. This time he swatted her pussy, not quite as hard as her ass but hard enough that it caused her to jerk in surprise.

Unbelievably, she came closer and closer to orgasm. She writhed beneath his swats, rubbing her mound against the furs, and she tugged at her restraints. A moan tried to escape around the ball gag. A moan from pain, pleasure and arousal.

He stopped and tossed the whisk aside and she slumped against the fur of the arch she was draped over. "You've handled your punishments well." Craig climbed onto the couch behind her and she felt the roughness of his jeans against her sore ass and thighs. But even better was the very naked erection he'd released from his pants that was now pressed against her ass.

Jessica struggled against her restraints, wanting to have him inside her. Her pussy was on fire, both from the swatting and from the need to come.

Craig leaned over her, his T-shirt brushing her back, and tickled her ear with his breath. It felt so good to have his hard body pressed against her. She liked the feel of his clothing rough against her bare skin and she moved her ass so that it would brush his erection.

His voice was deep and sensual and caused her to tremble with need. "You've earned a good fucking, baby."

Yes, God yes!

He rammed his cock into her pussy and she wanted to scream in ecstasy. But she bit the ball gag instead and whimpered.

"Don't come without permission," he said in a low growl.

Craig fucked her hard and fast. He drove in and out unmercifully, so deep and thick, and touching the place inside her that was making her crazy. This time the tears stinging at her eyes were from the need to come. She was so tightly bound as she was draped over the arch that she could barely writhe beneath him.

Her body wound tighter and tighter until she was so close to orgasm she was on an edge that made her feel like she was riding the crest of a wave before it crashed to the shore.

"You are so. Fucking. Tight," Craig growled as he held her hips and thrust in and out in a mind-blowing pace. His jeans scrubbed against her sensitive ass, and he moved his hands from her hips to her nipples, leaning over so he could pinch and squeeze them as he took her.

Jessica whimpered and cried, and fought against the orgasm that was rushing toward her. Craig drove her along that crest, along it, along it... Her entire body began to shake, her mind spun, her skin tingled.

"Now, baby!" he shouted.

Her orgasm slammed into her with such force she felt as if she could rip right out of the restraints and fly. Her whole body was on fire and she bucked as much as was possible the way she was pinned to the couch and bound. Craig didn't stop his pace and she wanted to scream as more waves went through her, one after another after another. It felt like they were never going to end. The pleasure of it almost turned into pain because she didn't think she would survive another orgasm.

Craig gave a shout and he squeezed her breasts hard. His hips jerked and he only thrust into her a few more times before he stopped and pinned himself tight against her ass.

It seemed like his body gave out as he sank against her on the fur-covered hump. Craig kept tweaking her nipples, causing more spasms to go off in her core, squeezing and releasing his cock inside her. She felt the pulse of his cock as it throbbed with his release.

Jessica moaned behind the ball gag and felt the restraints holding her wrists and ankles in place. She loved the feel of his body over hers and she never wanted to let go of the moment. Never wanted to let go of him.

Chapter Eight

ꟷ

The summer went by way too fast. Jessica sighed as she lay on the blanket on Ka'anapali Beach on Maui, just below their resort hotel. Craig was rubbing coconut-scented suntan oil on her back, paying close attention to her shoulders and neck and working his magic while he massaged her. Not that she was tense. With all the fabulous sex, she was sated and relaxed almost all the time.

They had spent every day of their summer vacation together. She had stayed at his house and they had talked about everything under the sun and did amazing things under the moon.

Her top was untied, but she was lying facedown on the blanket as he worked the oil onto her back. The sun was warm on her back, and his hands were so talented. Craig was now taking liberties, oiling the sides of her breasts and slipping his fingers beneath her to pinch her nipples.

Jessica laughed. "You are a naughty professor."

"Mmmm..." He leaned close and murmured in her ear, "I'd like to fuck you right here, right now, in front of all these people."

Tingling sensations went down her spine to the tiny little G-string bikini Craig had purchased for her. Her ass was completely bare, but from all the tanning they'd done going to San Diego, L.A., in Tucson and now in Hawaii, the pink marks from being spanked didn't really show. Her pussy ached and moisture dampened the scrap of cloth covering her folds.

"You have such a nice ass," he said as he began rubbing the oil first on one cheek then the other. "I'm so ready to fuck it again."

"And I'm so ready for you to," she said in a husky voice that betrayed how much she wanted him. Again. And again. She couldn't get enough of him, and it seemed he thought the same about her.

Craig pinched one of her ass cheeks that was sore from the spanking he'd given her for being a bad girl yesterday. She'd teased him on purpose, tweaking his cock in public without permission and rubbing her ass against his groin as often as possible to make him fully erect.

She grinned while he moved down to oil her thighs and calves. It had just been another excuse to spank her and fuck her hard, and she loved it. Sometimes she'd purposefully do things to get in trouble just so he'd punish her in some erotic way. She would even climax without permission just to get in trouble again.

Craig moved back up her body, rubbing her flesh as he went and moving his hands beneath her breasts to pinch her nipples. He leaned in close and she caught his scent of sun-warmed flesh and coconut oil. She could just imagine their slick bodies sliding against one another and her breasts ached even more as he fondled them.

"Let's go back to our room, Ms. Grayson." He nipped her earlobe hard and she gave a little cry. "It's time for me to punish you for not wearing any covering to the beach today and letting all the men see your gorgeous body." She usually wore a wrap around her waist so that her naked ass couldn't be seen since she only wore G-strings.

The ache between her thighs grew more intense. "I'm sorry, Professor. I won't do it again."

"Too late for that." He tied the straps of her halter-top then pinched her sensitive ass, causing her to give a low cry. "This time I'm going to come up with a new punishment."

Oh God. She couldn't wait.

Craig helped her to her feet, and his eyes were dark with arousal. With satisfaction, she caught sight of his huge erection just before he wrapped a towel around his waist. He shook the sand off the beach blanket and put it over his arm, along with her towel, before taking her hand and walking up the beach with her.

As her feet sank into the sand while they trudged up the beach, she looked up at Craig and met his smoldering gaze.

Oh, yeah, she was in for a wild ride.

After they'd washed the sand off their feet at one of the stations, they walked into the hotel. It was against the rules to walk around in a G-string without a cover, and she felt absolutely wicked going against the rules. They managed to make it to the elevators without getting caught. In just a few moments the elevator dinged and they entered it and Craig pushed the button for the twenty-fifth floor.

He shocked her when he shoved her up against the wall, dropping everything he'd been carrying.

"What—"she started when he released his erection from his trunks, pulled aside the scrap of material covering her pussy, and thrust his cock into her pussy.

"Oh my God," she cried out as he drove in and out of her, hard and fast.

"You're a tease, aren't you, Ms. Grayson?" he said as he fucked her.

"Yes. Oh God yes, Professor."

The danger of being caught in the elevator made her that much closer to reaching an orgasm faster than she ever had before. He continued to pump in and out and her breathing came hard and fast as the floors passed by.

"Almost there," she managed to get out, meaning both their floor and her orgasm.

"Come, baby," he demanded and she climaxed on command.

Her channel clamped down on his cock as new sensations spread through her, sensations caused by the threat of getting caught.

He gave a loud grunt and she felt his cock pulse in her core, his semen pumping inside her. She shuddered and Craig pulled out of her just as the bell dinged for their floor.

Her legs were so rubbery from the experience that she could barely stand as he gathered the towels, blanket and suntan oil. She fixed her G-string so that her pussy wasn't showing—just in time for the door to open and an elderly couple to be standing in the doorway.

Craig grabbed her hand. "Excuse us," he said with a nod to the couple. Jessica avoided their gazes. She knew they probably smelled like sex—of Craig's semen and her musk. This summer they'd both been tested so that he didn't have to wear a condom, and she was on the Pill, so the sex was better than ever.

He laughed and she giggled as they ran down the hallway to their room, him leading the way.

"What did you think of your punishment, Jessica?" he said in a low, rough voice as he pulled the keycard from the pocket of his swim trunks then opened the door with it. He dragged her inside and threw everything down again and pinned her up against the door when it closed. He took her mouth in a hard kiss then raised his head and looked at her. "Were you afraid of getting caught?"

She licked her moist lips and nodded. "Very."

"Good." He pressed harder against her as he untied the halter-top and each side of the G-string, pulled the bits of cloth away from her body and tossed them on the floor. "You'd better watch yourself or I'll find more ways to punish you."

Jessica nodded and he ground his erection against her belly. The man was insatiable. And so was she.

He kissed her hard and fierce, then his kiss became more sensual. He cupped her face in his hands and kissed the corner of her mouth, his lips traveling to her ear where he whispered, "I've got something for you."

Her curiosity piqued, she followed him into their luxurious hotel room. To her surprise there was a bouquet of white pink-tipped roses, a bottle of champagne chilling in a silver bucket, a platter of chocolate-covered strawberries and a present. The box was about the size of a toaster and wrapped with a big pink bow.

"What's this all about?" she asked, a little flutter in her tummy. The cool hotel room air brushed her naked skin as she moved toward the table.

He came up behind her and grasped her by the waist and rested his chin on her shoulder. "Today's our ten-week anniversary—from the day I found you naked in my office."

"Craig," she said, a lump crowding her throat. "I just can't believe you—"

"Open it," he said, holding her tightly around her waist.

Jessica bit her lower lip, wondering what in the world he'd gotten her to celebrate their ten-week anniversary. She pulled off the bow and tore off the wrapping paper, and lifted the lid off a white box. All she saw was tissue paper.

"Go on," he coaxed.

She started digging through the tissue and then stopped when she came to a black velvet jeweler's box—the size of a ring box. She stifled a cry as she lifted it from the tissue and held it in her hands that were trembling so badly she couldn't open it.

Craig released her waist to cover her hands and helped her raise the lid.

Jessica clapped one hand over her mouth and her eyes widened. Nestled in the black velvet was at least a one-carat diamond solitaire.

"I love you." He shifted so that he turned her in his arms and they were facing one another. "It's only been ten weeks, but I know what I want, and it's you, baby. We can have as long of an engagement as you want, but say you'll marry me."

Jessica leaned forward and pressed her face to his chest as she clutched the box. She raised her head and looked up at him. For once he looked a little unsure of himself and she found him that much more loveable.

She smiled, feeling giddy and shivery, and unbelieving. "Yes." She reached up and pressed her lips to his. "I love you so much, Craig. I can't say yes fast enough."

He grinned, took the diamond and slipped it onto her ring finger before he tossed the box aside. It fell to the carpet with a muted thump. As he walked her backward to the bed, she fell onto it and almost giggled. He slid between her thighs and entered in one hard thrust.

She took him inside her, welcoming him, feeling so much love for the man she'd lusted after for months. That lust had turned to such a deep love that she felt it throughout her entire being.

He kept the pace slow, making love to her like he never had before. His eyes never left hers, and when she crested the wave of ecstasy, he followed with her.

A feeling of peace and happiness eased through Jessica as he turned her into his arms and held her like he was never letting her go.

TAKING ON THE LAW

Author's Note

Taking on the Law incorporates only elements of Domination/submission and BDSM. It is not intended to accurately portray a true BDSM or Dom/sub relationship.

Chapter One

ꗃ

Erin Wilson gunned the engine of her little silver sports convertible as she flew down one of the darker back roads in Tucson. The powerful engine's noise cut through the night, and wind blew her hair around her face. She didn't care that the clip had fallen out or that the ends of the strands stung her eyes and her cheeks.

Goddamn him! That total bastard.

The backs of Erin's eyes ached and she ground her teeth. She would *not* cry over a bastard like Toby Wright.

She sucked in a breath of fresh night air and the lights of Tucson winked in the night like a glittering carpet. The road she was on wasn't exactly desolate, it just was a little farther out from town and where some of the nicer homes were built, sparsely situated so that there was a good mile between each house, if not more.

When she'd caught Toby in bed with her *former* best friend Wendy, Erin had stood watching for a moment, unable to believe what she saw. She'd stopped by Toby's place with Chinese takeout, let herself into his apartment with the key he'd given her—and heard noises coming from the bedroom.

Noises that sounded suspiciously like the headboard banging against the wall, and the sounds of moans and groans.

Everything had felt unreal. She set her purse on the couch, along with the food. Her ears had buzzed and skin felt stretched thin as she made it down the short hallway to the door of his bedroom.

Toby was in between Wendy's thighs, slowly fucking her. They were both naked and her best friend reached between their bodies and massaged his balls.

"That's it, baby," Toby groaned. "You're no cold fish in bed."

Wendy had giggled and then he'd kissed her as she drew her hand away and wrapped her legs around his hips.

Cold fish?

Cold fish!

Erin had grabbed the closest thing to her, one of his jogging shoes left in the doorway, the start to a trail of clothing leading to the bed.

She'd scooped it off the floor, and with all the fury built up in her, she'd flung the shoe straight at the asshole's head.

Erin grimaced with some satisfaction as she guided the sports car down the deserted road, edging over the speed limit by a good thirty miles per hour.

She'd clocked Toby a good one, hard enough to make him almost fall off Wendy and leaving an instant imprint on his cheek of the bottom of his jogging shoe.

"What the fuck?" Toby had looked momentarily disoriented until he looked at Erin and saw her standing with her hands clenched into fists. He held his hand to the side of his head. "You bitch!"

"Erin!" Wendy had shouted, trying to scramble from beneath Toby, but he pinned her down. "I can explain! Really!"

"You both go to hell." Erin was so pissed her entire body shook. "And I hope you enjoy one another's company while you rot there."

She had spun, grabbed her purse off the couch along with the bag of Chinese takeout, and slammed the door behind her.

Now the smell of the food sitting beside her on the passenger seat was making her stomach churn.

Fire and fury raged through her. She took her right hand off the wheel, grasped the paper bag of takeout and flung the bag of Chinese food out of the convertible, not giving a damn that she was littering. Everyone could go to hell.

Red and blue lights flashed behind her.

"*Shit*!" She resisted banging her head against the steering wheel as she slowed the car down. Great. Just what she needed.

Fuck. Fuck. Fuck!

Erin ground her teeth as she eased the car over to the shoulder, threw the convertible into park and killed the engine. She left the lights on and both hands on the steering wheel, clearly visible, like she'd been told one was supposed to do when stopped by a police officer.

Her heart pounded and only her rage at Toby and Wendy kept her from crying.

What a fucking great day.

From the very start. A coworker had come on to her again and she'd filed a sexual harassment complaint with HR; her brother and the sister-in-law she *hated* left a message they were coming from Spokane to stay with her for a week; her mother called about needing money again; and Erin had had a flat tire first thing in the morning and had been late for work. That had won her some brownie points.

Not. Her manager was a total bitch.

So, to top it all off, her best friend—*former* best friend—and her boyfriend were cheating on her, and now she'd been caught speeding. And probably littering, too.

Could things get any worse?

Don't tease God, Erin.

Her shoulders slumped and she waited for the cop to pull over and make her day even better. Dirt and rocks crunched under the cruiser's tires, and the flashing lights made her blink from the brightness. The red and blue flashes and bright headlights nearly blinded her in her rearview mirror, and the cruiser's engine had a powerful thrum as she saw the cop approaching the driver side of the car. She could make out his uniform but not his face.

The face of doom.

She moved her gaze from the rearview mirror and looked straight ahead into the darkness. The sparse house lights on the deserted road blurred and her eyes burned.

I'm not going to cry. I'm not going to cry!

"License and registration, ma'am," came a deep sexy voice that sounded…familiar. Too familiar.

She tilted her head up and her jaw dropped open.

Dave Bennett?

He lowered his clipboard and in the flashes of light she saw the hard planes of his face and his expression of surprise. "Erin?" He said her name in that way that had never failed to make her panties damp or her nipples hard.

"Hi, Dave," she managed weakly.

Yeah, she'd teased God and her day just got worse.

The cop she'd just been stopped by was the one and the same guy she'd dumped the end of their senior year in high school.

Dave Bennett's cock went hard at the sight of the All-American beauty who'd been his first sexual experience—both of them had been virgins in high school, but not long after they'd started dating their junior year, things had moved pretty fast.

He'd fallen in love with the blonde, blue-eyed girl. Real hard. After two years of dating, she'd wrenched his heart in two and stomped all over it when she said things were over between them because she was going back East to college and it would be too difficult to maintain a relationship.

All the planning they'd done—they were both going to go to the University of Arizona and then he'd enter the police academy. They would get solid jobs, get married and have three kids. The two of them had laughed and, at the time he thought, loved. But she'd torn that all apart when she left Tucson.

Right now she was looking up at him with those wide blue eyes that even now made him want to kiss her. Erin's hair was tangled around her face and the sweater she was wearing had drifted off her shoulders, exposing her upper arms where her sleeveless blouse ended—just enough flesh to intrigue a man. Her breasts were even more generous than he remembered.

Clipboard in one hand, he braced his palms on the door of her convertible and looked her over from head to toe. He remembered sucking the nipples that were now peaking beneath her blouse. It had been pure heaven sliding between those gorgeous thighs that were visible beneath a short skirt that had ridden up high enough that it barely covered her mound and a pussy he loved to fuck.

"Erin Wilson." Her name came out hard and she winced. "Back in town and out for a little joyride?"

Erin's throat worked as she swallowed. "It's good to see you, Dave."

"Uh-huh." Dave tightened his grip on her car door and set his jaw. "Thirty-five miles an hour over the speed limit, not to mention tossing a bag out the window right at my cruiser. Bet it's real good to see me."

"Sorry?" She bit her lower lip as he fixed his gaze on her. "I had the most screwed-up day of my life, okay? And now a couple of tickets will just round it off nicely."

He pushed away from the car. "Out of the vehicle."

"What?" Erin's eyes widened. "You're going to arrest me?"

"Do you want to be charged with disobeying the direct order of a police officer, Ms. Wilson?"

She closed her eyes briefly and then opened them. Her lovely breasts rose and fell as she gave a deep sigh. "Of course not, *Officer Bennett*."

Erin might not have intended to turn him on with the way she said his name, but his cock went from aching to rock-hard. He could just picture taking her home, handcuffing her and flogging her in his special bondage room. What would she think if he locked her up and fucked her through the cell bars? Or slid his baton up her pussy? He'd punish her for leaving him, and make sure she loved every minute of it.

Shit. This train of thought was killing him.

Seeing her—it opened up a whole floodgate of emotions that he'd long buried, fifteen years ago. The love he'd killed, the lust was obviously still there.

He backed up and Erin opened the door and climbed out. In the flashing red and blue lights he took in her deep red, tiny skirt that she had to tug down, and the red sweater over a sleeveless red shirt. Her legs were bare of any stockings, just the way he liked his women.

He set his ticket clipboard on the hood. "Spread your hands on the hood of your car, your stance wide."

"You're kidding!"

"*Now*."

Grumbling under her breath, what sounded like *sonofabitch*, she obeyed him.

When she was slightly bent, her stance wide, he went up behind her and just stood, letting her anticipate what he was going to do to her.

"Here for a visit, Erin?" he said as his gaze traveled the length of her backside, stopping to rest on her cute little ass.

"I live here now." She gave an audible sigh. "Just moved back from Boston to be closer to my mom, okay?"

His hands itched to touch her. God, how he'd missed her. He didn't realize just how much until right this moment.

"You're here to stay?" He kept his voice low, authoritative.

"Is this part of being arrested? Do you question the people you stop until they beg to be taken in?" Sparks might as well have been snapping in the lights of his cruiser just from the tone of her voice. She still had spunk, he'd say that much for her. He allowed himself a grin because she couldn't see his face, her back still to him.

Dave moved closer to her so that he caught a whiff of her soft powdery scent. After all these years she still smelled the same. Sweet and irresistible.

He barely resisted touching her. They'd done a lot of role-playing games when they were dating, and one of them was "frisk me", where he was the cop and she was the driver he'd pulled over. Or she was even a hooker he'd taken into custody. They'd had great imaginations back then.

She must have been thinking along the same lines, because she shifted her stance a little and her voice came out a little hoarse. "So, are you going to frisk me, Officer Bennett, or stare at my ass?"

A low growl rumbled up in Dave's throat and he almost reached out, grabbed her hips and ground his erection into her ass. "Do you want to be frisked, angel?" he asked, using the nickname he'd given her when they first started dating.

He heard Erin's sharp intake of breath. "It's been a long time," she whispered.

"Too long," he said before he could stop himself.

She turned her head and looked at him over her shoulder. In the flashing lights he saw that her lips were moist—she must have just run that pretty little pink tongue over them. Her gaze met his and held. "Frisk me," she said in a low, sensual purr that said "fuck me" and made him want to grab her and slam his cock into her pussy *now.*

Erin looked away from him, arched her back, tilted her face to the sky.

His heart thundered. His All-American girl looked more like a goddess right now. Her windswept hair a golden halo around her head with the car lights reflecting on the gloss of her hair. Her full breasts were raised high and firm, and her rounded bottom just begged for his hands—or his cock.

"Trying to get out of a ticket?" He rested his hands to either side of her on the car's warm hood, managing to keep his body from touching hers—barely.

"Of course not." Her voice trembled. "I'm just cooperating with the law."

Dave couldn't resist nuzzling her hair. She smelled so damn good.

Erin gave a little moan and moved back so that her ass came in contact with his groin.

Shit. He shouldn't be having the thoughts he was having. Shouldn't be doing what he was doing. He was a cop, for God's sake, and he'd never crossed a line like he would be if he did to Erin what his body was crying out to do. To make up for the last fifteen years.

He pushed himself away so that he wasn't leaning over her anymore, and she wasn't pressing her ass up against his cock. His breath came out harsh and uneven.

"Frisk me," she said in that low, seductive voice that had brought him to his knees all those years ago.

Chapter Two

ꟸ

Dave felt like his hands weren't his own as he reached up and started to frisk Erin—slowly. She gasped as he patted her down, starting under her arms at the sides of her breasts. He slid his fingers over the curves without going too far, but she caught him off guard when she arched into his touch and gave a soft moan.

"Dave, I—"

"Need to make sure you're not hiding a weapon in your bra," he said, his voice low and gruff as he moved his hands around her breasts, palms brushing her stone-hard nipples before he cupped them.

Oh, yeah. She had a pair of lethal weapons.

Erin leaned into his hands and pushed her ass back farther so that it pressed against his groin and his erection. A whimper rose up within her, just like the times he'd tease her before driving his cock into her core. As if remembering those same times, she ground her hips against his erection and he pinched her nipples *hard*.

She gave a startled cry but only wiggled her hips more, rubbing her ass along his cock. He pinched her nipples hard again before sliding his hands down the sides of her waist, then slid one palm against her flat belly to just above her mound.

"Oh God." Her words came out almost strangled. "I don't know if I can take much more frisking."

"That'll cost you." Dave leaned over her back, his weapons belt pressing into her lower back as he murmured close to her ear, "I think we're talking jail time."

"Wha—"

Her words were cut off by a moan as he palmed her ass then squeezed the tight globes. He skimmed his fingers along the edge of her short skirt from the backs of her legs to the front, just below her pussy. He'd bet she was soaking wet if he stroked her between her thighs, but he was intent on teasing her, punishing her in his own way for leaving him all those years ago when they were teenagers.

But this older Erin Wilson was, if possible, even more gorgeous than she had been before, not to mention her body was more developed and she was sexy as hell.

Dave continued his exploration, ignoring her pussy and instead sliding his hands down her legs to the strappy heels she was wearing. The vivid image of her on her back, wearing only those heels, just about made him come in his uniform pants.

"There's only one place I haven't searched for weapons," he said as he eased back up her body, his hands slowly sliding over her firm thighs, up to the tiny skirt.

Erin trembled beneath his palms as his fingers neared her pussy. "Are you going to resist arrest, Erin Wilson?"

"Depends."

"Oh?"

"On whether or not you intend to make me come, or if you're just teasing me."

He held back a chuckle. "Are you bribing an officer of the law?"

"No," she gasped as his fingers neared her panties. "Maybe. *Yes*!"

"That'll definitely cost you," he murmured before he slipped his fingers into her wet folds.

She cried out and brought one of her hands from the hood of her car to cover his and press it tighter against her pussy. He thrust his hips against her ass at the same time he circled her clit.

"Dave…oh God, I missed you." Her body trembled beneath his and he caught the smell of her musk. "I want you inside me. I want you to fuck me." He stilled and she whimpered again. "Please," she begged. "I need you."

"I don't have a condom," he said, his cock nearly bursting from the seams of his uniform slacks.

"I'm on the Pill." Her breathing came in heavy pants. "And I trust you."

The fact that she trusted him sent a warm bolt through his chest that combined with the lust raging through his body.

Technically he could call it a day, but he hadn't yet. He was still on the job.

"I need you," Erin whispered. "I need *this*."

Before he could even stop himself, he unzipped his slacks and freed his erection. He pushed Erin's skirt up and over her ass so that all he could see was a thong and her bare ass cheeks, and he nearly shuddered. He pulled the scrap of cloth to the side with one hand and used his other to steady his cock at the opening to her core.

She moaned and leaned back, trying to take him inside her.

He grabbed her hips and drove his cock home in one hard thrust.

Erin screamed. He stopped, holding himself inside her, feeling the tightness of her pussy holding onto his cock like a fist. Goddamn, she felt good.

"Please." Erin wriggled her hips. "Don't stop."

Dave started fucking her, feeling like he'd just found a lost treasure.

Erin was so lost in the sensation of having Dave inside her that she could barely think. Red and blue lights continued to flash, exposing them if anyone was to drive by. His weapons belt and gun dug into her flesh as his cock rammed into her core.

Over all of these years, no one had ever lived up to Dave, and he seemed impossibly bigger and thicker than he had as a teenager.

He moved his hands up her hips to her blouse and pushed it up, over her skimpy red lace bra. He pulled the cups of her bra down, exposing her skin to the cool fall air. Her nipples ached in a pleasurable way as he pinched them and fucked her at the same time.

"Definitely bribing an officer of the law," he said as he slammed harder against her. "Looks like you need a little punishment to teach you a lesson you won't forget."

"P-punishment…" Erin felt like her mind was floating away. "I un-understand, Officer."

"Do you?" He stopped for a moment, his body flush with hers. "This means solitary confinement with me as your jailor."

"Please don't stop." She gasped, his erotic words floating somewhere with her mind. "Whatever you want, Officer. Just fuck me."

He rotated his hips so that his big cock worked magic inside her and she wanted to scream. "I'll be taking you into custody as soon as I finish 'frisking' you, Ms. Wilson. Do you understand?"

A thrill tumbled through her belly. "Anything you require of me, Officer."

He gave a sound of satisfaction and began pumping in her hard and fast, slamming his hips against hers, his balls slapping her ass.

Erin's body shuddered with the need to come. She climbed higher and higher, her mind still floating as if she were a balloon, barely tethered to the ground. Her entire body felt light, her oncoming orgasm lifting higher and higher.

Out of nowhere her climax slammed into her and she shouted.

She came so hard her arms collapsed against the warm hood of the car and she found herself resting her head on her arms. She felt disconnected from reality as her body shuddered and her core clamped down on his cock.

Dave gave a low growl just before she felt his semen spurting inside her, his cock pulsing while her pussy spasmed. He thrust a few times more, letting her body milk the rest of his come from his cock.

"Angel." He pressed his groin tight against her ass. "You don't know just how much trouble you're in."

Trouble? Hell, if this was trouble *bring it on,* Erin thought as Dave drew his cock out of her and she heard him zipping up his uniform slacks. Who'd have thought her day would end up like this?

"You might get time for good behavior," he said in his deep, sexy voice as his hands clasped her wrists. "But we'll have to see."

Her cheek pressed against the hood of the car as he drew her hands behind her back too fast for her to react—and he *handcuffed* her.

"Dave!" she cried out as she pulled at the metal handcuffs that bound her hands behind her back. "What the hell are you doing?"

"Resisting arrest, Ms. Wilson?" he asked as he drew her to a standing position. He didn't bother to pull down her blouse or her skirt.

"What—no, I—" She did resist stomping on his booted foot. "What are you doing?"

He leaned so that his lips were close to her ear and he reached around and pinched one of her nipples. She moaned and felt more moisture dampen her thighs. "Jail time, remember?"

"But—"

He turned her toward his cruiser, the red and blue lights flashing across her bare breasts. Her skirt was still above her ass and she felt the chill fall air on her breasts and every other body part that was bared. If she weren't so hot and horny from Dave fucking her, she'd be cold. Thank God this was Arizona.

Dave actually read her the Miranda Rights as he opened the back door of his cruiser and shoved her into the seat, his hand pushing down on her head. Her naked ass hit the cold vinyl of the seat and she shivered. What was he doing? Taking her in? After *that*?

Erin's heart pounded as he slammed the door shut behind her. She didn't know what was happening, but he couldn't take her in like this.

Through the grill separating the backseat from the front, she saw him fiddling with her car, raising the convertible's roof and turning off the headlights. When he ducked his head into the car, he took a moment before bringing something from inside. It looked like her purse, then he slammed the door closed. As he walked back to the cruiser, her car's lights flashed indicating he'd used the remote to lock the doors. He slipped her keys into her purse and closed it.

Dave reached the cruiser, climbed inside, tossed her purse onto the seat beside him and killed the flashing lights. She just sat there numb from shock as his headlights remained on her little convertible and he closed the front door behind him. Her body still felt his touch, still remembered the fullness of having him inside her. But now she was handcuffed, her body mostly bared, and sitting in the back of his police car.

The numbness turned into a slow burn of anger that began to rise within her. "What the fuck is going on, Dave?"

"I'm taking you into custody." He threw the car into gear and turned the vehicle around so that they were headed in the opposite direction—toward town.

He spoke into his shoulder radio, but she didn't hear or understand a word he said.

Her entire body started shaking. "Is that what you do, *Officer Bennett*? Fuck the women you stop for speeding, then take them into custody?"

By the dashboard lights, she saw the corner of his mouth curve. "Only you. I think we have a little interrogating to do."

Erin was at a total loss for words. She felt so vulnerable, yet for some stupid reason, she felt amazingly turned on. It was like one of their teenage role-playing games had come to life—only this time she didn't know what to expect next. Would she turn *him* in for sexual harassment like she had earlier today with the guy from her office?

This went a little beyond sexual harassment.

But how she'd wanted it. After the day she'd had, it had felt so good having his calloused hands on her, his big cock inside her.

God, she was going out of her mind.

They reached another street on the west side of town, not too far from where she'd been driving and she wrinkled her brow in confusion. There were very few houses on the street, separated by large lots. He drove up into the driveway of a house and the garage door opened.

A whoosh of relief rose up from her chest. Dave had no doubt taken her to his home.

Even after all these years, she completely trusted him—and despite the handcuffs. After he'd turned off the powerful engine he lowered the garage door and got out of the cruiser. He opened the back door, took her by the upper arm and helped her out of the car.

Thrills bounced around her belly after he closed the door behind them and he paused to look down at her, his beautiful brown eyes meeting hers. It was the first time she'd been able to see his eyes all night and she caught her breath. They were the same chocolate brown with long dark lashes and his dark hair short in the kind of cut you'd expect a cop to have. From what she could tell with his uniform on, his body was even more fit than it had been when he'd played high-school football, and he'd filled out. He was all man now, that was for sure.

His gaze moved from hers and slowly traveled to her exposed breasts. He ducked his head and latched onto one of her nipples with his warm mouth and suckled. Erin caught her breath then let out a soft whimper when he moved his lips to her other nipple. She wanted her hands free from the cuffs to run her fingers through his short dark hair.

He raised his head and looked at her again. Her nipples were hard, aching and a little chilled from the dampness and the cool garage temperature.

Their eyes met and locked. "Damned if I haven't missed you," he said as he cupped her face in his hands. "Fifteen years, and just seeing you makes me feel like you never left."

She swallowed. "I feel the same way. Can't believe it, but I do."

"I haven't even kissed you yet," he murmured as he held her face in his palms. "Welcome home."

Dave's mouth met hers in a soft kiss that was so different from their wild lovemaking out on the side of the road. Her body knew him, welcomed him, wanted him.

Their tongues met and she sighed into his mouth. His familiar taste and the way he kissed brought back so many memories. The sweet nights they'd shared, learning one another's bodies, then the wild, untamed sex that blossomed the more they came to know each other and the more they'd learned.

When Dave raised his head, her breathing had elevated and she felt flushed from her head to her toes. "Take off the handcuffs. I want to touch you."

He shook his head. "You're still in custody, and I've got some interrogating to do."

Erin's belly flip-flopped at the rough way he said it, while at the same time his eyes held such sensuality. She let him lead her into his home, through a laundry room that had a pile of dirty clothing, and into a large, airy combination kitchen/family room.

It was a really nice home, but definitely looked like a bachelor pad. A pair of jogging shoes sprawled by a coffee table that had a couple of empty beer cans and a half-full cheese puff package. Across from the leather L-shaped couch and coffee table was a large-screen TV, and she could just picture him kicking back and watching sports. Back when they'd dated, he'd been into every kind of sport imaginable and she'd always enjoyed sitting next to him while he got into the games, and she'd laugh when he'd get to his feet and shout at the players on the screen. No doubt he hadn't changed in that regard a bit.

Dave guided her to a square oak kitchen table in the kitchen, seated her in one of the chairs and sat across from her. The light that hung over the table was stained glass, causing reflections of various colors to freckle the walls. A few dirty dishes were scattered on the counter and there was a dish drainer full of clean ones.

Her shirt was still up and over her breasts, her bra below them, causing her breasts to be raised high. She felt exposed, vulnerable and a little more than turned on. "My arms are starting to ache," she said as her gaze met his. "*Please* take off the handcuffs?"

He shook his dark head. "Not yet, Ms. Wilson. You've got some answering to do."

She raised an eyebrow. "Should I call my lawyer?"

The corner of his mouth quirked before his expression was serious again. "Why did you leave me like you did when we graduated?"

Erin leaned back in surprise. She hadn't expected that question. "I, well—"

"The *truth*." His expression was grim. "Did you stop loving me?"

She squeezed her eyes shut for a moment and thought back to the day she told him she was leaving. It was the hardest thing she'd ever done. "I was scared." She opened her eyes as the words came out of her mouth. "We were so young, and I—I wasn't ready, Dave."

"You could have stayed." His big palms were splayed out on the table. "I would have given you all the time you needed."

"I know." It came out in a whisper. "But you were all I'd known for two years, and I wanted to make sure I wasn't missing out on what life had to offer. I didn't want to have kids or even think about them. Whenever we used to talk, I'd get a funny feeling in the pit of my stomach."

A hurt expression flashed across Dave's face, to be replaced by the firm mask again. "Why didn't you tell me instead of just breaking it off? I just asked you, did you stop loving me? Because I sure as hell couldn't forget you."

"I didn't date for the first couple of years," she admitted, "because I couldn't get over you."

"Why didn't you come back?"

She sucked in her lower lip as she remembered those days when she'd missed him so badly it hurt deep inside. "After the way I left—I didn't think you'd want me."

"It took me a couple of years to get over you, too." His gaze pinned hers and she couldn't look away. "But I finally did. I finally moved on and you became a part of my past."

Erin's chest ached, and she wanted to cry. She'd been stupid to throw their love away. She'd realized it too late—or what she'd thought had been too late.

"And now you walk back into my life and it's happening all over again." He shook his head. "Goddamn, Erin. I want your—I want your body even more than I did then."

And my heart? She quelled the thought before it went any further. That was over. All there was left was lust.

Dave gripped his hands into fists and gritted his teeth even harder. He was admitting things to Erin he hadn't admitted to himself in years. He'd told her what he wanted was her body, when a part of him yearned for her heart again, too.

It's been fifteen goddamn years, Bennett! *What the fuck are you thinking*? *She left you.*

"Things have changed a lot since then." His voice was hoarse, betraying some of his emotion, and he wanted to kick his own ass.

"I know," she said softly. "And you don't know how sorry I am."

"Just how sorry?" He rose and withdrew the key to the handcuffs and held it up where she could see it.

Thank God he was going to take the cuffs off. "*Real* sorry."

"Good." He pocketed the key again.

"Hey!" She narrowed her brows. "You promised."

He shook his head. "No. I told you I was taking you into custody, and that's exactly what I'm doing."

Erin flopped against her seat, an expression of disbelief on her face. "We talked. What more do you want from me?"

"A lot." He took her by the arm and helped her to her feet. She tried to jerk her arm away, but he gripped her tight as he guided her to the one room he'd wanted to take her to all night.

They walked down the hallway to the farthest—and largest room, and he opened the door.

Chapter Three

ꟙ

Erin's jaw dropped and her eyes widened as Dave closed the door behind them. *Un-freaking-believable.* She'd been introduced to a little bondage and domination by one of her boyfriends, but nothing like this.

He had a table with floggers and other devices, a stool with restraints, what she was certain was a sex swing, chains hanging from the ceiling, some kind of machine with a metal ramp, and at the top of the ramp were grips and arm- and belly-rests, all leather padded. There were wrist restraints at the grips and restraints at the bottom of the ramp. The thing that really got her attention, though, was the tall metal cage against one wall.

"Um, Dave?" She looked up at him and licked her lips. "What are you planning to do to me?"

He cupped the side of her face with one of his hands and brushed his lips over hers. "It's not want I intend to do *to* you, it's what I intend to do *with* you."

Her stomach flip-flopped once again. "How do you know I want to?"

He moved his lips to her ear and gently nipped. "All those sexual games we played when we were teenagers…we've grown up and so have our toys. And you want to try them out. You want me to fuck you in every way imaginable. Admit it."

Dave released her arm as he raised his head and looked into her eyes. At the same time he brought his hands to her nipples and squeezed, causing her to gasp from the sheer pleasure of it. She tried swallowing, but her throat was dry.

Erin's pussy ached and her nipples grew harder as he cupped her breasts and squeezed her nipples between his thumbs and forefingers. She had to admit it did feel so erotic having her wrists handcuffed and being at Dave's mercy.

He moved his hands from her breasts to her ass, raised her skirt and massaged the naked globes, pulling them apart and releasing them again. "Are you ready to play?"

"Yeah." She shocked herself by how easily she answered him. "I'm ready."

The corner of his mouth turned up in a devastatingly sexy smile. "Pick a safe word."

Safe word. Safe word. Oh, yeah, that ex-boyfriend who had introduced her to a little bondage and domination had mentioned that people heavily into BDSM chose a word they could use any time they thought things were getting too out of hand.

Memories of earlier this evening hit her hard. "Dirty, stinking, lying, cheating bastard and bitch." A moment's fury was in her words at the memory of her *ex*-best friend, and her *ex*-boyfriend.

Dave looked taken aback. "Uh, angel. That's a bit much. Maybe you'd better tell me where that came from."

Erin's shoulders slumped and she shook her head, still unable to believe what she'd walked in on. She told Dave about her day from hell and how it ended finding her boyfriend with her best friend.

In the meantime he unfastened her handcuffs, put them back into the pouch on his belt and massaged her wrists.

"Of course that was before you stopped me for speeding and littering," she said as he rubbed the slight ache in her shoulders.

"Your day sucked." He kissed the top of her head. "And I'd like to kick that sonofabitch's ass. But wouldn't you say it ended up pretty well?"

She smiled up at him. "Getting fucked by a cop on the side of a road was definitely hot."

He raised an eyebrow. "Any cop?"

Now that her arms were free, she wrapped them around his waist and snuggled against his chest. She breathed deeply of his masculine scent. He smelled so damn good. "Definitely not just any cop would have done."

Dave gave a soft laugh. "Now about that safe word. How about you choose just one."

"If you insist," she said with a smile as her cheek rested against his chest. "Ballerina. I always wanted to be one when I was a little girl."

When she tilted her face up and met his gaze, he had a serious expression on his face. "You know how this works, I'd bet."

Erin shrugged. "Not really." She had a feeling it wouldn't go over well if she admitted to indulging in a little bondage with an old boyfriend. "It's just one of those things I've learned about over the years."

"Uh-huh."

"Really." She did her best to look innocent.

He swatted her on the ass, hard, and she yelped. "Always tell me the truth or you'll be punished."

Her face flushed as he rubbed one of her ass cheeks with his palm. "An old boyfriend used to tie me up every now and then, but we never got into BDSM."

"You have several punishments coming to you." He was now rubbing both ass cheeks. "Five counts. Speeding, littering, bribing a police officer, lying…and leaving me."

At his last words she caught her breath and met his gaze. He lowered his mouth and took hers in a hard kiss that made her head spin. He mastered her mouth with his tongue, his teeth and his lips. By the time he finished kissing her she was so dizzy she almost couldn't stand.

When he finally raised his head and she managed to catch her breath, he said, "You're to refer to me as Officer Bennett, or Officer at all times. Do you understand?"

Wow. This went a little more than beyond what they would play when they were teenagers. It made her hot enough that moisture dampened her thighs and her nipples ached in the cool air of the bondage room.

"Five punishments, Officer?" she asked, coming back to her senses. *Five*?

"More if you deserve them." He took a step back. "Strip—but leave your heels on."

Erin's pussy was positively aching now. She slipped out of her sweater and he took it from her, along with the other pieces of clothing she stripped out of. When she wore nothing but her heels, he gave a smile of pure male satisfaction.

He went to a long, oak table that was built into the wall and set her clothes on it. While she watched him, he went to a tall safe, unlocked it with a combination, then took off his weapons belt and put it into the safe, along with any other equipment he had on, like his shoulder radio. He finished and shut the safe door before turning to the table and looking it over—she saw that he'd kept a hold of the handcuffs, though.

Uh-oh.

As he looked over his table of "toys" he finally settled on something that looked like a chastity belt—but had both a dildo and a butt plug on it.

She shivered as he approached her with a tube of what she was sure was lubricant, along with the contraption.

When he reached her, he trailed one of his fingers down her spine to her ass. "Ever been butt-fucked before?"

Erin thought about lying, but knew he'd see right through her and it would mean punishment number six. "A couple of times." She stared at the butt plug. "But I don't think anything *that* big has been up my ass."

"This is punishment number one—for speeding." He took the tube, squeezed out some lubricant and applied it liberally to the plug. "You'll wear these at all times until I take them out of you."

Whoa. "Yes, Officer."

He had Erin place her hands on a padded raised table and had her stand with her legs wide. She felt so open and vulnerable to him—and really, really *hot*. She gave a sharp cry then a groan as he pushed the plug up her ass. The tight ring of her anus didn't want to let it in, but he slipped the plug in until she felt packed full and she wanted to squirm from the sensations.

Next he took the dildo—no need to lube it as wet as she was—and he thrust it into her pussy, this time causing her to gasp at the sudden invasion. He strapped the harness so that both the dildo and the plug were kept snug inside her. While she was getting used to the feel of them, he left to put the lube back onto the table with all his toys.

"Punishment number two is for littering," he said as he returned to stand in front of her. "No orgasm without my permission. Do you understand?"

"Yes, Officer." Erin was practically trembling with the need to come *right now* because of the plug up her ass and the dildo in her pussy. Not to mention she was naked with only her high heels and a harness on—in front of her former high-school sweetheart who had turned out to be one hell of a good-looking man *and* was a cop.

He drew her away from the padded table and slowly walked around her. "Damn, you're beautiful. You're even more gorgeous than you were when we were in high school."

"I was thinking the same thing about you, Officer Bennett," she said when he was facing her again.

He gave a slow smile. "Now for punishment three." His gaze roved the room and settled on the tall cage. "For bribing a police officer, you definitely need to serve some jail time."

Her heart started thundering. "You're going to lock me up, Officer?"

"You bet your sweet ass I am." He pinched one of her ass cheeks as if to make his point and she yelped. "I read you your rights, I've processed you, and now I'm going to lock you away."

Dave took her by the arm and she nearly stumbled into him as they went to the jail cell that was about four by four feet square. The bars were shiny, thick, square-shaped, and the cell was over six feet tall.

Erin's belly twisted as he put her into the cage and bolted it shut behind her. He walked around the free-standing cell and came to a stop on the opposite side from the door.

"Come here," he ordered and she obeyed, feeling the plug and dildo with every step she made. "Put your arms through the bars." Again, she did as he told her and he had her handcuffed to the cage in two seconds flat.

She looked up at him, feeling enslaved, yet hot and excited all at once. "What are you going to do to me now, Officer Bennett?" she asked with a tremor in her voice.

He started to unfasten his uniform slacks. "On your knees."

Erin knelt, the links connecting the cuffs making a rattling sound as they hit the bar above her that went crosswise all around the cage. It caused her arms to be way up over her head. Before Dave finished unfastening his slacks, he reached down and pinched her nipples. "Beautiful," he murmured.

She arched into his touch and moaned at all the sensations bombarding her at once. He released her nipples and finished unfastening his slacks so that his cock and balls were freed. With both hands he reached through the gaps and brought her face lightly against the bars at the same time he pressed the head of his erection against her lips.

The sight of his cock made her squirm and she eagerly parted her lips and accepted him into her mouth.

Dave groaned as Erin began swirling her tongue over the head of his cock and along his length.

Shit. Just the feel of her mouth on his cock was bringing him close to a powerful climax. He hadn't wanted to come just yet, but she felt so good and looked so fucking hot, naked in just her heels and the harness. He knew she had to be close to orgasm just from the way she squirmed and the whimpering sounds she made as she went down on him.

He fisted his hands tighter in her hair, loving the silky strands against his fingers. His All-American girl was turning out to be an All-American sex toy that he intended to play with as long as he could. She looked up at him with her big blue eyes and he watched his cock slide in and out of her mouth.

This morning he never would have thought he'd have Erin Wilson in a cage at his mercy and with her excited at the prospect of everything he wanted to do to her. With her.

Damn, but her mouth was so hot, so wet. She sucked harder and a rumble rose in his throat. He pumped his hips a little faster and she made soft sighing noises that caused more sensation to build in his groin.

He actually felt a little lightheaded as his angel sucked his cock. She was more experienced now and the thought caused a stab of jealousy in his chest. Erin should have been his all these years. No one else's.

Dave ground his teeth and focused on the feel of her lips wrapped around his erection. The sight she made, handcuffed, on her knees and taking him deep was so erotic that his climax came roaring toward him like a freight train.

He shouted as it slammed into him and he had to release her hair and hold on to the cell's bars to keep from dropping to his knees. She continued sucking his cock, drawing out every bit of his semen until he couldn't take it anymore.

Dave's breathing was hard and heavy as he pulled his cock out of Erin's mouth. She looked up at him with those innocent blue eyes and licked her lips.

"Long time no see, Erin," came John's voice. Dave glanced over to see John casually leaning against the doorframe, an aroused look on his face.

Erin squealed and yanked her handcuffs against the bars of the cage, her whole body turning an enticing pink.

Dave tucked his cock and balls back in his uniform pants and zipped them up. He and his brothers had shared women before. Dave had spent a pretty hot night with Craig and Jessica before the two of them became engaged. Now Jessica was off-limits, and rightly so. Dave's other two brothers, John and Drew, were both still single and they all liked to share their toys.

But this was different. This was Erin.

"Feel like letting me join in tonight, bro?" John said as his eyes lingered on Erin's body.

She gasped and shot her gaze up to meet Dave's. He smiled at his brother, but it wasn't friendly. For the first time when one of his brothers wanted to join in, what he felt was dominance and possession.

"Not this one," Dave said. "She's mine."

Chapter Four

ꟗ

Erin wanted to slide through the floor, taking the cage and handcuffs with her.

Oh my God. John, Dave's brother, was looking over her naked body with definite desire in his green eyes, and a good-sized bulge outlined against his jeans. He was almost as gorgeous as Dave but with blond hair and a leaner, muscular build.

This, however, was not exactly the position she wanted to be in when seeing John again after fifteen years—

On her knees, her wrists handcuffed over her head so that her breasts were exposed, with a butt plug and dildo harnessed to her. Not to mention he'd probably just watched her giving Dave head.

And John had mentioned *sharing*?

"You sure you're not into letting me have a taste?" John said with a sexy grin that would probably make most women melt. "It's never been a problem in the past."

Her heart pounded and she shot her gaze to Dave who was wearing one hell of a scowl. "I told you. Erin's mine. Get the hell out of here."

John pushed away from the doorframe and his grin broadened. "Just stopped by to pick up my golf clubs. I'll grab them and head on home."

"You do that." Dave's scowl hadn't lessened.

"Good seeing you, Erin." John's gaze raked over her one last time, in a slow, sensual perusal. "*Real* good."

Dave growled and John chuckled. "Later, bro."

After the door closed, Erin banged her head on the bars of the cage, wincing from the pain. "I can't believe your brother just saw me like this."

Dave crouched, reached through the bars and stroked her hair. "Sorry, angel."

She tilted her head and looked up at him. "Have I served out my sentence?"

"Yeah." He dug the handcuff key out of his pocket. "Now for your fourth and fifth punishments."

She shook her head. "And here I thought I'd get time off for good behavior, Officer."

"Not a chance."

Dave took off her cuffs then let her out of the cage. He was so much taller than her that she felt petite when he gripped her elbow and led her to the chrome and leather bench she'd seen earlier. Her heart throbbed when they reached it.

"Knees there." He pointed to a pair of leather-covered pads on the incline of the contraption. "Your belly here, forearms on these pads and grip the handholds."

Erin shivered as she complied. It was like being doggy-style, only her belly and arms were higher up. Her knees were so far apart she was spread wide for Dave's viewing pleasure. He strapped her wrists down with the attached leather cuffs, also her ankles, and in addition a belt around her waist. She could barely wiggle, much less move.

He went back to the table and Erin's breathing ramped up a notch when she saw him retrieve a leather flogger—and what she knew was a policeman's baton.

"Count four—lying. One of the worst offenses." Dave set the flogger and baton on the nearby padded bench. "Are you ready for your punishment?"

Not. "Um, yes, Officer." She held her breath as he unfastened the harness resting around her hips, then she gasped when he pulled out the plug and the dildo. The sensations made her pussy and her ass clench with mini-spasms, and she felt empty with them gone.

And jeez, she needed to come.

He set the harness on the padded table then rubbed her ass cheeks with both of his hands, massaging them so that she relaxed a little even as her arousal grew. And grew.

When Dave bit her ass cheek, she cried out in surprise. He'd bitten her hard and the pain made her eyes water. He rubbed his palm over the mark and more moisture flooded her pussy. Damn, this was unbelievably hot. Another yelp escaped her when he bit her other ass cheek, but the pain quickly faded as he rubbed it with his palm. Instead of pain in the places he'd bitten her, she felt an arousing ache.

He slipped his hand into her slick folds. "Turned on?"

No fucking kidding. She moaned. "Yes, Officer."

He thrust a couple of fingers inside her and she felt the need to come increasing and increasing. "Just how turned on are you? What do you want me to do to you?"

"Fuck me." She moaned again and rocked as much as she could while he thrust his fingers deep enough that his knuckles hit her folds. "Please, Officer."

"Not until all of your punishments have been dealt." He pulled his fingers from her pussy and she groaned in disappointment.

Dave went to the bench where he retrieved the baton and the flogger. Just exactly what was he going to do with that baton? But worse, just how hard was he going to flog her?

Dave laid the flogger across her back, causing a shiver to race up her spine in anticipation. Then she felt the warm wood of the baton as he slipped it into her pussy.

Erin gasped and tugged against her restraints as he thrust the baton in and out of her core. He was taking it so deep she felt as if he was hitting her bellybutton. It hurt a little, but at the same time it was driving her crazy with need.

"How's that?" he asked as he continued to thrust the baton in and out of her pussy.

"Good," she managed to get out. "Really, really good, Officer."

"Let's see how you like this." He pulled the now very slick baton from her pussy and placed it to the tight ring of her anus.

She bit her lower lip and shut her eyes, her body tensing automatically.

"Relax." He stroked her ass cheeks and kissed one of them. "It'll go in easier if you're not so tense."

Erin tried, she really tried, but still her anus clenched. He pushed the baton in, causing her to cry out at the invasion. He slid it in just far enough that she felt it deep, but not too deep.

Just right.

Wow. *You've come a long way, baby.*

It was such a different feeling to have the baton in her ass instead of her pussy. The length, the width, the smoothness of it. Different…and *exciting*.

She eased into the steady thrusts of the baton and rocked back against it. Unbelievable. The ache in her core intensified and her whole body felt electric.

"Enjoying being butt-fucked by a policeman's baton?" Dave asked as he slid it in and out.

Erin nodded. "Yes, Officer."

He withdrew the baton and she sighed. Everything he was doing and had done to her body was ramping up her desire. More than anything she wanted *him* inside her.

Her mouth grew dry as he set the baton on the bench and returned to take the flogger off her back. "Don't cry out," he said as he rubbed her ass cheeks with his palm again. "Or we'll go for punishment number six."

"Yes, Officer." Her heart rate picked up again. She was going to have a heart attack as many times as her heart had been pounding the whole night. "Is this punishment number five?"

"No." He kissed one of her globes. "That'll be after your flogging."

What did he have planned for her final punishment?

The first lash fell on her ass and she almost screamed. It stung! But then Dave trailed the flogger over her back and ass and thighs in a sensual tease, and she felt the sting blend into a pleasant burn. Everything he was doing to her made her want to climax even more. She couldn't believe how much she enjoyed the pain and pleasure of it all.

Dave flogged her again, catching her off guard, and again she barely restrained a cry. He struck the other ass cheek, each thigh, and under her ass, close to her folds. Her eyes watered and her desire to reach orgasm had her entire body shaking.

Finally—or was it too soon?—he stopped and tossed the flogger aside. He got down on his knees and rubbed her ass, then trailed kisses over the hot flesh, easing the burn. Erin sighed as she relaxed into his mouth and tongue on her ass and her thighs, but tensed when he neared her pussy. She wanted his mouth on her so badly she was quavering from the desire.

"I haven't tasted you in so long," he murmured, and she silently agreed that it had been way too long.

Butterflies danced in her belly as he positioned her to be even more spread out for him and moved himself so that he had his mouth close to her pussy. She could feel his warm breath on her folds and she shivered in anticipation.

"Remember," he said. "Don't come without permission."

The first flick of his tongue would have sent her straight off the bench if she hadn't been restrained. She cried out and squirmed as he laved her folds and dipped his tongue into her core. She didn't know if she could take much more without climaxing—she'd been on the edge all night and it had been a fight to keep from losing it.

When he sucked her clit, she thought she was a goner. She cried out and clenched her belly and tried to still her trembling thighs. Dave chuckled and moved away from her and she whimpered.

"Now for punishment number five," he said as he came around to where her head was resting on the leather padding.

"I don't know how much more I can take, Officer." Erin was breathing hard and her voice quavered. "I'm so close to coming."

"But you're not going to." His voice was firm, a definite command.

"Of course not, Officer," she said through gritted teeth. God, it was so damn hard to hold back!

He unfastened her restraints at her wrists, ankles and her belly. When he helped her to her feet, she was trembling. All the sensations were almost too much. Everything he'd done to her made her nerves and her entire body feel raw. She needed him so dam much.

"Time for number five." Dave grasped her around the waist, and before she knew what he was doing, he flung her over his shoulder.

Erin squealed in surprise. Her hair fell over her face, all the blood rushed to her head, making her lightheaded. Her bottom was right up in the air, her pussy pressed against his shoulder. He swatted her on the ass and she squealed again.

"Dave!" she cried out. "Er, Officer. What are you doing?"

"You'd just better be on your best behavior," he said and swatted her bottom. She managed not to cry out, but her butt cheeks smarted from the flogging and now the swats.

She had a good view of his tight ass as he started walking toward the dungeon doors and she took advantage of her position and grasped both cheeks in her hands and squeezed through the material.

"Hey." He rubbed her stinging flesh with his hands. "No touching."

She giggled and he gave a laugh and she imagined him shaking his head.

The living room passed by in a blur as he walked through it to a hallway on the other side of the house. When he reached the bedroom, her tummy did a little twist. She laughed when he slipped her off his shoulder and let her drop to the bed so that she bounced on the mattress.

He stood and looked at her for a long moment, a serious expression on his face, and she sobered.

His eyes were dark and intense. "Undress me."

With pleasure.

"Yes, Officer." Erin held back a smile as she got up from the bed and approached him. She reached up to his shoulders and ran her palms over his uniform shirt to the top button. Slowly she unbuttoned his shirt, brushing her knuckles against his naked flesh as she revealed it, inch by inch. When she reached the waistband of his uniform slacks, he sucked in his breath as she purposely stroked his taut abs.

She pulled his shirt from where it had been tucked into his slacks. "Teasing me just got you another punishment," he murmured as she pushed the shirt off his broad shoulders. He slid it the rest of the way off and tossed it aside.

"Sorry, Officer," she said, but knew she didn't sound sorry at all. She paused to run her hands over his hard chest from his shoulders to the planes of his abdomen. "You must work out a lot."

"You're taking too long," he said in a warning tone and she tried not to smile.

"We need to get your boots and socks off, Officer." She pushed him toward the bed and he sat with a grunt.

Dave watched as she crouched and took one of his boots in her hands, unlaced it and tugged it off then flung it to the side. Next went his sock, followed by his other boot and sock.

When he was left only wearing his slacks, he stood. Erin unbuttoned them, purposefully brushing her knuckles over his cock and felt his erection twitch. She unzipped his pants and his large cock and balls slipped out, and she couldn't resist running her hand over its length, feeling its hardness beneath the soft skin covering his erection.

In a fast movement, he dropped his pants, kicked them off and had her in his arms. He kissed her hard before leading her to the bed. This time he sat, and to her surprise he pulled her down and laid her across his lap, her ass in the air, her belly pressed against this erection. She gave a little cry as he draped her over his thighs and rubbed her ass. Once again her hair was around her face and blood rushed to her head.

"This is your final punishment," he said in a deep voice, thick with lust. "This one is for leaving me, angel."

The huskiness and the meaning behind his words made her breath catch.

But then she gasped and cried out when he slipped the fingers of one hand into her pussy and stroked her clit. Her whole body trembled and her mind spun with the need to climax. When his other hand landed hard on her ass, she almost lost it.

He was spanking her!

Dave continued to swat her ass with his palm while he fingered her pussy. In between each swat he leaned over and kissed the place he had spanked her.

Erin thought she was going to die if she didn't come. He thrust his fingers inside her, kissed and spanked her ass. The more he did it, the more she needed to climax. She whimpered and squirmed on his lap.

"I'm so close to coming, Officer." Her tone was breathless. "Please let me come!"

"Bad girls have to earn their orgasms." He swatted her again. "You've almost earned yours."

She grew lightheaded from the blood rushing to her head from hanging over the side of his thigh, not to mention the swats and the need to climax.

When he finally stopped and raised her up so that she was sitting on his lap sideways, her body pressed against his naked chest. The depth of his desire for her was in his eyes, and she was sure were in her own as well.

"You've served your time." He brushed his lips over hers. "Now for your reward for good behavior."

Chapter Five

ꝏ

Erin held her breath as Dave carefully moved her so that she was settled on his bed sheet, his pillow beneath her head. The other covers were already tossed aside, his bed unmade. The sheets had his masculine scent that filled her, made her want him more.

She released the air in her lungs as he eased between her thighs, his eyes focused intently on hers. She spread her thighs wide, taking him fully against her so that his cock was pressed to her belly and he was real and solid in her arms. He braced one hand on the bed and used his other to guide his cock into her channel.

Inch by heavenly inch he slipped inside her. So different than the fast and hard fucking he'd given her on the side of the road. That had been incredible, but this felt…special.

When Dave's cock was fully inside her, Erin gave a soft moan and wrapped her legs around his hips to take him even deeper. His ass flexed beneath her legs as he started to move in and out.

His lovemaking was slow and deliberate, his eyes never wavering from hers. She brushed her palms along his powerful back to his waist and up again as he pushed in then pulled out.

When he kissed her, it was soft and sweet. He never stopped the rhythm of his strokes as he tasted and explored her mouth with his tongue and nipped at her lower lip. The kiss was so sensuous it made her already dizzy mind spin even more.

All the sensations she'd experienced tonight heightened the sensitivity in her body and she felt it in every fiber of her being. When Dave raised his head, she couldn't take her gaze from his. All night it had been like that. As if they couldn't get enough of looking at one another.

Every part of her started to tremble and she fought back the need to come. "Please, Officer, I need to climax."

"Dave." He brushed his lips over hers. "Right now we're Dave and Erin."

His words sent a burst of warmth inside her that did nothing but raise her level of need higher.

"Please, Dave." Her skin tingled from head to toe as she came closer and closer. "I need to, so badly."

"You can come," he said softly. "Come now."

Erin let loose with a cry that probably shook the walls. A hundred explosions seemed to go off in her body at once. She bucked against him and her entire being shook. Lights even flashed behind her eyelids, and the dizziness never stopped. She felt like she was in a whirlpool—or more like a hurricane with thunder and lightning.

Her climax seemed to go on forever and she barely heard Dave's murmur, "That's it, my beautiful angel."

He started to thrust harder and faster and spasms continued to rock her body. Perspiration had broken out all over her skin, and she saw beads of sweat on his forehead as his jaw clenched and his strokes increased.

After several thrusts, Dave's entire body tensed and he shouted as he came inside her. His cock pulsed, causing more contractions in her channel that clenched down on him. He pressed his groin tight against hers and he actually trembled between her thighs.

With a loud groan, he lowered himself so that most of his weight was on her, pinning her to the bed. It didn't hurt her at all. She enjoyed the solid feel of him against her, reveled in it even. He felt so comfortable, so real…like he belonged right where he was. And that she belonged right where she was, too.

His chest rose and fell against hers and she almost laughed as she thought about her "heaving breasts" like what she'd read in old romance novels. They were heaving all right.

He gave one last shudder, rolled onto his side and drew her into his arms. He held her tight, her head under his chin. His cock was still inside her, still making her feel full and setting off little spasms in her core. Having her face pressed up against his chest slowed the dizziness in her mind until she felt the world gradually slow and her breathing calmed.

For a long time they just cuddled, like they had once upon a time. Right now it felt like the years had fled by as if they'd never been separated. And at this moment she wondered how she could have let this go—let *him* go. Sure, they'd had their arguments when they were in high school, but in a healthy relationship that was normal.

She'd just been so young, and so scared.

Erin had always believed that things were meant to happen for a reason. Maybe they weren't meant to be together until now.

Whoa. She had to stop that train of thinking. This was one night, and could very well be just a good fuck to him.

Their gazes met, and he pulled her closer to him so that his naked body was flush to her sensitized skin.

"You can stay right here with me," he murmured into her hair, "or you're free to go."

She tipped her head up, looking at him in surprise. "Free to go?"

He brushed his lips over hers then kissed her softly. "Only if you want to."

Dave's words echoed in Erin's head as their eyes met and held. Right now, even after one night, she felt so firmly his that it was difficult to imagine the world around them.

She took a deep breath and smiled. "We'll see," she said.

A serious look was on his expression and he pushed a lock of her blonde hair over her shoulder. "It doesn't seem like so much time has passed."

"No, it doesn't." An ache deep inside her rose up. Again she wondered—had she thrown away something real, honest and true? Something that couldn't be replaced?

So many emotions whirled through her as she met his chocolate brown eyes. And so many memories.

The first time they'd made love—beneath the Christmas tree, while his parents were at a holiday party, and Dave's brothers had been out with some friends. It had been so magical, so special. The pain of that first slow entry had faded into the most incredible pleasure as they both lost their virginity. They fumbled, they laughed, they explored, but the love they had made had been true.

Tears wanted to spill from Erin's eyes and she buried her face against his chest. She squeezed her eyes shut for a moment, letting the loss weigh her shoulders down.

Dave rubbed her back in slow circles and his voice was low and soft. "We can make up for lost time and get to know one another again. If you want to."

She opened her eyes and tilted her face to look at him again and smiled. "I'd like that."

Dave trailed his fingers down her spine to her buttocks and up again, causing her to shiver. "I'd like to ask you out on a date."

Erin laughed. "You don't think we're already beyond that point?"

The corners of his mouth tipped up in a grin and he brushed his knuckles over her cheek. "This doesn't mean our dates are going to be anything like high school." He leaned down and kissed her before drawing back. "Although you have to admit, some of our dates were pretty damn hot."

"Two horny teenagers." Erin returned his grin. "Now two horny adults."

He brushed his knuckles across her cheek again and his expression softened. "I'm serious. Dinner and a movie tomorrow night?"

The sweetness of his proposal made her melt. "You're on."

* * * * *

Erin couldn't believe how nervous she was as she prepared for Dave to pick her up for their "date". Lots of those crazy butterflies flew rampant in her belly as she slipped into a little black sleeveless dress with a scoop neckline, the hem of the dress hitting her mid-thigh. She usually didn't wear heels over two inches, but she'd gone shopping and bought three-inch heels, the dress and a sleek little black purse.

She'd twisted her hair up into an elegant style and clipped it, and applied makeup as well as wearing her favorite jewelry—which included a gold interlocking heart necklace Dave had given to her in high school. A lump formed in her throat as she clasped it around her neck. It had been nestled in her jewelry box all of these years. She hadn't been able to let it go, just like she'd never been able to let the memory of Dave slip away.

After a night in each other's arms, Dave took Erin to her to her car and gave her a soft kiss before she left for her condo. She hadn't wanted to leave him, but she was excited at the prospect of actually going on a date with him. It made her feel giddy and girly, and she couldn't wait.

When the doorbell to her condo finally chimed, Erin made it to the front door in record time. When she opened the door, she wanted to fling herself into his arms, but restrained herself.

He looked so damn hot in a pair of black dress pants and a white shirt that complemented his muscular figure without being tight, and it tapered down to his waist. His brown hair was so sexy she wanted to run her fingers through it and mess it all up. She'd save that for later.

And he was even holding a bouquet of red roses with baby's breath and a bottle of champagne.

Dave looked her over from head to toe and she noticed a definite bulge in his slacks. "I don't know if we're going to make it out of your place, as gorgeous as you are," he said before brushing his lips over hers.

She smiled and used her finger to wipe away the light smudge of lipstick at the corner of his mouth from kissing her. "You look pretty great yourself, Officer," she said as she let him in.

When the door closed behind him, he caught her in his arms, crushing the bouquet between them and kissed her hard. Erin fell into the magic of his kiss, giving soft moans of pleasure as his tongue explored her mouth and she explored his. It was such a sensual kiss that it made her heady. This time he drew away and she managed a smile when she wanted to swoon like a heroine in one of those romance novels. She grabbed a tissue and dabbed his lips with it. He was wearing much more of her lipstick this time—he had to have kissed it all off her.

She crumpled the tissue in her hand as he brought his fingers to the heart pendant at her throat. His voice sounded hoarse as he lightly touched the hearts. "You still have it."

"Of course I do." She brought her hand to his. "I've never forgotten the night you gave it to me."

"Your seventeenth birthday." His eyes met hers. "We made love in my bed."

"And almost got caught." She laughed. "Your parents came home a little earlier than we expected."

Dave drew his hand away from the pendant. "Those were good times."

Erin whispered, "Special times."

He placed the bouquet into her arms and held up the champagne bottle. "Where's your fridge?"

She led him to her little kitchenette that had a homey feel to it with a spring flower décor and a breakfast nook in a bay window. After she tossed the tissue and put the champagne in the fridge, she found a vase for the roses and put them in the middle of her table.

"They're so beautiful." She touched one of the velvety buds with her fingertip then looked up at him. "Thank you."

"I'm going to take you right on the table if you don't stop looking at me like that," Dave said with a dark look in his eyes.

For a moment Erin considered it, but then shook her head and smiled. "That would make us late for our dinner reservations."

He drew her to him. "Then we'll just save it for dessert."

Those crazy feelings stirred in her belly again as he took her by the hand, his fingers large and warm in hers. She grabbed her purse and a wrap to keep the chill off her shoulders on the way out before locking the door behind them. He'd parked his truck in front of her condo's walkway, and she got a good look at it for the first time—she vaguely remembered seeing it when they were in the garage, but she'd been rather, er, preoccupied.

It was a king cab custom truck with a lift and was metallic tan and brown. Because it was so high, he had to help her into the passenger side, and he took advantage of it by placing his palm on her bottom to help her into the seat. Unfortunately, her bottom still ached from last night's spankings and she winced. She looked at him and he winked before closing her door, going to the driver's side and climbing in.

Ignoring the stinging pain in her ass, Erin used the lighted mirror to put a fresh coat of lipstick on. "I'm just going to kiss it off again," he said as he glanced from the road to her.

She gave him a teasing smile. "The better the excuse to wear it, then."

The restaurant Dave had chosen was elegant with a romantic atmosphere. They were seated in a secluded corner, his chair close to hers, and he ordered a bottle of chardonnay. She breathed deeply of his spicy, masculine scent that had away of seeping inside her and making her feel so good.

"I thought you were strictly beer and pretzels," Erin teased. "I don't seem to remember fine wines and romantic restaurants."

He glanced up from his menu. "I don't remember having any money back then. My job as a ranch gofer didn't pay a whole hell of a lot."

She smiled and returned her gaze to her menu. "Hey, you never heard me complain. Pizza and sodas were perfectly fine with me."

Their gazes met as she raised her eyes again. "Yeah," he said. "Perfectly fine."

Erin shivered from the look he gave her and she had to fight to focus on her menu. So many memories bombarded her, from dating in high school to the erotic things they'd done last night.

She wondered exactly what he had planned for tonight, sore ass and all. She couldn't wait.

After they ordered their appetizer, Dave held out his hand. "I got you something I want you to use tonight."

"Use?" Erin raised an eyebrow and took the small black cylindrical object in her palm. "What is this?"

It started to vibrate in her hand and she jumped. The vibrations tickled her palm before they stopped. Her eyes met his and he held up what looked like a remote control. "Go to the bathroom. You're going to enjoy this night more than you expected."

Her pulse skipped and heat rushed over her. "I'll be right back."

It didn't take long to insert the remote-controlled vibrator in her core, and she returned to her seat. She expected it to start vibrating immediately but Dave just looked at her with a glint in his eye.

"Half the fun is in the anticipation." He took a drink of his wine before setting it down. "You'll never know when I'll use this little remote."

She squirmed. She felt the vibrator inside her and she was already hot and wet and ready for the fun to begin.

After a few moments, the waiter approached them. Just as he started to take her order, Erin gave a little cry of surprise and jumped in her seat as vibrations went off inside her—much more intense than when she'd held it in her palm.

Heat rushed to her cheeks as she looked up at the waiter, embarrassment flooding through her at having yelped in front of him. God, she hoped he couldn't tell what was going on. The waiter just looked at her with a questioning expression.

"Um…" She tried to get her voice and her senses under control as the vibrations continued. "I'll—I'll take the petite filet, the baby potatoes, with broccoli for the vegetable. And make the side salad a Caesar."

Dave ordered the cowboy steak along with his choice of sides. When the waiter walked away, the vibrations stopped.

"Are you out of your mind?" Erin placed her palms on the table. "That waiter probably knew exactly what you were doing to me."

With a grin, Dave leaned close. "Are you going to need another spanking for misbehaving?"

She blinked then tried to keep a smile from her lips. "What do you consider misbehavior?"

She quivered as he placed a hand on her thigh and slowly moved it up to the hem of her dress. "Climaxing without my permission. Questioning anything I do or tell you to do."

Erin's panties were already damp from the vibrator, but grew even wetter from the sensuality in his voice, along with his commanding tone. "Yes, Officer," she whispered, and he smiled.

She was on edge all night. The next time he used the remote was when she took a drink of her chardonnay, and she almost choked as she swallowed. That one earned him a glare, but he just acted like nothing had happened.

He left it turned on the entire time they ate dessert, and she was certain she was going to climax right in the restaurant, and she wasn't going to be able to hold back the cry building in her throat. She didn't know whether to be relieved or disappointed when he stopped the vibrations.

The dinner had been sexually nerve-racking, yet at the same time, one of the nicest evenings she had ever enjoyed. The chemistry between her and Dave was so strong that Erin wanted to just take him home and be with him all night long.

When he wasn't making her squirm from the vibrator, they talked about the past and the present and even what they were each working toward in the future.

He was sorry to hear that her father had passed away—Dave and her father had always gotten along well, especially when it came to watching sports. Erin's mother was ill and Erin did everything she could for her. She told Dave about her life on the East Coast and her marketing career. She now worked for a marketing firm in the downtown area of Tucson—she'd returned to help take care of her mother.

Dave talked about his parents, who had moved to Florida for their retirement. His brother Craig was a college English professor at the university and was engaged to one of his former students. Drew was a personal trainer, and John was the CEO of his own corporation in Tucson.

At the mention of John, a flush stole over Erin. She still couldn't believe John had watched her giving head to Dave while she was handcuffed in a cage with the harness holding in the butt plug and the dildo. She wasn't sure she'd be able to look him in the eye again.

When Dave noticed how embarrassed she looked when he brought up John's name, he took her hands in his and kissed her fingers. "Angel, that will never happen again. You belong to me."

Chapter Six

ꙮ

Dave watched the flicker of wariness mixed with desire in Erin's gaze. He didn't care if she felt a little skittish about his claim on her. This time he wasn't going to let her get away.

While the waiter took care of their bill, Dave put his hand on Erin's bare thigh beneath the table. He raised the hem of her dress higher, until it barely covered her mound.

"Dave, stop," she hissed and put her hand on his, trying to keep him from going any further.

"Remember what I told you." He pushed his hand a little farther until his fingers touched the leg band of her underwear. Bikini underwear, if he wasn't mistaken. "Questioning anything I do will get you a punishment."

Even in the dim lighting he could see her cheeks turn pink and he held back a grin as he rubbed the damp cloth between her thighs and turned the remote on. Erin startled again, jerking against his hand. She bit her lower lip, as if trying to hold back a complaint or a cry, he wasn't sure which.

The waiter returned and Erin looked positively mortified as he let the vibrator continue and he stroked the panties over her folds. Dave didn't think the waiter could see, and he enjoyed seeing Erin squirm.

When they were ready to go, he turned off the vibrator and removed his hand, and she practically slumped in her seat. "You are so naughty," she managed to get out in a breathless voice.

"You haven't seen anything yet," he said and she gave him a sensual look that told him she was ready for anything he had in store for her.

The movie he took her to was an action-adventure. Neither one of them had ever enjoyed watching chick-flicks or anything sappy. They were action junkies and Erin was definitely pleased with his choice.

"I feel like a teenager again," she said as she took a delicate bite from the bag of popcorn he handed her. "I haven't done dinner and a movie in forever."

"We should try the drive-in." He walked close to her as they carried their popcorn, sodas, and red licorice. Her surprised gaze met his. "Lots of old memories there," he said.

"It's still open?"

"You bet. Maybe we'll make that our next date and bring back more old memories."

Erin's cheeks turned pink again. He took her to the very top row of the theater, in corner seats, just like they had when they were teenagers. Damn, she looked so hot tonight in her sexy, short little black dress and heels. Her scent of roses and wildflowers drove him crazy, and he had to fight to keep from having a constant hard-on.

The entire time they watched the movie, he had his arm draped around her shoulders and she squirmed as he let the vibrator run.

"Remember," he murmured in her ear. "No climaxing without my permission."

"Yes, Officer," she said through gritted teeth and he chuckled.

When the movie was finally over, Dave took her hand and they left the theater into the chilly night and he helped her put her wrap around her shoulders.

His cock was already aching when they arrived at Erin's condo. He wanted to be inside her more than life itself, but he intended to make her wait.

Dave used her key to let them in and shut the door and locked it. Before she could move away from him, he caught her to him and kissed her with all the passion that had been building between them all night. Her lips were soft, her mouth so pliable beneath his.

She gave sweet, soft whimpers and moans and he crushed her to him, pressing his powerful erection against her belly. She slipped her arms around his neck and teased the short hair at his nape. He groaned and kissed her harder before reaching up and pulling the clip out of her hair. The clip he tossed aside and he slid his fingers through her loose hair.

When he drew away, he was almost dizzy with need for her and wanted to strip her naked right in her foyer. "Champagne," he said, his voice rough with desire. "To celebrate."

Erin nodded even though she didn't move for a moment. Her blue eyes were dark, her moist lips parted and her blonde hair in a wild tumble around her shoulders. God, how he wanted to pin her against the wall and take her hard and fast.

As she walked toward the kitchen, he watched her sweet little ass sway, her toned legs flexing beneath the hem of her short dress as she walked in her high heels. The images of the two of them naked in her bed grew more intense and he ground his teeth. To distract himself—and her—he flipped on the remote just as she opened the fridge.

With a little cry, she stepped back, but held on to the handle of the refrigerator to steady herself. She shot him a look of pure sensuality as he let the vibrator continue and she reached into the fridge and withdrew the bottle of champagne.

He took the bottle from her while she searched her cabinets and brought out a pair of champagne glasses. Images went through his mind, of her in his kitchen, her in his bed, always.

Dave shook his head. Twenty-four hours and already he was planning on her moving in with him.

The pop of the cork was loud and Erin laughed as foam spilled over the sides of the bottle. He filled each glass and set the bottle down before they each took one of the champagne glasses.

For a long moment they looked at one another, their glasses ready to make a toast. "To finally finding one another again," Erin said softly, her words echoing his feelings.

"To us," he said before touching his glass to hers and taking a long swallow.

She laughed as he drained the glass. "You're supposed to savor it."

He took her glass from her and set both on the countertop before taking her into his arms. "I intend to savor you." He kissed her again, intending to do just that. Her breath was warm against his mouth as he murmured, "Show me where your bedroom is."

She carried the champagne glasses while he grabbed the champagne and one of the red roses from the vase on her table. He followed her up the stairs, enjoying the view as he watched her shapely ass and long legs. When they reached the landing, he followed her down a short hall to a bedroom that was uniquely Erin. It was filled with mahogany antique furniture from the vanity to the dressers, to a love seat and a couple of chairs. Impressionist oil paintings on the walls, crystal bottles of all sorts, sizes and shapes on her vanity dresser, pictures of family and other people scattered on every available surface and vases of colorful flowers on her bureau. And to his extreme pleasure, she had a four-poster bed.

Perfect.

By the time they reached her bed, Erin was a bundle of raw nerves. They were in her territory now, but he still had control.

Dave set the champagne bottle and the red rose onto the nightstand beside the bed. He took his empty glass from her, topped off her half-full champagne glass and refilled his own.

Once he set the champagne bottle down, he raised his glass again.

"To making new memories," he said in a rough voice, and Erin clinked her glass against his.

This time she downed the champagne as she watched him over the rim of her glass. Their eyes held until they both drained their glasses.

He took hers and set them both aside. "Do you have any scarves?"

Erin raised her eyebrows. She had a feeling she knew exactly what he wanted to use those scarves for, and the idea made her body go crazy.

From a lower drawer in her vanity she pulled out a bundle of scarves of all sizes, shapes, textures and colors, and handed them to Dave. He tossed them on the bed and approached her.

"Turn around," he said, even as he took her by the shoulders and moved her so that her back was to him. She shivered at the feel of his fingers brushing her spine as he lowered the zipper to where it ended at the top of her buttocks.

With gentle hands, he pushed the material from her shoulders and let the dress slide to the floor, leaving her in only her heels, the new lace panties and the bra she had purchased for tonight. She stepped out of the dress and was pleased when Dave picked it up and carefully laid it on one of the antique chairs in her room.

The champagne was starting to take effect and she felt a little woozy as he returned to her. He rubbed her shoulders and slowly looked her over from head to toe. "You are so beautiful."

She reached for him and he didn't stop her as she unbuttoned his shirt. The champagne caused her to fumble a bit but she made it all the way to his waist. He pulled the shirt out of his slacks and shrugged out of it before he tossed the shirt aside. Erin wanted to run her palms over the muscles of his chest, abdomen and his biceps. She wanted to explore every bit of him.

But he was busy shucking off his shoes, peeling off his socks and dropping his slacks as if he couldn't wait any longer. When he was naked she reached for him and ran her fingers over his erection that seemed impossibly bigger than it had last night.

Erin gasped when he slipped his fingers into her bikini underwear and into her folds. He reached her core, withdrew the vibrator that was slick with her juices and set it on the nightstand.

She gripped his cock tighter, hoping he would slide inside her, where his fingers and the vibrator had been. But he gave a low rumble, scooped her up and carried her the short distance to her antique four-poster bed. She giggled from the quick movement and from the effect the champagne was having on her.

Dave settled her on the middle of the bed and lightly kissed her before he reached for one of her satin scarves. Shivers racked her body as he brushed his lips over the inside of her wrist before tying it securely to the bedpost. He took another scarf and walked to the other side of the bed, kissed the inside of her wrist and then bound that arm. She couldn't get enough of watching his naked body as he tied her up. Every muscle flexed with his movements and his cock arched against his belly, telling her how much he wanted her.

Erin was so intent on watching him that she barely noticed him kissing the inside of each ankle and fastening the ankle to the bedpost. He was so purely male, so fluid in his movements that she couldn't get enough of looking at him.

When he finished and she was spread-eagled on the bed, he sat on the edge of the mattress with the rose in one hand. He touched her nose with the bud then slowly trailed it over her lip, her chin and down to the hollow of her throat. His sensuous attention caused a part of her to fall back in love with him a little more.

She knew she was tumbling fast toward that point, and she wondered if he had forgiven her and cared about her again the same way she was growing to care for him.

To love him again.

Dave laid the rose on her belly then pulled her delicate lace bra down and under her breasts so that they jutted up, her nipples aching for his mouth.

"You're more beautiful than ever," he murmured as he leaned forward, then flicked his tongue over one of her nipples.

Erin moaned and arched her back, thrusting her breasts in his face. He gave a soft laugh then licked the other nipple. Instead of sucking them, he raised his head and brushed the rose over each of the damp peaks, which caused her to whimper from the exquisite sensations.

He continued his slow, sensual movements with the rose, dragging it down her belly to the inside of each of her thighs. He lightly brushed the bud over the cloth covering her pussy and she gasped and pulled against her satin restraints. "Dave, *please*."

"What do you want, angel?" He trailed the rose down over one of her thighs to her knee. "Tell me."

"I want your mouth on my pussy." Erin had no problem telling him exactly what she desired. "Then I want your cock inside of me."

"Mmmmm..." He slid the rose down to the inside of her ankle and it tickled her, causing her to struggle against her restraints again. "Can't always have what you want," he said and she groaned.

He continued his slow, sensual torture, sliding the rose down the bottom of one foot, tickling her, then went to the other foot and did the same. Erin's eyes watered from being unable to move as he teased every nerve ending until her whole body felt alive.

Dave took the rose and ran it up the inside of her other leg, and she thought she was going to die. The softness of the petals stroking her skin made her ache, made her want to come with a fierceness she had to tamp down.

Again he swept the rose over the damp cloth covering her pussy, and again she jerked against her restraints. He brought his nose to the panties and audibly inhaled. "Damn, you smell good," he said just as he gripped the edge of her panties and pulled the material aside.

Erin would have come off the bed from the first swipe of Dave's tongue if she weren't restrained. Her cry echoed in the room and she arched her hips up, begging for more. He made a low, rumbly sound as he inserted his tongue in her channel then laved her folds.

"Let me come, let me come, let me come," she begged, tears of need and frustration leaking down the corners of her eyes.

Instead of answering her, he nipped at her clit and she cried out again. Tight coils of sensation built in her body, intensifying what she'd felt all night with the vibrator inside her. Her body flushed with heat as he inserted his fingers into her channel while continuing to lave her clit.

The heat in her body caused perspiration to cover her body in a light sheen, and she felt as if she were on fire. She tossed her head from side to side. "Daaaaaaaave! Please!"

He rose up, an intense look on his handsome features as his cock nudged her channel. He braced his hands on the bed, to either side of her chest.

Yes, yes, yes, yes, yes, yes!

With a feral look in his eyes, Dave slammed his cock home.

Erin shrieked and struggled against the hold the scarves had on her wrists and ankles. Everything felt so right with him inside her. Like they were two halves that finally made a whole again.

He thrust in and out in slow, measured strokes, and she bit her lip to keep from crying out and begging him again to let her climax.

His lips met hers in a powerfully dominating kiss.

A kiss of ownership.

The feel of him inside her, his body moving against hers, his masculine, spicy scent—all of it combined to intoxicate her far beyond the effects of the champagne.

She looked into his eyes and his expression was fierce, intense. "You belong to me again, angel. Say it."

"I'm yours and you damn well are mine, Dave Bennett," she said with no hesitation.

He smiled, a spark in his eyes and he began to thrust harder and faster. So hard the headboard banged against the wall and she felt him deep, so deep. She wanted to hold him, to wrap her legs around him. But the sensation of being tied down added to the growing need to climax.

Her need must have been her eyes because he leaned close and whispered in her ear, "Come, angel."

Those two soft words set off a chain reaction that had her crying and screaming. The fire that had been raging in her body was so hot she thought the scarves might just burn off her ankles and her wrists.

Spasm after spasm went off in her core as Dave continued to drive in and out of her. Then he growled out his climax as his body shook between her thighs and his cock pulsed in her core. After a few more strokes, he pressed his hips tight to hers and took her mouth in another claiming kiss.

She was breathing hard as he eased off her and untied each of the scarves in a matter of moments. As soon as she was free, he wrapped her in his embrace, her head under his chin, his thigh pinning her hips down, and her cheek pressed to his chest. They smelled of sweat and sex and she'd never felt so loved, so protected…not since…

"I meant what I said." He held her tighter as he spoke. "This time I'm not letting you go."

Chapter Seven

ꝏ

Christmas lights twinkled and Erin watched them, mesmerized by their brilliance. She was curled up beside the tree, her legs tucked up under her. She was wearing a sexy little red dress Dave had picked out for her, along with a pair of strappy high heels. Dave was in the kitchen, preparing each of them a mug of hot chocolate. He looked great tonight in black jeans and a red shirt that matched the color of her dress.

It was Christmas Eve and they had spent the day with Dave's brothers—John, Drew, and Craig—as well as Jessica, Craig's very young fiancée, along with their parents who'd flown in from Florida. Erin's mother had also joined the group, but left early since she wasn't feeling well. Her brother and his wife Tammy had spent the holidays with Tammy's family.

Erin couldn't believe how fast the past couple of months had flown by. She and Dave had dated like they had when they were teenagers, and they'd had so much fun together. They'd gone to drive-in movies and had sex in the backseat of the king club cab of his truck, went to pizza houses and ice cream parlors, had dinners at fine restaurants, spent time with his cop friends watching games, drinking beer and eating munchies, and got together with some of her coworkers as well.

She sighed and her skin tingled as she thought about all the fun they'd had in Dave's bondage room. He could take her into custody *any* time. So long as they made sure the door to the bondage room was locked.

It had been no problem whatsoever in getting over what's-his-name. And she considered the friendship she'd *thought* she'd had with Wendy not a friendship at all. Friends don't fuck friends' boyfriends.

But if it hadn't been for them, she never would have been pulled over by Dave…

Erin shifted on the floor as she looked up at the sparkling tree in Dave's family room. Beneath the tree were two more presents they hadn't unwrapped. One was from her to Dave, and the other from Dave to her. She wondered what was in the box he'd wrapped in red foil with a metallic green bow. It was about the size of a shoebox, and she just had no clue what was in it.

The living room lights dimmed and the Christmas lights sparkled even brighter. She heard footsteps crossing the carpet and she looked up to see Dave with two cups topped with a mound of whipped cream. He looked so handsome that she wanted to put whipped cream on him instead and eat him all up.

He smiled as he handed her a mug. She took a sip of the cocoa that was just the right temperature so that she didn't burn her tongue. She caught the taste of something strong and glanced up at Dave.

"Okay, what'd you put into this?"

Dave laughed. "You have a whipped cream mustache," he said just before he leaned forward, kissed her and darted his tongue out over her upper lip.

"Mmmmm…" Erin sighed as he drew away. "I think I'll make sure I have whipped cream on my face all the time."

Another kiss was her reward before they went back to drinking their hot chocolate laced with brandy.

When they were finished, Dave took their mugs and set them on an end table near the leather L-shaped couch. He settled on the floor next to her and took the two presents from beneath the Christmas tree.

"I want you to open your present last." His expression was serious, but there was a spark in his eyes.

"What did you get me?" she said with a grin. "My own flogger?"

"How did you guess?" He met her lips again in a soft kiss before moving back and looking at her with his dark, intense gaze.

Erin handed him his gift. "I hope you like it."

"You could give me a pair of socks and I would love it." He pulled off the gold bow and tore off the silver wrapping paper. For a long moment he was quiet as he looked at the framed photograph she had given him.

"Thank you, angel." His voice sounded thick when he wrapped his arm around her shoulders and squeezed her close to him.

It was a photograph of the two of them together—him in his football jersey, and Erin in her team spirit shirt. They looked so young, so in love as they stared up into one another's eyes.

How could she have let that go?

Dave kissed her, a soft loving kiss that told her how much he appreciated her gift.

When it was her turn to open the present from Dave, her hands shook. She didn't bother taking it off slowly, she ripped off the paper with enthusiasm.

It was a shoebox beneath the wrapping paper—hers, in fact. She looked up at him and cocked her eyebrow.

"Open it," he said, gesturing to the box.

Erin lifted the lid—to find a pair of airline tickets nestled on top of a bed of tissue paper. Her hands shook even more as she opened one of them. "Paris?" She grinned at Dave, feeling like she was going to bubble over with excitement. "We're going to Paris?"

"Look in the box, under the tickets," he said with a smile.

For some crazy reason her heart started to pound even harder than when she'd discovered the tickets to Paris. She moved them aside, dug through the tissue—and found a small red velvet jeweler's box.

A lump crowded her throat and she fumbled as she opened the box to discover a gorgeous marquise-cut solitaire. Erin held her hand to her mouth and tears started to roll down her cheeks. She was trembling so hard she almost dropped the box.

He cupped her face in his hands, turning her head to face him. "Marry me, Erin Wilson."

Erin found it hard to speak. She felt overwhelmed, dizzy, like this was happening to someone else. For a long moment she just stared into his eyes, realizing all her hopes, dreams, and happiness, lay with this man.

"Yes," she whispered. "God, yes."

Dave crushed her to him, hugging her so tight she could barely breathe. "It's about damn time," he said and she laughed and brushed away a tear.

Her fingers continued to tremble as he slipped the marquise diamond on her ring finger. It sparkled, catching the Christmas lights as they winked in and out.

"Honeymoon in Paris?" She smiled up at him. "When's the wedding?"

"I love you, angel." He squeezed her hands in his. "I think we've waited long enough. I booked the trip for the first two weeks of January. I hope you don't mind that I worked it out with your boss, and arranged for an intimate wedding the day before we leave."

"I love you so much." Erin wrapped her arms around Dave's neck. "I couldn't have asked for a better Christmas present than you."

He took her down to the carpet so that they were nearly lying beneath the Christmas tree. "I'm the lucky one."

"We both are." She traced her finger over his firm lips. "If you hadn't stopped me..."

"Thank God I did."

Dave began unwrapping her like a Christmas present, almost reverently uncovering every inch of her. The warmth of the air in the room brushed over her bare skin as she waited for him to strip out of his own clothes. He wasn't so slow at that. Before she knew it, he was in between her thighs and she had her legs hooked around his thighs.

"Our first time was under a Christmas tree," she said as she looked up at him.

Dave clasped his hands with hers. "And I intend to make love to you under the tree every year for the rest of our lives."

Erin gasped as he penetrated her as slow as if she were still a virgin. This time it was pure pleasure as her soon-to-be husband filled her and made her feel whole again.

The double heart pendant that she now always wore felt cool against her bare skin and the ring was snug on her finger. He pumped his hips in and out, building up the sensations in her body that threatened to overcome her.

"Come with me," he said as their eyes held.

The room itself seemed to sparkle with glittering Christmas lights as she hit her climax. Her whole body felt as if she was glittering along with them.

He gave a loud groan as he came. He pumped his hips several times, then gathered her in his arms so that she was lying almost on top of him.

"You're home now, angel," he said as he held her tight.

She sighed against his chest. "And I'm here to stay."

TAKING THE JOB

ꟈ

Author's Note

ꕥ

Taking the Job incorporates only elements of Domination/submission and BDSM. It is not intended to accurately portray a true BDSM or Dom/sub relationship.

Trademarks Acknowledgement

ꕥ

The author acknowledges the trademarked status and trademark owners of the following wordmarks mentioned in this work of fiction:

Jaguar: Jaguar Cars Limited

Chapter One

ꟙ

Rain pounded down on Elsie Meyers as she hurried into the towering office building where Bennett Consulting offices were located in downtown Tucson. She loved rain and its clean scent, but right now she'd give anything for it to have been a nice, dry desert day.

"Damn, damn, damn!" she muttered as she reached the glass doors and yanked one of them open. In the space of time it had taken her to get from her car to the building, she became totally drenched. Her cream silk shirt was plastered to her skin, and her mauve linen skirt kept hiking up her thighs, damn near exposing her garters, her guilty little secret—wearing such sexy underwear beneath her clothing.

Thank goodness she'd swept her hair up and fastened it with a clip so at least she wouldn't look like a drowned poodle. The natural curl in her red hair went nuts when it got wet. It was bad enough she was going to be attending her job interview looking like she'd taken a shower in her clothing.

Both the security guard on duty and the information desk clerk looked at her with interest, but she ignored them and took quick strides to the elevator bank. She inhaled a deep breath as she waited for the car and her nerves jumped when it dinged. On the way up she hitched the strap of her black, faux alligator briefcase up on her shoulder and tugged down on her skirt, hoping she looked halfway presentable. She'd really wanted to impress the owner and CEO of the company with a professional appearance—so much for that.

Once she got off at the floor for Bennett Consulting, she'd find a bathroom and touch up her makeup. God, why didn't she think of that when she was on the bottom level?

Because you're going to be late if you don't hurry, that's why!

John Bennett had agreed to an early evening interview because her current work schedule wouldn't allow her the time it would take to sit down and discuss her qualifications with him. She was a software design consultant and her contract was going to expire soon.

When Elsie stepped off the elevator, she came up short. *Damn!* It opened right to the reception area, not a hallway where she could run to the restroom and check out her makeup.

She touched her upswept hair and found that an errant curl or two had escaped and she gave a frustrated sigh.

A gray-haired woman about the same age and build as Elsie's grandmother rose from her chair behind the receptionist's desk, her eyebrows cocked, making Elsie wonder if her skirt was on backward or if her makeup had melted all over her face.

"Just leave a wet T-shirt contest?" the woman said with amusement in her tone.

"Wha—" Elsie looked down at her silk cream blouse and felt heat rush to her cheeks and to the roots of her hair. The silk was practically invisible against her skin, her satin bra standing out as clearly as if she was wearing nothing over it. And, "Oh, my God," she said as she saw her nipples hard and pointed through the material.

She looked at the receptionist in horror. "I-I—"

"Ms. Meyers?" came a deep male voice from her left.

Her skin prickled with more heat. If it was John Bennett, she was going to die of embarrassment. The floor might as well swallow her up right now.

Don't let it be Bennett! Don't let it be—

"John Bennett." He held out his hand as she slowly swiveled toward him and her eyes met his. "Right on time."

"Uhhh," was the only sound she managed to get out as heat flooded her body.

A zinging sensation zipped straight to her belly when he shook her hand. Something flashed in his blue eyes but quickly vanished as he released her. God, the man was gorgeous. Neatly cut blond hair, broad shoulders beneath an expensive business suit and a blue tie that matched the blue of his eyes.

And he looked somewhat familiar…

He politely kept his gaze on her face and not on her wet blouse as he released her hand.

"Are you leaving for the day, Theresa?" he asked the older woman who still wore an expression of amusement.

"If you won't be needing me, Mr. Bennett," the woman he'd called Theresa said, "I'll head out into that lovely storm. The rest of the staff has already left for the day."

Bennett nodded and smiled. "Enjoy your grandkids while your daughter's in town."

"I will—the little monsters." Theresa swept by Elsie with a smile. "See you Monday."

As Theresa punched the button for the down elevator, John gestured toward a tall mahogany door at the corner of the expansive room filled with cubicles. "The heat's on in my office, so you should warm up, Ms. Meyers."

Not that her body wasn't on fire already with embarrassment and from the intense look in the gorgeous man's eyes—and the fact that she was practically naked from the waist up. Thoughts of him warming her up, personally, filled her mind and her cheeks were on fire.

Elsie took a deep breath as she clutched her briefcase strap with one hand and walked ahead of him as he'd indicated. She imagined the heat of his stare on her back as she preceded him to his office.

After she entered, she felt like an automaton as she walked through the door then seated herself on one of the thickly padded arm chairs in front of his desk. She perched on the edge of her seat, her back ramrod straight, her briefcase at her feet. Water droplets trickled down her spine, ending at the waistband of her skirt. She was going to leave a damned wet spot on the chair when she stood up.

And if her libido didn't calm down from being close to John Bennett, the wet spot wasn't going to be just from the rain.

His office was all mahogany with rich navy carpeting and upholstery. Everything from the globe by the window to the shelves of books with various forms of artwork. It was everything she imagined an executive's office would look like. Through the large windows the rain could be seen pouring down on the city and fat droplets splattered on the panes. The room smelled of polish, wood and new carpeting.

The sound of the door shutting met Elsie's ears and her heart thumped in her throat at the soft footfalls coming up from behind her before he reached the chair beside her. To her surprise he sat in it rather than behind his desk.

When Bennett was seated he still saved her from further embarrassment by not staring at her chest. He leaned casually in the chair and gave her a devastatingly handsome smile that had the effect of making her nipples tighter and her folds grow wetter.

Oh my God.

Even though her nipples had to be standing out like mountain peaks, she cleared her throat and sat up even straighter in her seat, if that was possible. "It's a pleasure to meet you, Mr. Bennett," she said, managing to get words out of her mouth for the first time.

"Yes, a pleasure," he echoed, "but call me John. May I call you Elsie?" He eyed her as if making a monumental appraisal while not staring at her breasts. "I've seen you somewhere before, but I can't quite grasp the occasion."

"You look familiar to me too." Good, words were coming from her head to her mouth. Maybe she could do this. "And Elsie is fine."

Goddamn, the woman was gorgeous. Without being obvious about it, John took in her upper body, her slim shoulders, the graceful curve of her throat and her delicate features. Her hazel eyes seemed to almost shift colors, and the curls that had escaped her upswept red hair looked so damn sexy. When he'd followed her in, he'd watched the way her small ass swayed and had studied her long, toned legs. He wondered exactly what she wore beneath that skirt. Thanks to the rain, he knew what she wore above it.

Now that he was face-to-face with her, there was no missing that her nipples were hard and obvious through her transparent shirt—*thank you, rain gods*—and the curves of her large breasts made his mouth water and his cock harden.

He shifted in his seat, trying to ease the pressure against his zipper, and hoped she didn't look at his lap. Images flashed through his mind of his collar around her throat, her ass pink from his whip and driving his cock in and out of her pussy from behind as he bent her over a spanking bench.

Fuck. He had to get his thoughts and erection under control.

On top of that, some serious sexual undercurrents snapped between the two of them like an electrical wire. By the look in her eyes and the tentative way her tongue darted out to touch her bottom lip, he was positive she was as attracted to him as he was to her.

Just by looking at her and her mannerisms, he had no doubt she would make an excellent submissive.

To gain some semblance of control, and to ease the tension, he commented about the weather and said he was sorry she'd had to come out in such bad weather—even though he wasn't, sorry that was. She looked too damn delicious with her shirt plastered against her chest.

He asked her if she enjoyed her current position.

"It's been challenging," she said in her bedroom voice that made him think more and more about what she would be like naked, maybe even tied down to his bed. "But I've truly enjoyed it. I'm sorry the project is coming to an end."

"Why are you interested in a position with my consulting firm, Elsie?" he asked, letting her name slide over his tongue and enjoying the taste of it.

She still sat rigidly in her seat, and he wondered how to get her to relax. "I've made the decision that I would rather work with a consulting firm than strictly on my own," she said.

"Why is that?" He was tempted to rub his cock with one of his hands, it ached so badly. Wild fantasies of marking her as his own continued to spin through his head. Jesus Christ, he couldn't remember being this affected by any woman.

Elsie's eyes shifted from hazel brown to green as she tilted her head to the side. He wondered if she made that movement consciously. "I'd rather be consistently in the field than having large breaks in between consults."

"Reasonable." He leaned forward and braced his forearms on his thighs. "Would you be interested in an inside consulting position? I'm looking for a software designer for an in-house project." Hell, he'd make up a job to keep this woman nearby. He'd made it a rule to never be involved with any of his employees, but if she worked as a consultant, she wouldn't technically be an employee…

"Yes," she said without hesitation and his cock stirred. Having her close…that would be dangerous and challenging all at the same time.

"What are your qualifications?" he asked.

"Let me give you my résumé." Elsie leaned down to pick up the black briefcase she'd brought with her.

As she started to sit back up, he watched her fumble with the catch as if her hands were shaking. The clasp made a clicking sound as it opened.

In the next moment she gave a little cry as the briefcase slipped out of her grasp, and the contents tumbled out and rolled across his carpeted floor.

"Let me help." John got out of his seat and knelt beside Elsie as she frantically scooped up items and put them into one of the briefcase's pockets.

"Really, I'm fine." A strangled sound came from her throat when she looked up to see him holding a suede flogger that had fallen out of her briefcase.

It was at that moment he remembered exactly where he had seen her before.

"Uhhh..." Elsie's face flamed while she tried to form a coherent sentence as her brain took a holiday from sheer embarrassment.

She was still on her knees as he crouched beside her, just inches away. He didn't give her the black and red leather flogger. Instead, he gripped the handle with one hand and ran the fingers of his other hand through the strips of suede.

He was so close she felt his body heat, and her heartbeat ratcheted up a notch from the way he was holding the flogger—as if he knew his way around one. What if he...

Elsie cleared her throat as he stroked the flogger then met her gaze. "Fetish Ball, Las Vegas, two months ago," he said in a dark, dangerous, sensual voice.

The briefcase slipped from her fingers again, but she barely noticed the contents rolling away.

Oh. My. God.

Not a single word would come out of her mouth, not that her heart would let any words pass.

He suddenly seemed closer than he had before and the spicy scent of his aftershave caused the furious churning in her belly to increase.

John took the flogger and traced it down the side of her face and she closed her eyes. He moved the soft leather straps lower, along the curve of her neck to the opening of her blouse as he spoke.

"You were wearing a black leather corset that barely kept in your breasts, and a black leather thong that showed off your ass perfectly." As he continued she shook from the sensuality in his words and the way he stroked her with the flogger. Her eyes still closed, she pictured everything he was saying as it had been that night. "You had on the sexiest high heels that showed off your long, gorgeous legs as you were spread out, strapped to a St. Andrew's cross. God, you looked beautiful as you were being flogged. Your ass so pink and perfect for fucking."

Elsie gasped and he paused and rested the flogger at the curve of her neck. "You were wearing another Dom's collar."

She licked her lips and opened her eyes but she couldn't meet his gaze. He knew. God, he knew.

"Do you still have a Dom, Elsie?" he asked in that deep, penetrating voice that made her thong even more soaked.

She shook her head. The relationship between her and Terry had ended not a month after that fetish ball.

"Good." John caught her off guard with his statement and she raised her gaze to meet his. He stroked the flogger from the curve of her neck to the opening of her blouse, but this time moving it beyond. "Are you looking for a new relationship, a new Dom, Elsie?"

She opened her mouth then shut it. She remembered him now. He'd been standing off to the side, watching her being flogged by Terry, her Dom. John had been wearing the same sexy but dark smile that tipped the corner of his mouth now, and he'd been dressed in tight black jeans and a sleeveless black suede shirt. She could still remember his finely carved biceps that were now hidden by his suit jacket.

"Are you, Elsie?" He repeated her name each time he spoke to her, as a Dom would. "Answer me."

His voice was so compelling, so masterful, that she couldn't have stopped herself if she tried. "Yes," she whispered.

John traced the flogger around one of her nipples, causing her whole body to heat more than it already was. She gasped and nearly lost her balance from where she was kneeling, but caught herself by grasping one of his arms. His biceps flexed beneath her fingertips as he skimmed his hand up her shoulder and her neck to cup the back of her head.

"I'm going to kiss you, Elsie." His mouth was so close to hers now that the warmth of his breath feathered across her lips. "Unless you tell me no."

Her heart dropped from her throat to pound like crazy against her breastbone.

"Tell me what you desire, Elsie." He nuzzled the corner of her mouth. "I want to hear you say it."

It took a great deal of effort but she finally got the words out in a whisper. "I-I want you to kiss me."

A smile of pure male satisfaction curved his lips before he claimed her mouth with his own.

The moment his lips touched hers, she moaned. His tongue delved into her mouth, expertly touching and teasing and experimenting with her and their kiss. He held the back of her head firmly with one hand while the other grasped her ass so tight the flogger he still held dug into her flesh.

The moans rising up within her grew as he intensified the kiss, mastering her. She completely and totally gave herself up to him.

Before she knew what was happening, he had lowered her onto her back on the carpet while he was still kissing her.

One of his knees slid between her thighs, spreading them and causing her skirt to hike up, almost to her pussy.

John groaned as he continued to tease her, tempt her, taste her with his kiss. As he straddled her, he began to explore her body with one of his hands, palming her breasts one at a time through her wet silk blouse, then pinching each of her nipples, almost as hard as she liked it. She arched up into him and gave a cry into his mouth when he pinched her nipples so hard they hurt. Yeah, that was it.

Elsie's moans became louder as he slid his hand down from her breast to her thigh. He slid his fingers up and over her stocking to her garter belt, and he smiled against her lips.

John moved his hand higher up her thigh, and she caught her breath as he whispered against her lips, "Oh, sweetheart, what have we got here?"

Elsie stilled beneath John's touch, but her rapid breathing and the darkness of her hazel eyes when he raised his head told him she wanted this.

Shit, this was crazy. He was crossing into taboo territory by taking things so far with a woman he was interviewing. But it felt so right. So good. And she seemed to feel the same way.

She audibly caught her breath as he skimmed his fingers along the bare skin of her thigh beside her garter, pushing her skirt up higher. He moved slowly, giving her every opportunity to put a stop to what they were doing.

Instead, she slid her hands up around his neck and brought his head closer to hers so that their lips met. He kissed her softly then drew away. "That's not how the game goes, is it, Elsie," he stated. "You do what I tell you when I tell you."

Her eyes widened but she didn't argue.

Some of the things that had fallen out of her briefcase rolled under his desk as he adjusted himself so that he was more firmly on top of her.

"I want to see your hair down." He moved his hand from her thigh and traced her lips with his fingertip.

"But the rain will have made it all curly—"

He shook his head. "Don't make me tell you twice, Elsie. Do you want to be punished?"

She bit her lip and shook her head as she reached up and tilted her face to the side so that she had access to the clip. She slid it free, and a few of the curls started to escape. He smiled and knelt between her thighs so that he could use both hands to fluff out her hair and spread it behind her like a fire-red halo. It was long and curly, and adorable around her face.

John looked down at the place he had hiked her skirt up to her upper thigh—to where he could almost see her mound. He braced his hand to the side of her head and studied her. Her cheeks were pink, her parted lips swollen from his kiss, her eyes heavy-lidded and dark with desire.

He braced one hand to the side of her head and brought his other back beneath her skirt, where he pushed it up farther while keeping his gaze focused on hers. She gasped as his fingers crept higher.

"Put your hand on mine, Elsie." His words came out deeper and gruffer than he'd intended. "Guide my fingers to where you want me to touch you."

Her eyes widened and she hesitated. He gave her a firm look, meant to tell her to follow his instructions. If she was a good submissive and wanted him to be her Dom, she would need to obey him without pause.

She eased her hand down to cover his and he could feel her trembling fingers as she guided his from her garter to her mound.

Jesus Christ. She wasn't wearing any underwear.

The curls of her mound tickled his palm as she moved his hand down until his fingers rested on her folds.

His heart pounded a little faster and his cock ached beyond measure. How he wanted to unfasten his zipper and plunge into her pussy now—he could barely restrain himself.

He teased the outside lips of her folds with his fingers, not delving into her wetness yet. And he knew she'd be wet. "What do you want me to do now, Elsie?"

The way her cheeks turned pinker made her look even more desirable. "Touch me. Rub my clit."

John gifted her with a smile of approval and slipped his fingers into her slick folds. "You're so damn wet, Elsie." He stroked her clit and she gave a soft moan. "Do you want me to fuck you?"

Again she stilled, her lips parted as another moan escaped her and she locked gazes with him.

"Do you?" he repeated. "Say it, Elsie."

"I—" Her voice came out in a harsh whisper. "I-I want you to fuck me, John."

He smiled, slid two fingers into her slick channel and began pumping them in and out so that his knuckles met her folds. She cried out and arched her back, raising her chest and drawing his attention to her large breasts beneath her wet blouse. He lowered his head and bit one hard nipple through her shirt and bra and she cried out from the pain of his bite.

"Did you like that, Elsie?" he murmured as he moved his mouth to her other nipple.

"*Yes*." She gasped as he bit her other nipple. "A lot. I like everything you're doing to me."

He gave another satisfied smile and pounded his fingers in and out of her pussy at the same time he bit and sucked her nipples through her shirt and bra. She moaned and grasped his biceps, digging her fingers into his suit jacket.

"Oh God." Her whole face was flushed as she writhed beneath him. "I'm so close to coming."

"You know how it works, Elsie," he said as he slipped his fingers from her core. "No orgasm without my permission."

She shuddered and whimpered as he brought his fingers from between them and slipped them into his mouth. He sucked her juices and drank in the scent of her musk while he watched her.

"You taste so fucking good, sweetheart." He braced both hands to either side of her chest. "Unbutton your blouse."

Her throat worked as she swallowed, but her fingers moved from his biceps to the buttons of her blouse at once. She fumbled with the buttons but gradually her blouse fell to the side as she pulled the hem out of the waistband of her skirt. Her bra barely restrained her breasts that almost overflowed the cups. When her blouse was unbuttoned, he helped her rise up as much as she needed to so that he could slide the material off her shoulders and fling the blouse on one of the chairs.

God, he loved when a woman wore a front clasp bra. He unfastened it and she bit her lower lip as he eased it completely off her, setting her breasts free so that she was naked from the waist up.

"Damn, you're beautiful," he said just before he leaned down and licked one of her nipples. She gave a sound between surprise and pleasure, then moaned when his mouth covered her nipple and moaned again as he bit the taut bud.

He loved the taste of her skin, her juices. And right now he wanted to taste all of her, especially her pussy.

Chapter Two

ཽ

Elsie's mind was spinning. She couldn't believe what was happening. She'd come to John Bennett's office for a job interview, and now she was beneath him as he suckled her nipples and teased her clit again with his fingers. His mouth was hot against her chilled skin and the warmth was spreading throughout her.

She didn't even know this man, but it felt as if her body did, and she couldn't have stopped all of this from happening if she tried. She didn't *want* to stop it.

He went from biting and sucking her nipples to sliding his mouth down the center of her belly, closing in on the waistband of her skirt. "Arch your hips," he said as he licked a path along the material.

When she obeyed, he reached behind her and unfastened her skirt, eased the zipper down and slid her skirt down her hips. The sparks in her belly became more frantic as he stripped her of her skirt and tossed it aside. Now all she was wearing was her stockings, garters and her heels. Her pussy and the rest of her were completely bared for him. She was nervous, yes, but she liked the way he looked at her and she didn't feel the need to cover herself. No, what she wanted was his mouth and hands on her and his cock inside her core.

He studied her with obvious approval and pressed her thighs apart with his palms, spreading her wide. "That's better."

As his gaze took her in, he shrugged out of his suit jacket and threw it on top of her skirt. He loosened his tie, took it off, and it ended up on top of his jacket. He undid the first couple of buttons on his shirt, just enough to tease her with a glimpse of his golden skin and his muscles bulging beneath his shirt.

"I want you naked too, John." Her pussy was growing wetter beneath his scrutiny.

He shook his head. "Only when you've earned the right. I *am* going to have to punish you."

She looked at him in surprise.

John gave her a wicked look. "For fucking a total stranger."

Elsie opened her mouth to respond, but words failed her once again, this time as he went down on her. He buried his face against her pussy, running his tongue from the sensitive spot between her anus and her clit. Without realizing what she was doing, she buried her hands in his soft hair and held onto him as he licked and sucked her folds and her clit. He shoved fingers from one hand into her core and began ramming his knuckles against her folds as he had earlier.

And then to her shock, he slipped a finger from his other hand into her anus.

She gasped and arched her hips as he pounded inside her pussy and anus while licking her clit. Her whole body was on fire and she writhed beneath his welcome assault.

John raised his face from her folds long enough to say, "Pinch your nipples, and I want you to pinch them *hard*."

He watched as she did as he instructed and cried out as he began licking her clit and pounding inside her from both directions.

Moans spilled from her throat as she pinched her nipples and watched him between her thighs. Fireballs ignited from the sparks in her belly and she could feel the heat at every nerve ending in her body.

"John." She couldn't stop moving as he mastered her body. A climax was building up so fast in her body she was afraid she would explode from it. "I'm going to come. Please let me come."

"No, sweetheart." He raised his head and she wanted to cry because he wasn't licking her clit. "You're an experienced sub. You know how to control your orgasms."

Elsie thought she was going to scream. Yeah, she'd become good at holding back her orgasm until her Dom gave her permission to come, but she didn't remember being this on fire, having this same need ever before. Maybe it was the situation, that she didn't even know John. Maybe it was the way he took command of her body. Whatever it was, he had her writhing and ready to climax at any moment.

She pinched her nipples even harder, the pain both a distraction and an addition to the torture he was inflicting on her.

"Put your palms on the carpet, Elsie." He raised his head again. "And don't move."

Don't move? Is he insane?

Her entire body trembled with the need to come as she placed her hands down on the carpeting. She bit her lower lip and struggled not to move as he continued pounding his fingers in and out of her anus and her pussy while licking her clit. Tears formed at the backs of her eyes, the need to climax was so powerful.

John stopped and withdrew his finger from her ass and his others from her pussy before pushing himself to his feet. She shuddered from the loss of contact and from relief that she didn't have to fight off her orgasm. As he unfastened his belt and pulled it from its loops, the firestorm in her belly intensified. Was he going to fuck her now? Or punish her?

"On your knees, Elsie," he said, holding the belt in his hands.

She eased up so that she was on her knees in front of him, her heart pounding like crazy. He walked behind her and she tensed, a tremor running up and down her spine, waiting for the spanking she was certain was coming. Instead he brought her arms behind her back, wrapped the belt around her wrists and fastened it. She tugged at the restraint, but he had her bound tightly.

He moved so that he was standing inches from her face. He unzipped his pants and released his long, thick cock.

John felt like his erection was bigger, harder, and ached more than it ever had before. Something about this woman drew out the beast in him. He had the primitive urge to throw her down and fuck her until she screamed loud enough for the security guard ten flights down to hear.

He grasped Elsie's wild red mane in one fist and brought her lips close to his cock. She moaned as she swirled her tongue around the head of his erection and he couldn't hold back a groan. He nudged her closer and she slid her mouth over his. "That's it, sweetheart," he managed to get out. "Take me deep."

Jesus, but her mouth felt so hot and wet. She made little whimpering sounds of pleasure as she applied suction then licked the circumference of his cock. He clenched his fist tighter in her hair and began thrusting in and out, fucking her mouth but taking care not to go too far.

He looked down to see the bound woman looking up at him with her hazel eyes, the color having shifted to look almost blue. The pain in his cock only increased as he watched his erection slide between her lips.

Goddamn, but he was getting close to climaxing, and that was something he couldn't do. He was the Dom, he was in control, and he wasn't about to let her see him lose it.

When he took all that he could of the velvet wetness of her mouth, he drew his cock out and tried to catch his breath and keep his body shaking from need without looking like that was what he was doing.

Maintain, Bennett. Keep your cool.

She looked so beautiful with her hands bound behind her back, only wearing garters, stockings and heels, her face tilted up, her lips parted and her hazel eyes dark with desire.

He couldn't take much more before he had to be inside her, had to fuck her with everything he had. But first things first.

"Kneel on that chair, Elsie." He gestured to the one she'd been sitting in, what was it, minutes, hours ago? "Facing away from me and leaning over the back of it." Her eyes widened as he scooped up her red and black suede flogger he'd discarded earlier. "It's time for your punishment."

Elsie still couldn't believe he was going to punish her for having sex with a stranger, when *he* was the stranger! But at the same time she anticipated the sting of her flogger, the slow burn that would eventually take her to heaven.

And she had no doubt that he knew that's what she wanted.

John took her by the arm and helped her stand. She got to her feet as gracefully as she could with her wrists bound behind her back and she moved to the chair. He assisted her as she climbed onto the seat and knelt so that she was half hanging over the back of the chair. The smooth wood was cool but hard beneath her belly.

Shivers wracked her body as she felt the soft touch of the flogger at her nape before he trailed it over the curve of one of her shoulders, then the other. He lightly brushed her spine with the suede straps, lulling her into relaxing, even though she knew what was coming soon.

His slow movements continued as he seemed to caress every curve of her body. He reached her ass and lightly swatted her, just teasing, sensual slaps of the leather over her ass. She bit her lower lip in anticipation of that first hard slap of the flogger.

"You have such a fine ass." He moved the flogger back and forth over her skin in a movement that increased her desire to reach climax. "You've been fucked in the ass before, haven't you, Elsie." It was a statement.

"Yes," Elsie admitted with no problem. She enjoyed the different sensations of fullness.

He moved the flogger lower so that he was caressing her thighs. "Have you ever been fucked by more than one man at a time?"

She shook her head, her long hair whispering across her bare shoulders. "No."

"But you've fantasized about it." Again, a statement.

Elsie hesitated and he paused in his movements with the flogger. "Yes." The word came out in a hoarse whisper. "I've been curious what it would be like."

The flogger reached the backs of her knees and she found herself trembling. "Would you like me to arrange for your fantasy to come true, Elsie?"

Her breath caught in her throat. Did she? It was something she'd imagined more than once—what would it feel like to have two men inside her at the same time?

"Answer me, Elsie," he said as he moved the flogger back up to her ass. "Do you want to be fucked by me and another man? I want to hear you say it."

She swallowed. "Yes," she managed to get out. "I want to be fucked by two men at the same time."

"We'll see," he said before the first lash fell across her ass and she screamed.

Sparks of heat erupted from the pain of the first lash. The heat traveled like a wildfire through her body, racing to the roots of her hair. Even her ears tingled.

And it almost made her climax at the same time.

Shit, he'd struck her harder than she'd expected. Tears stung the backs of her eyes as she waited for the slow burn of pleasure that rolled over her in the next wave as he rubbed her ass with his palm. His touch made it hurt more, yet soothed her at the same time.

"You've misbehaved, Elsie." John leaned over her back and she felt his rough clothing against her bound wrists and her soft skin. "You shouldn't be naked in the office of the man you were interviewing with, about to let him fuck you." She shivered as he pushed her thick hair over one of her shoulders and kissed her nape. "Isn't that right, sweetheart?"

She nodded and moaned at the same time from the featherlight movements his lips made over her neck.

"Answer me, Elsie." He palmed one of her breasts and kissed a path down her spine.

"Yes." Her pussy grew wetter with every touch, every movement he made. "I shouldn't be here."

"But you want it, don't you, Elsie." A statement again.

Her whole body vibrated with the need to come. With the need to have him inside her. "God, *yes*."

He gave a soft laugh that tingled along her spine. "You definitely deserve your punishment. Don't you think?"

"Yes." She squirmed and tugged her wrists against her bonds as his lips skimmed the place he had struck on her ass. "I need you to fuck me, John. Please."

"Uh-uh." He darted out his tongue and licked her still stinging skin. "That's not the way it works."

He drew away and before she even had time to tense in anticipation, he snapped the flogger against the other side of her ass. She cried out again, heat flowing through her body and her pussy growing wetter. It was all she could do to hold back her climax as pleasure followed pain.

Again he stroked the spot he had flogged, and again he pressed light kisses against her burning skin. "You should see how beautiful your ass looks when it's pink from your flogger." He licked her ass cheek. "Why were you carrying one in your briefcase, Elsie?"

The heat in her body magnified. "I-I picked it up from Terry's house—my old Dom—and kept forgetting to take it out of my briefcase."

"Or did you leave it on purpose, I wonder."

She looked over her shoulder in time to see him move back and raise the flogger.

John was magnificent. His short, dark-blond hair complimented his high cheekbones, and his broad shoulders and chest looked powerful beneath his dress shirt. His re-fastened pants hid his cock that she so badly wanted inside of her.

His gaze met hers. "Face away from me, Elsie."

The tenseness in her body magnified even though she knew she should relax her muscles. It was going to hurt a lot more if she didn't.

Too late. He snapped the flogger between her ass and her thigh, once on each side in rapid succession. She screamed and moisture flooded her eyes. The burn intensified when he didn't pause and struck the backs of her thighs, then her ass again, in places he hadn't flogged her before. Each time it was in a different location.

She perched on the precipice of her orgasm with every stroke, every burn and the resulting sting of pleasure.

When he finally stopped, she sagged in relief. Fire raged through her body. The tenseness coiled in her belly and the ache in her pussy had her so on edge it wouldn't take much to throw her over.

Elsie heard the rustle of clothing and the sound of something being torn open. Her folds grew wet enough that she felt moisture on the insides of her thighs.

She moaned as he molded his body to hers, his clothing scratchy against her burning skin and his chest pressing her bound hands tighter to her back. He kissed the curve of her neck as he rubbed his erection in her folds.

A shudder of desire wracked her body. She needed his cock inside her so badly she could almost scream.

"What do you want me to do now, Elsie?" he murmured as he dropped kisses down her shoulder.

"Fuck me." A moan rose up inside her from the contrast of his sweet kisses and her burning flesh. "I need your cock."

"It's time for your reward," he said just before he slammed his cock into her core.

She cried out at the exquisite feel of having him inside her, stretching her, filling her. Terry had nothing on this man, and she'd thought Terry had been big.

Slowly, John began thrusting in and out of her and she whimpered with every movement he made. She burned from the lashes, burned from need, burned from the way he felt inside her.

"Ever been fucked during an interview before?" he asked as he kept up his maddeningly slow pace.

The thought was incredulous. "Of course not." The words were a gasp as they came from her throat. "I've never even had sex with anyone I've worked with."

John's thrusts increased and he gave a sound of satisfaction as his balls slapped against her pussy. "Why me, Elsie?"

"I don't know." She moaned and wished her hands were free so that she could grip the chair and push back against him to meet each of his strokes.

He slowed. "Don't you?"

"I—uh." Her mind was whirling from the need to come and every sensation bombarding her all at once. "The—the moment you took my hand I felt something."

He moved his palms up from her hips and grasped her breasts as he picked up his pace again, pumping in and out of her at a faster rate. "I wanted you the minute I saw your blouse plastered against your skin, your nipples poking against your bra. I wanted to fuck you right then and there."

Elsie moaned. The way he put the emphasis on "fuck" made her all the hotter. And she was already about to burn out of control.

The sparks in her belly had rolled into the fire consuming her body. Perspiration had broken out on her skin and she was breathing hard and fast. Her whole body shook with the need to climax as he pumped in and out of her. His cock was so big and hard, so filling and long. He reached every sensitive spot inside her.

"I need to come. Please, John," she moaned. "Let me come."

"Hold, sweetheart." His thrusts became harder, deeper.

Oh God. Could she last much longer? In the last couple of years as a submissive, she had learned how to hold back her orgasm. But this was different. It was John, and he was taking her to limits she'd never felt before.

He pinched her nipples hard and whispered by her ear. "Come, Elsie. Come now."

She screamed. Her orgasm hit her so hard she thought she was going to fall over the back of the chair. The heat she'd been feeling swirled into a maelstrom of fire in her body and in her mind.

Everything that they were doing and what he'd done to her magnified the impact of her orgasm. The fact she was fucking the man she was interviewing with and only wearing heels, stockings and garter belt, the burn of the lashes against her ass and thighs, her hands bound behind her back, the rough feel of his clothing against her, his fingers pinching her nipples, and his cock ramming in and out at a furious pace—everything was driving her out of her mind.

He slammed into her so hard he forced her belly against the back of the chair. Her mind continued to spin and fire never stopped flaring in her body. Wave after wave of her orgasm traveled over her from toes to head and her orgasm wouldn't stop, not with him continuing to slam into her.

A sob tore from her throat. She couldn't take it. He was driving her further than she'd ever been.

When she thought she was going to scream again, John shouted. He pressed his hips tight against her burning ass and she felt the throb of his cock inside her core. Her pussy spasmed and spasmed, clenching down on his cock.

With a loud groan he moved his hands from her breasts and braced them on the back of the chair, to either side of her. His weight pressed against her bound wrists and her back. He felt comfortable, solid, but heavy.

After a moment, he drew away and she looked over her shoulder to see him dispose of a condom in the garbage can beside his desk. His eyes were wild and his shirt wrinkled as he tucked his cock back into his slacks and zipped them up. She sighed in disappointment that he hadn't been naked with her, but at the same time it had been erotic feeling the roughness of his clothing against her sensitive skin.

Her pussy went on spasming while she looked at him and the feral gleam in his eyes as he reached for her. She didn't know what to expect as he helped her to her feet, and was pleasantly surprised when he took her mouth in a wild, possessive and dominating kiss.

Again his tongue mastered her, claiming her, and it was all she could do to stand. Her perspiration-coated body was smashed against his body as he grasped her by the ass and ground his growing erection against her belly. Smells of sex and sweat and his spicy male scent filled her senses.

John reached around her and unfastened the belt binding her wrists as he kissed her. The belt fell to the floor with a soft thud. Her wrists and arms were sore from being behind her. He brought them between them as he broke the kiss and started massaging her wrists and working his way up to her shoulders. She was already boneless from her orgasm and everything else she'd just been through, and his massage made her want to drop into a puddle of liquid heat.

His smile was so damn sexy as he looked down at her then brushed her forehead with his lips. He was a good six inches taller than her five-foot six-inch height. Only his big hands on her arms kept her standing.

As he massaged her he nuzzled her hair and audibly inhaled. "Some kind of flower—orange blossoms maybe? Whatever it is, you smell so damn good, sweetheart."

Elsie just released a deep, shuddering sigh and leaned against him, enjoying his hard, muscular chest against her soft breasts. His shirt had a clean, starched smell that lingered with his spicy scent.

John worked his hands up her shoulders to her neck and then cupped her face. "You are so beautiful, Elsie." He brushed kisses over her nose, her cheeks, her jawline, to her ear. When he backed away he slipped his fingers into her curtain of hair and fluffed it over her shoulders. "I love your hair down." He let his hands trail from her hair to her neck. "And I love the sprinkling of freckles on your shoulders," he said as he ran his palms up and down, from her upper arms to her throat.

As she looked up into his blue eyes, she gave a sated sigh again. "Where do we go from here?" she said softly.

He brushed his mouth over hers and tickled her lips when he spoke. "Are you a lifestyle sub or a bedroom sub?"

When he drew back to look in her eyes she smiled. "Definitely only when it comes to sex. Otherwise, watch out."

With a grin, he said, "The flogger triggered your response to me."

"My body was already responding to you." She gave a soft laugh. "But I never dreamed *this* would happen."

John cupped her cheeks and kissed her again. "We played that I was your Dom tonight. Will you be my sub?"

She didn't even hesitate when she responded, "Yes."

"Good." He raised his head and looked at her. With a wink he added, "By the way, you're hired."

Elsie laughed. "When do I start?"

"As soon as possible."

Chapter Three

ꟸ

John could hardly maintain his focus as he pumped iron in his home workout room, working on his biceps. All he could think about was Elsie Meyers and all that they had shared last night. Goddamn, it had been incredible.

After he'd helped her dress and pick up *almost* all of the items from her briefcase, he'd walked her out to her little blue sports car and gave her one last kiss. It had been dark by the time they made it out of his office building, only the yellow glow of the parking lot light illuminating her wet features. It had still been raining, but neither of them seemed to care as their kiss lingered on.

Reluctantly he let her leave and stared in the direction her car had headed long after it disappeared from sight. He'd asked her to spend the last night with him, but she'd refused. Instead, she promised to go with him tonight.

Sweat trickled down his spine as he set the pair of dumbbells down. He flexed his biceps then picked up her flogger from off one of his workout benches. He ran his fingers through the straps as he remembered how deliciously pink her ass had looked and then how hot and tight her pussy had been around his cock. The orgasm he'd had—shit, he didn't remember anything so fucking intense in all his life.

It was Saturday and a bondage party was taking place later at his friend Aaron Richard's home, starting around eight. Tonight he was going to fulfill Elsie's fantasy of two men at the same time—and then he wasn't so sure he wanted to share her anymore. He owed his brother Drew—the only one of his three brothers who was single now—for the time with the Nelson triplets, a night almost as hot as what he'd experienced with

Elsie right in his office. Amazing how one woman could outshine every other sexual experience he'd ever had.

Just thinking about tonight had his cock coming to full alert and pressing against his gym shorts. At least the material had some give—yesterday his business suit hadn't and he'd felt like his erection was being strangled as he'd dealt out Elsie's punishment and pleasure.

He adjusted his cock and tossed the flogger back on the bench before picking up a dumbbell to work on his triceps. One glance at the clock on the wall of the workout room told him it was closing in on noon. It was going to be a hell of a long day.

* * * * *

Sparks continued to bounce around in Elsie's belly as she glanced at the clock again. John had said he'd pick her up around eight, and it was getting close to the time he would arrive. She didn't know what to do with herself before he got there. She'd eaten a little something since he said there would just be hors d'oeuvres at the party he was taking her to. He'd suggested they go out to dinner before the party, but she'd already promised her sister they'd go clothes shopping—which had given her the perfect excuse to pick out her ensemble.

Her fingers trembled a little as she brushed down the skirt of her little green halter-style dress that made her hazel eyes seem greener, set off the creamy color of her skin and showed the sprinkling of freckles on her shoulders that John had appeared to like. Just remembering the way he had skimmed his fingers over them made her shiver and the ache between her thighs intensify. She'd arranged her hair up in an elegant knot, and imagined him pulling the pins out and setting her hair free again.

She still couldn't believe she'd had sex with the man she was interviewing with for a job. Instead of discussing her qualifications as a software design engineer, they'd ended up exploring her qualifications as a sub.

Considering how take-charge and independent she was in life, sometimes it struck her as strange that she was so submissive when it came to sex. The moment she was near her Dom, her sub qualities came forth and she reveled in letting him take control. She'd only had two Doms before John, and they'd lasted only about three months each. For some reason neither man had filled a need inside her that she still couldn't identify. They'd parted ways amicably, and she still considered Terry and Jason as friends.

When the doorbell gave its familiar trilling sound, Elsie nearly jumped out of her skin. She looked in the mirror one last time, used industrial-strength hairspray to hold back a lock that wanted to escape, and then dabbed on her orange blossom perfume.

She took a deep breath, squared her shoulders and headed to the front door. She opened it and about melted on the spot. John wore his devastatingly sexy grin, along with black jeans and a black leather sleeveless shirt, like what he'd been wearing when they'd seen one another at the fetish ball in Las Vegas. She had a feeling he wasn't into silver studs. It just wasn't his style.

"Hello, gorgeous," he said as he took her by the waist and softly kissed her.

Elsie sighed and barely restrained from sinking against him and wrapping her arms around his neck. She could kiss this man all night long. "Want to come in for a sec?"

John followed her inside to her spacious kitchen where she drew out a bottle of Merlot and two wineglasses. He hitched his shoulder up against the doorway as he watched her pour them each half a glass.

He took the glass she offered him and she said, "To floggers."

With a chuckle, John shook his head and clinked his glass to hers. He swallowed, letting the Merlot warm his throat. Then he set the glass down and reached into his back pocket. "I have something for you."

She raised her brows then her lips parted as he brought out a long, thin jewelers box. "I can't accept anything, John," she said as he took her hand and pressed the box into her palm. "We've barely met."

"And fucked," he said with a teasing glint in his eyes. Her cheeks heated immediately. "Just open it."

Face still warm, she lifted the lid of the box and gave a soft gasp. "It's beautiful. But—"

"Do we need to start counting punishments already?" He raised an eyebrow.

"No, but—"

"This is your collar." He took the box from her and extracted the gold filigree choker that was about an inch wide and long enough to fit around her neck. "I want you to wear it to show that you're mine."

Elsie opened her mouth then closed it again as he moved behind her and slipped the choker around her neck. It fit snugly. And it felt right.

John took her by the shoulders and turned her around to face him. "Beautiful," he said in a voice husky with primal desire. "Will you wear my collar, my sign of ownership?"

She brought her fingers to her throat and touched the delicate choker. "Yes."

Another sexy smile tugged at the corner of his mouth. "I like your hair down," he said and reached up as if to take out her pins.

Elsie took a step back and shook her head. "Not yet. We'll save that for later."

"All right." His stare was intense as he reached for her. "But come here."

Instinctively she obeyed, stepping into his embrace and wrapping her arms around his neck. He grabbed the silky material covering her ass. "You don't know how much it turns me on to see you wearing my collar."

"Show me," she said as she reached up to kiss him.

John took possession of her lips, thrusting his tongue deep inside her mouth as he rubbed his erection against her belly. She grew wet between her thighs and even more so when he slid his hands beneath her dress and palmed her naked ass.

"Jesus Christ." He pulled away from her and looked into her eyes. "You're only wearing a garter again. Damn, woman. I don't know if I'm going to be able to wait to be inside you."

She gave him her naughtiest grin. "Maybe you should fuck me right now?"

It obviously pained him to shake his head, saying no with that movement. "You have to wait for your reward, and you know it."

A teasing pout started to form on her lips when he slid his hand in front of her and slipped his fingers into her wet folds. Elsie gasped and grabbed onto his biceps to hold herself steady as he rubbed her clit, raising her need so powerfully that she was ready to climax already. She knew he wouldn't let her, so she kept it to herself and just squirmed against his hand.

He finally drew his fingers from her folds and brought them beneath her nose so that she could smell her own musk. The sparks went crazy in her belly again and more moisture flooded her pussy when he slipped his two fingers into his mouth and sucked. The mere act made her knees weak as she imagined him going down on her again.

With a smile of pure satisfaction, he leaned down and kissed her, and she tasted herself on his tongue. He palmed her bare ass again. "We'd better go before I throw you across your kitchen table and fuck you right here, right now."

*****

John's gut tightened when they reached Aaron's place. The closer he came to the time to share Elsie, the more he felt like resisting. Strange. He glanced at her and she seemed a little rigid as she sat against the butter-soft leather seat of his Jag. She was so Goddamn beautiful, it was like a punch to his solar plexus to look at her.

The way she'd swept her hair up exposed her delicate neck, making him want to explore it with his mouth and fingertips. Her makeup was applied just enough to accent her high cheekbones, and her full lips were a glossy deep red, begging to be kissed.

Aaron had an expansive home in the Foothills and a hefty bank account from his talent for stock trading. He'd ridden the last wave to its peak and bailed before the market had crashed. John managed to pull out before it was too late, but not quite as soon as Aaron had. The man had enough cash to have the most "interesting" parties.

John parked the Jag off to the side of the wide, circular driveway, behind a row of other vehicles. Most were luxury cars, as the guests ran in the same circle as Aaron and John. What happened in Aaron's home stayed in Aaron's home. No one who participated in these particular get-togethers had any intention of sharing their activities with anyone outside their circle.

John walked around the front of his Jag to the passenger side of the vehicle, opened the door and helped Elsie step from the car. It took all his restraint not to pin her against the car and fuck her on the hood, voyeurs be damned. Considering she was wearing no underwear beneath that sexy little dress, all he'd have to do would be unzip his jeans, pull out his cock, throw her on the hood while pushing up her dress and drive into her core.

He shook the images off, took Elsie's hand and headed across the cobblestone driveway to Aaron's home.

Elsie held her free hand to her belly and gripped John's hand tight as they walked into the foyer of a gorgeous home that looked as if it had come right out of the pages of a magazine. A chandelier glittered overhead and in front of her spread a luxurious room with a sweeping staircase, oil paintings gracing the walls and fine works of art arranged throughout the room.

People mingled, sipping glasses of wine and eating tiny sandwiches, crackers with pâté, cheeses of all varieties, fruit and elegant miniature desserts. John introduced her around and some men kissed the back of her hand where others simply shook it. Laughter and chatter whirled around her and the room smelled of perfumes, cologne and food.

It was like no kind of bondage party she'd ever been to, especially with the way these people were dressed. They looked like they were simply at an upscale social event with lots of sequins, diamonds and other jewels. But there were subtle differences. Such as women wearing extremely short dresses that barely covered their asses, incredibly plunging necklines and obviously no bras as many of the women's nipples were large, hard and obvious. Beneath some dresses she could tell they had on nipple rings from the soft outline of the material. She wondered what else these people might be wearing under their clothing.

Another clue was that a number of women wore collars, but so were some of the men. Most of the men wore jeans or nice slacks or black leather. There were no obvious piercings or other signs that these people were involved in the fetish world.

The home was two stories, and she noticed men and women coming from upstairs looking a bit rumpled and walking a little funny, as if they'd just been paddled.

Thoughts of what might be going on up there made her wetter between the thighs. Maybe she should have worn underwear.

John guided her through the crowd, his hand at the small of her back. His touch felt warm and sizzled through her. She found it difficult to believe she'd just met the man yesterday and had sex with him!

"My brother Craig and his fiancée Jessica," John said, bringing her back to reality as he introduced her to a man about John's age, and a woman who looked like she couldn't be *that* far out of high school. Maybe a couple of years into college at the most. She was gorgeous with long dark hair and brilliant green eyes. Jessica had a smile as brilliant as her eyes—it was no wonder Craig had fallen for the beauty.

As they walked away, John told her that Craig was a college professor—and Jessica had been one of his students. Elsie grinned and shook her head, wondering how *they* had gotten together.

After she'd met his brother Craig, John introduced her to another brother, Dave, who happened to be a police officer. He was newly married to the blonde, blue-eyed woman with him, whose name was Erin. She was friendly and outgoing, and Elsie liked her immediately.

Elsie began to wonder how many brothers John had when they came to a stop before a gorgeous hunk of a man who just about took her breath away. As far as she was concerned, John was more handsome, but this guy wasn't bad at all. He had wavy blond hair that reached his shoulders and coffee-brown eyes. His body was sculpted, absolute perfection.

"My brother Drew," John said as the man reached out and took her hand. "He's a professional personal trainer."

No wonder he had the body of a god.

Elsie tilted her head up to look at John and smiled. "Just how many brothers *do* you have?"

"You've now met them all. Drew's the only one who's not married or engaged." John took her hands in his. "And you're going to get to know Drew better than any of them."

Elsie's eyes widened. "Wha—"

John silenced her with a swift kiss then murmured against her lips, "I promised to make your fantasy come true."

She could so easily lose herself in his kisses, but her mind was whirling. Was John really going to—to share her with his brother?

When he raised his head, Elsie's lips parted to say something when Drew took her by the waist, brought her around to face him. And took her mouth in an absolutely scorching kiss.

Oh. My. God.

The man knew how to kiss, and as he pressed his body against hers, she felt his erection press hard against her. She pulled away, gasping for breath, and he winked.

Her heart pounded so hard her chest ached as John took her hand and led her toward the sweeping staircase. Drew walked on her other side and her belly twisted as the three of them made their way to the second floor. Her knees were shaking now, enough that she wondered how she was even walking.

At the top of the stairs on the landing, John grinned and grasped the hand of another great-looking man. "Elsie, this is Aaron, the owner of this magnificent playground."

Aaron was even taller than the Bennett brothers who stood a good six-two or so. Aaron must have been six-six, had eyes as gray as clouds before a storm, and the build of a professional basketball player, lean and powerful. He took her hand, and instead of kissing her knuckles, he turned her palm up and kissed the inside of her wrist. He darted his tongue out against her skin and she shivered.

When he released her, she was trembling from the sexual tension the three men exuded as they surrounded her. She looked up at John who now had a stormy look in his blue eyes as he looked from Drew to Aaron and back to her.

"Why don't I show you to my favorite room?" Aaron asked with a sinfully delicious smile.

Oh shit.

John wrapped his arm possessively around her shoulders as they walked down a long hallway, but Drew cupped her ass in one hand and she knew John couldn't see his brother more than copping a feel.

Elsie had been to plenty of bondage parties where things were more open. She'd never had sex in front of anyone, had never allowed her Dom to do any more than flog her in front of a group of people. Being spanked in front of a crowd had always turned her on and her sex with Terry had been absolutely incredible once they'd left.

Here the doors were closed and everything was private. She could still hear orders being shouted, cries of ecstasy as well as screams, but all the sounds were muted. As they walked down the corridor, they passed several people who looked sated and well-fucked.

Her mind was now spinning out of control as the four of them rounded a corner and entered a beautiful room that was all rich burgundies and cream.

Elsie jumped when Aaron shut the door behind them and she heard the click of the lock. She backed away from John and looked at the three powerful men who had feral looks in their eyes...and she felt like their prey.

She swallowed and looked at John who took her in his arms and kissed her forehead. "Is this what you want, sweetheart?"

From the tingling between her thighs to the carnal thoughts flowing through her mind, her body was more than ready. But she wasn't so sure her mind was. She'd had anal sex before but had never been with more than one man at a time. And three?

Three very gorgeous, hunk-a-licious men.

The opportunity of a lifetime.

"We'll take it slow, Elsie." John rubbed his palms up and down her shoulders. "Any time you want us to stop, you can say your safe word and you and I will go back to your apartment."

She met his clear blue eyes and hesitated before she slowly nodded. "Computer," she said. "My safe word is computer."

John kissed her like he'd never get enough of her. At the same time she felt one man's strong hands undoing the ties to her halter top while the other man palmed her ass and squeezed her globes.

"Damn, she has a great ass," came Drew's voice from behind her, and she knew it had to be him kneading the cheeks.

"Fucking gorgeous," Aaron murmured as the ties fell away and he took her by the waist and started trailing his lips along her nape to her spine.

John continued to kiss her, his chest pressed to her breasts, keeping the halter top from falling down just yet.

Her body was on fire, her mind whirling and whirling. She was lost in a storm of emotions, touch, taste, and sound. The whole of it nearly overwhelmed her.

Computer! Computer! Computer!

No… No, no, no!

She *wanted* this, and John was gifting it to her.

His mouth was hungry as were the hands and mouths of the men touching her from behind.

Drew kissed her on the opposite shoulder than where Aaron was teasing her with his lips and tongue.

Her skirt was raised up and over her ass and Drew said in a rough voice, "Holy shit. She's not wearing anything under this dress."

"Not a fucking thing but those stockings and heels," John murmured against her lips. He pulled away from her and let the front of the halter dress fall to her waist.

Heat rushed through her at the feel of six male hands on her body, exploring, worshipping her.

"Nice and pink. Good work, bro." Drew spread her ass cheeks wide. "I can't wait to fuck you in the ass, baby."

Tingles prickled her skin at Drew's statement then she made a strangled sound of surprise when Aaron slid one of his hands around her thigh, through the trimmed curls of her mound and into her slick wetness.

"Damn, she's wet," he said as he stroked her clit.

John palmed her full breasts and pulled and pinched her nipples *hard*, causing her to moan even louder than she already was.

Someone tugged on her dress and it whispered down to land around her heels.

"Perfect." Aaron nuzzled her ear as he continued to stroke her clit. "She's so damn perfect."

John's mouth took place of one of his hands, the warmth and wetness adding to the fury of sensations raging through her body. He continued to pinch and pull the other nipple while his free hand glided down her belly and between her thighs where he shoved two fingers into her core and began slamming his knuckles against her folds.

"Oh...*God.*" Elsie couldn't say anything more as the men took total control of her body.

She grasped her hands in John's hair as he suckled her other nipple and continued to pump his fingers in and out of her pussy.

Aaron withdrew from her folds and clasped her face in both hands, turning her head slightly so that she was looking to the side and she was looking into his slate gray eyes. He gave a groan before he kissed her hard, savaging her mouth with his. He tasted different than Drew and John—all three men had their own unique masculine flavor. And she could almost tell them apart by the feel of their hands.

Drew slowed the exploration of her body as Aaron kissed her. Drew's lips slowly moved up her body as he pressed them against the back of her knee, slid along her thigh, and then he bit her ass cheek, hard.

Elsie cried out into Aaron's mouth, but he swallowed the cry and only kissed her harder.

She gave another cry as Drew moved one of his fingers to the tight ring of her anus and pushed his way inside her. Even without lube, his finger felt so good as he reached inside her for that sweet spot. She'd been butt-fucked by her other Doms—but this...all she could think was, *Oh my God,* over and over again.

Aaron kept kissing her but moved one of his hands back to her folds and began stroking her clit, rubbing circles around it, then flicking it in ways that made her shudder with need.

She was under sensory overload. John suckled and pinched her nipples while finger-fucking her pussy. Aaron kissed her while rubbing her clit. Drew played with the curls of her mound with one hand while ramming his finger in and out of her anus with his other hand. He nipped at her ass cheek and John bit her nipples. Aaron even sucked on her lower lip hard enough to hurt.

Her whole body shook and she could feel her orgasm sweeping toward her like a great storm.

"I'm going to come," she cried against Aaron's lips. "Please let me come."

"No." John's words were definite, powerful. "If you do, you'll be punished."

Elsie fought against her orgasm but the men never let up. When she couldn't take it any longer, all she thought was, *Who gives a fuck about being punished...bring it on!*

Chapter Four

ꕥ

Elsie ripped her mouth from Aaron's and climaxed with a scream that must have torn through his entire home. The orgasm hit her with the strength of a tsunami and she felt as if she was being dashed against the rocks with the water's powerful force. She felt a swoosh in her head and her entire being wanted to dissolve and splash on the floor as if she was made of water.

But she couldn't let go and collapse into that boneless mass like she wanted to. Her body bucked and she thrashed against the three men, trying to get them to stop everything they were doing to her.

But John dropped to his knees, moved Drew's hand out of his way and started licking and sucking and laving her pussy and lapping up the juices flooding from her body.

The sonofabitch! He wouldn't let up and tears rolled down her face and she sobbed from too much sensation. Too much, too much!

"Pl-please," she begged. "I can't take any more."

Wrong thing to say to a Dom. If you told him you couldn't take it any longer, he'd show you just how much more you *could* take.

That damned Drew kept butt-fucking her with his finger and Aaron was now palming her breasts as he kissed her.

Finally, when she was certain she was going to die, John let up and stopped licking her pussy. He stood and took her face in his hands, stealing her from Aaron and kissing her hard. The other two men stopped their assault on her body and she totally lost it.

She sagged against John and started to fall, but he caught her by her upper arms and held her. The scents of her musk and the smell of testosterone and cologne seeped through her senses.

John brushed curls that had escaped her clip out of her face. "You were such a bad girl, Elsie, that I'll have to find the perfect punishment for you."

All that came out of her mouth was a soft whimper. He scooped her up in his arms and she let her head loll against his chest. What had they done to her? They'd sapped her strength as if they had taken it as their own.

Vaguely she realized the men were all still clothed as she watched Aaron and Drew walk ahead of them, and felt John's soft suede shirt against her body. There was no way she was leaving this house under her own steam. He'd have to carry her home. Right now she didn't even care if she was naked when he did it.

But he took her into an enormous bathroom, everything in granite, mahogany and the richest fixtures she'd ever seen. Candlelight flickered from every available surface. A huge whirlpool took up one corner of the bathroom and Aaron was already filling it with water and the whirlpool gave a low hum as he started the jets. The spot lighting was low and she gave a tired and very sated smile as she looked at the three hunky men. How could a girl get so lucky?

Her gaze fixed on John as he looked down at her. Yeah. How'd she get so lucky as to find *him*? Forget everyone else, as long as she could be with John.

Lazily she watched Aaron and Drew remove her high heels. Somehow they figured out how to unfasten her garter belt and rolled it down, along with her stockings, and tossed them onto her shoes.

John settled her onto one of the benches in the granite whirlpool. It was a good thing the surface she was sitting on was textured because otherwise she would have slid right down beneath the water.

"Mmmmm..." slipped from her lips as she watched the men undress. All those muscles and firm bodies.

Her eyes widened. *And oh my God! Look at the size of those cocks!*

All three men were hung so well that she didn't think she'd be able to take all three of them at once. 'Cause she knew that's exactly what they had planned.

If that kind of experience was *anything* like what they'd just put her through, there was no way she was going to survive. Not to mention John planned to punish her. What exactly was he going to do to her?

The men eased into the tub, John on one side of her, Drew on her other and Aaron directly across. The whirlpool was large, yet intimate.

John put his arm around her shoulder and kissed the top of her head. "Are you all right?"

"Sure." She sank against his side. "If feeling like you've been hit by a tsunami and washed out to sea is feeling all right."

He gave a low laugh. "Oh sweetheart, we haven't even begun yet."

The way Elsie looked up at him with her lips parted and her eyes widened made him harden even more beneath the water. Such beautiful hazel eyes that looked so green in the candlelight.

She started to open her mouth as if to say something, but closed her mouth, holding back any words that might have come out. Smart girl. She knew if she begged for leniency she'd only get more.

If he didn't know they'd taken her to Heaven and back, he wouldn't push her. But he had no doubt she'd enjoyed everything they'd given her.

He kissed her softly, then more urgently. As her kiss increased in tempo with his, he could feel and sense her body come more alive, could feel her strength returning. She wrapped her arms around his neck and held on to him as he deepened the kiss and she made soft little whimpering sounds.

When he pulled away, her lips formed a small pout.

"I have something those lips can wrap around right now," he murmured. Elsie raised one eyebrow then looked at him with hungry eyes as he raised himself on the next bench seat up so that his fully erect cock was out of the churning water of the whirlpool.

He took Elsie by the shoulders and moved her so that she was positioned on her knees between his thighs. She reached up and grasped his erection with her small hand and brought her mouth closer to it. Her eyes remained fixed on his as she slipped her mouth over his cock.

John gritted his teeth and held back the instant need to climax in her sweet mouth. Goddamn she felt good, like wet silk. Slowly she began moving up and down his length like she had in his office. She played with his balls in one hand and then noticed Drew had moved closer, taken her other hand and wrapped it around his cock.

"That's it, baby," Drew said as she moved her hand up and down his erection and continued sucking John's cock.

Aaron moved to the other side of them and grasped her other hand, bringing it to his cock so that she was running her hands up and down both Drew's and Aaron's erections and sucking John's.

"Just right," Aaron said in a low voice as he tilted his head back.

John felt an insane possessiveness over Elsie but kept it to himself as he enjoyed the feel of her sucking and licking his cock. To try to take his mind off the orgasm building inside him, he grasped the back of Elsie's hair and pulled the pins out. He tossed each one aside and they clattered on the bathroom floor. Then he fluffed her red hair out so that it fell to her shoulders and tumbled down her back. All she was wearing was his gold collar and her creamy skin was bared as was the light sprinkling of freckles across her shoulders. God, she was beautiful.

When he knew he was on the fine edge of self-control, he brought his hands to her face and cupped her cheeks. "That's enough, sweetheart."

Drew took her hand and easily brought her to him in the buoyancy of the water. "My turn," he said as he grasped her hair and brought her lips to his erection. As she took him inside her, John wanted to kill his brother. Such an intimate act by Elsie should be his and his alone.

She gave a soft moan as she concentrated on sucking Drew's cock, John distracted himself by lowering to the next seat and pinching and pulling Elsie's nipples. She groaned around her mouthful of cock and John increased the pressure on her nipples.

Aaron eased behind her, moved her thick hair aside and kissed her nape before letting his hands roam her body. John looked at his brother Drew, whose jaw was tense and his hands fisted in Elsie's hair. Suddenly Drew jerked his erection from Elsie's mouth. "That was so good, baby," he said through clenched teeth. "But I have other plans for my cock and where I plan to put it."

John let out a low growl and Drew looked at him with an expression that turned amused, probably because he could see the possessiveness in John's gaze.

Aaron was already bringing Elsie between his thighs and John's gut clenched as she went down on him. Her head bobbed and her hair floated on the whirlpool's roiling water.

"Where'd you find her?" Drew said as he eased back down so that his cock was underwater again. "She's a fucking babe."

It took a great deal of self-control to calm the jealousy raging through him but John forced a nonchalant look on his face. "She came in for a job interview yesterday. Things went…well. Better than either of us expected."

Drew gave a low whistle. "I'll say. She can interview with me *any* time."

John clenched his fist under the water and Drew grinned. "There's something about Elsie that's gotten under your skin. I've never seen you look or act like this."

John sucked in his breath but didn't bother to say anything. Instead he glanced at Elsie going down on Aaron. That only made the pain in his gut more intense.

He moved behind her and pulled her away from Aaron who raised an eyebrow and settled down lower in the whirlpool. John brought her to the opposite side of the whirlpool and held her in his arms.

Elsie tilted her head up to look at him and smiled. He brushed his mouth over hers and trailed his lips to her ear. "I think you've had too much fun, enjoyed sucking their cocks too much. I might just have to punish you a little harder than I'd planned."

Even though it was warm in the bathroom, Elsie shivered. All three men were wiping her down with the softest, thickest towels she'd ever remembered feeling. By the time they finished, the ends of her hair were toweled dry and her skin was only slightly moist.

"I've decided on Elsie's punishment." John looked at Aaron then Drew. "She needs to be spanked by all three of us as she came without permission when we were pleasuring her."

And torturing me, she thought as her belly sparked with fear and anticipation. She could always use her safe word if it was too much, but she wanted to live out this fantasy, this one time, too much to let it go.

"You've got it," Aaron said as he went to a stocky velour-covered chair. She watched in surprise as he flipped it and folded it in half so that it was positioned like a spanking bench. He moved some hidden pieces of wood and arranged a place for her to kneel.

She glanced up at John, her heart beating a lot faster now. His expression had turned stern, the expression of a Dom ready to deal out punishment. "In position, Elsie."

Automatically assuming the role of a sub, Elsie said, "Yes, John," and immediately crossed the room to the velour-padded spanking bench. She was acutely aware of her nakedness, the only thing on her body was the gold filigree collar marking her as John's.

She knelt on the padded board and leaned over the back of the A-framed bench. Her belly pressed against the apex and her ass was high in the air. She still felt sensitive due to her flogging from last night, and she knew this was going to *hurt.*

"Do you know why you're being punished, Elsie?" John asked as he stood close to her and rubbed his palm over one of her ass cheeks.

Elsie nodded, trying to relax her body as she prepared herself for what was to come. "I climaxed when you ordered me not to," she said, her face turned so that her cheek rested against the padded velour. Blood was rushing to her head and she was starting to feel a little lightheaded.

"That's right," he said just before his hand landed on the ass cheek he'd been rubbing.

Elsie screamed and then again when he spanked the other side of her ass. It burned so damned bad. The heat flushed over her, starting as a sizzling pain where he spanked her to spread through her body and reach face, her arms, her legs.

One slap after another landed on her ass and she cried. She didn't dare beg him to stop or he'd just have her spanked more. Gradually the pain evolved into sweet pleasure too that made her pussy wet and a tight sensation grow in her belly.

She took a breath of relief when John stepped away, but tensed again when he said, "Drew, your turn."

"My pleasure."

Elsie waited for the first slap, but instead she felt his lips and tongue on her stinging ass, soothing her in one spot. And then he bit her.

The pain was intense and caused her to cry out. He made soft growling sounds as he bit her again, sucked her flesh then bit her again. Even more tears rolled down her cheeks. It always amazed her how pain could turn into pleasure. She'd never had a man bite her ass after being spanked before, and despite the pain it was somehow erotic.

Drew stopped biting her and placed soft kisses on every spot he had bitten, which caused her to moan. He pulled back, and in a low voice said, "She's yours now, Aaron."

Elsie sagged against the spanking bench. How much more could she take?

Aaron didn't wait. He spanked her fast, unlike John's slow, methodical slaps. Aaron's were short, sharp, and stung with every contact against her ass and her thighs. She cried, hurting but wanting to come all at the same time.

Abruptly the spanking stopped and Elsie felt strangely exhilarated despite the pain radiating throughout her body. Her pussy ached for John to be inside her. She wanted to feel that fullness again as he stretched her wide and took her deep.

He helped her back to her feet, caught her as she stumbled and brought her around to face him. His kiss was strong and urgent, his mouth taking hers and for a moment she lost herself in the swirl in her mind from his kiss.

John broke their kiss and she caught him around the neck as he grabbed her by the thighs and raised her so that she could wrap her legs around his hips. Her thighs burned from her spankings where he touched. Over his shoulder she saw Aaron and Drew, both men with intense desire in their eyes. Aaron's a smoky brown while blond-haired Drew's brown eyes looked almost black.

When they reached the bed, John turned and eased them both on the enormous bed so that she was straddling him and he was looking up at her. She caught her breath. She'd never had her Dom allow himself to be beneath her. They'd always been in the dominant position.

His blue eyes were intense as her folds cradled his cock, wetting it. A foil package landed on the bed beside them and Elsie glanced up to see Drew already sheathed and spreading a generous amount of lubricant over his erection. She swallowed, looking at Aaron's naked cock, knowing what was coming next.

With shaking fingers she took the foil package that she picked up off the bed, tore it open with her teeth and drew out the soft rubber. Heart pounding, she eased back so that she could roll the condom down John's erection. She was so wet, so horny, so ready for this moment.

"That's it, sweetheart," John said as she rose up and he grasped her waist. She caught her breath as he slowly slid her down his cock, thick and long and filling her completely.

Automatically she started to ride him, loving the feel of him moving in and out of her pussy. She loved him there, loved him inside her.

Then Aaron was in front of her, kneeling on the bed, and Drew behind her, his cock nudging the tight ring of her anus.

She tensed and her eyes widened. This was really happening.

But John said, "You can do this, baby. You can do it and you're going to love it."

Elsie groaned as Drew brought her ass cheeks wide and started to fill her from behind. She'd had plenty of anal sex and had had plugs inserted, but nothing as big as Drew's cock. Her muscles clamped down on him as he pushed his way into her and she groaned louder when he completely buried himself deep inside her. Her ass burned from the contact of his hips against her sore flesh, but the pain of his entry and the pain of her spankings blended into sweet pleasure.

"Oh God," she moaned. The two cocks were so deep inside her she felt as if they were almost touching.

Drew and John began to slowly fuck her and she moaned with every thrust. It was unlike anything she'd ever experienced or had expected to experience in her lifetime.

John brought her face down to his and kissed her hard before Aaron fisted his hands in her hair and drew her up so that his cock was pressed to her lips. She opened her mouth and let him slide inside her. He gripped her hair tight as he fucked her mouth and John and Drew fucked her pussy and ass.

They moved their hands over her at the same time they kept up their slow, rhythmic strokes. The sensations were wild, intense, unbelievable. The three men filled her up so completely. Her ass and thighs stung, adding to the pleasure of the moment.

Her orgasm was coming toward her, another thunderstorm even bigger than the last. She knew when she came this time that she was going to lose all control.

The men began to fuck her faster, building up what was already at an alarming high inside her. Without thinking she began to fight them, fight what they were doing to her.

"Hold on, sweetheart," John said as he drove up, harder and harder.

Her eyes watered and her moans were swallowed with Aaron's cock deep inside her mouth.

"That's it." John gripped her stinging hips as Drew continued to pummel her ass. "Hold on, hold on."

Elsie was close to crying. Her whole body was tense and she felt like she was going to explode.

"Come now, sweetheart," John said, and that was all it took.

Elsie's body felt like it was coming apart. Aaron grunted and his come filled her mouth and she automatically swallowed as she thrashed. When Aaron pulled his cock from her mouth, she let out the scream that she hadn't been able to let loose until that moment.

She felt both Drew and John climax, their cocks pulsing inside her as her body clenched around them both. It seemed to go on forever, the pleasure and the pain, until finally she collapsed as they rolled to the side and she was sandwiched between Drew and John.

Darkness slipped over her and she faded away.

Chapter Five

ꕥ

Elsie snuggled up to John as they lay in his bed. He had his arm around her, and her face rested against his muscular chest. She was absolutely exhausted from the "party" last night. The fact that she'd had sex with three men just blew her mind.

But right now she was cuddling the man she truly wanted to be with. He smelled so good, so masculine. After she'd passed out last night, she'd woken in John's arms and Drew and Aaron were gone. He'd helped her dress and they'd left and gone straight to his home. She'd felt kind of tipsy, as if she'd had too much to drink, and she hadn't had any alcohol.

Once they reached John's home they took a luxurious bath and then he tucked her in bed, his big arms wrapped around her, holding her tight. The scents of clean linens and soap from their bath last night was comforting along with John's masculine scent that made her feel as if she was home.

"Good morning, sweetheart," John said in a gravelly voice as he pressed his lips to her hair.

"It is." She snuggled closer and discovered it could be a *very* good morning if the size of his erection was any indication.

John pumped his hips, rubbing his cock against her belly, and she gave a soft moan. He matched her with a loud groan as he rolled her onto her back and slid between her thighs. Being on her back made her ass burn deliciously from last night's spankings, adding to the wet heat in her pussy.

He nuzzled the curve of her neck. "I wish I could fuck you with nothing between us," he murmured.

She was on the Pill, but she never took chances no matter how much she trusted a man. Not until they were both fully vetted.

John reached into the drawer of his nightstand and pulled out a package. In moments he had his erection sheathed and drove straight into her before she had a chance to prepare to take him in.

With a loud gasp she arched her back and wrapped her thighs around his hips. He pumped his cock hard and fast and Elsie gave soft cries with every thrust. The feel of him inside her and the continual burn of her ass and thighs drove her closer and closer to a powerful climax.

This time she let the energy shoot through her, skyrocketing to tingle at every nerve ending of her body. She shouted loud and long and John followed her moments later with a load groan, a few more slams of his hips and the pulse of his cock inside her core.

John sank against her, his weight heavy but welcome. Elsie gave a contented sigh and he raised his head and gave her a sensual smile. His blond hair was sleep rumpled, his blue eyes heavy-lidded, his muscles corded and powerful as he braced himself above her and he had the shadow of a beard—she'd never seen anyone as sexy as he looked right at that moment

* * * * *

It was only a matter of days before John knew he was head over fucking heels in love with Elsie. Love at first sight? *Bullshit*, he'd always thought. Now he couldn't imagine life without her and her sweet personality, the ever-changing colors of her hazel eyes and her flame-red hair. So elegant and refined during the day, and so hot and wanton at night.

He'd had plenty of relationships, and mostly throwaway where he and the woman would have a fling and part ways amicably. He'd never wanted more than that. There were too many good-looking women to enjoy to be tied down to one.

As he stared out his office window he wondered what Elsie was doing right at this moment. They'd decided it *wasn't* a good idea for the two of them to work together. They'd be going at it like fucking bunnies all the time. He rubbed his cock through his slacks. That pink rabbit with the drum had nothing on them.

The sky was cloudy, threatening to rain like it had the day she'd first walked into his office. What was it? A week ago? God, it seemed like it had been months instead of days.

Right this minute she was still at work consulting for the company where her contract was about to run out in the next week or so. She'd told him that often between jobs she'd take time off—usually her contracts were lucrative enough that she could afford it.

He just needed to convince her to take that time off now and spend it with him instead of spending it looking for a full-time position, or even another contract job. He hadn't taken a vacation in who knew how long, and he had an efficient staff that could manage without him for a couple of weeks. Hell, a month even.

John drew his cell phone out of its holster and pressed the speed dial number he'd programmed in for Elsie's cell.

She answered on the third ring, her voice breathless and low as she said, "Hi, John," in her sexy fuck-me voice that made him harder than ever.

He adjusted his raging hard-on through his slacks. He could picture her in his office now, on her knees, sucking his cock.

"What are you doing, sweetheart?" His words always seemed to be low and husky when he spoke to Elsie. He felt like he was in high school again. It was like he could barely speak around her.

John imagined her twirling a strand of her red hair around her finger. "Staring at a computer screen and thinking about you."

A groan rose up in his throat that he barely held back. "And what were you thinking?"

"About going down on you in your office with your whole staff on the other side of that door." Her words made him groan again. "It would be so hot just knowing they had no clue what we were doing—or maybe they'd be trying to guess if I was fucking their boss."

"You're being a very bad girl, Elsie." He couldn't stop rubbing his erection through his slacks. "Teasing me will only get you punished."

"Who, me?" she said and he pictured her doing her best to look innocent. "I would never tease you about wanting you to come here, where I'm working, and do me in this backroom."

"Oh, I definitely think you've earned a punishment…or two." He leaned forward and toyed with a pen on his desk. "Any plans for the first couple of weeks in February?"

He imagined her tucking the strand of hair behind her ear. "Well, no."

"How about skiing in Colorado?" To his surprise he actually felt *nervous* about asking her and what her response might be.

A pause. "I—well…I don't know how to ski."

He smiled. She wasn't saying no. "I'll teach you, sweetheart."

"I'm scared to death of anything fast, John."

"Bunny slopes," he said, thinking of that pink rabbit and almost laughing. "We'll keep things slow and easy until you're ready to move faster."

Like their relationship. Zero to sixty as far as his heart was concerned, but he knew he'd have to take it slower with her.

"Sure," she said after another pause, and he blew out a breath of relief. "But I'll warn you in advance that I'm not crazy about snow."

"How about hot chocolate and popcorn on a bearskin rug in front of a warm fireplace?"

She laughed. "Okay, the idea definitely has merits."

"Good. I'll make arrangements," he said before she blew a kiss over the phone to him and he grinned like a fool.

* * * * *

A snowball exploded in John's face and he wiped icy snow out of his eyes with the back of his gloved hand. "Wench," he said with a grin, the warmth in his chest heating any chill the snow could cause. "You'll pay for that."

"Wench?" Elsie nailed him again, dead on, before he had a chance to scoop up his own snowball. "I was captain of the softball team." She planted one between his eyes, but not before he got her in the chest. "Starting pitcher."

"Yeah, well I was first string offensive tackle," he said just before he dove for her and tackled her into a snow bank.

Elsie giggled as she squirmed beneath him and tried to free herself. As he looked down at her, she took his breath away. Her cheeks were pink from the cold, her lips red, and her ever-changing hazel eyes almost blue like the sky.

Snow slammed into the side of his head and he jerked back to see that she'd taken advantage of his momentary lapse and got him good with a handful of snow.

She wriggled and laughed some more, but he held on and pulled her down so that she was beneath him again and he had her gloved hands pinned above her head in the snow.

"Hey, no fair," she said with a gleam in her eyes.

"All's fair in love and war, sweetheart," he said as he started to tickle her through her ski jacket, under her arms. He'd discovered she was *extremely* ticklish.

Elsie laughed and screamed as she fought against his hold. "Noooooo." She was laughing so hard she could barely get the word out.

"That's your first punishment," he said as she giggled so hard she was having a hard time breathing. He let up on her and stopped tickling so she could catch her breath.

Her breath rose and fell beneath her ski jacket. "What f-f-for?" Her lips were starting to turn blue from the cold. He'd take care of that.

Instead of answering, he kissed her slowly, letting his mouth warm her lips before he kissed her more deeply. Elsie sighed into his mouth and relaxed her body. He released her lips and cupped her face in his gloved hands, holding her still so that he could take her more thoroughly. His ski pants strangled his cock and he ground his hips between her thighs. She made soft little moans and wrapped her arms around his neck.

He picked her up by her ass that was probably still sore from a spanking last night—it had been at least a week since her last one. She wrapped her thighs around his hips and smiled at him as he carried her toward their cabin.

They were in Aspen and staying at a cabin owned by John's friend. It was huge—could hardly be called a cabin by traditional standards—but it had a cozy feel to it.

When they were in the cabin, John got a fire going in the massive fireplace that also served as a fireplace in the master bedroom. She had peeled her gloves off and was shivering while he stoked the fire. Even though they'd had a ridiculous amount of fun the last couple of weeks in Aspen, snow still wasn't her favorite thing. With Elsie, anything was his favorite, as long as he spent the time with her.

He was in such deep shit when it came to Elsie. Way over his head.

When the room was toasty—aided by the state-of-the-art heating system his friend had installed in the luxury cabin—John helped her strip out of her snowsuit. She was still chilled and as he slowly took her clothing off he kissed every cold part on her body he could find.

He pushed away her hood and released her hair. Elsie sighed as he started with her nose, kissing it before moving to each of her ears.

"John," she said on top of a moan. "You're a useful man to have around."

"Am I?" He brought his mouth to her lips and warmed them with a kiss.

"Definitely."

He raised an eyebrow and pulled back. "And how is that?"

"Shall I count the ways?"

"I'd love to hear them."

She pinched her brows as if deep in thought. "Let's see… You have excellent interviewing skills and you handle group situations almost as well as you work one-on-one."

John grinned and shook his head.

Her eyes turned a smoky gray. "Not to mention your ability to control a heated…situation."

He took her down to the soft, faux bearskin rug in front of the fireplace so fast she gave a yelp of surprise. He tugged down the zipper of her snowsuit then pulled off her boots, peeled off her snowsuit, her flannels next, then her underwear.

She twisted a lock of her hair with one of her fingers while she stared up at him, naked and beautiful in the firelight. Every time he looked at her like that, she stole his breath. Her red hair was spread out in a wave of fire against the brown bearskin, firelight flickering on her pale, creamy skin. The only thing on her was his gold collar, which to his pleasure she wore all the time. Her freckles sprinkled delicately across her shoulders and her breasts were large, her nipples hard and ripe for tasting. His gaze lingered on the fiery curls between her thighs. Speaking of tasting…

"You're dripping," she said with a teasing smile, and he looked down to see that he was still in his snowsuit.

He solved that problem in a hurry. In no time he was naked and between her thighs. Together they'd taken care of being tested, so they no longer needed any kind of barrier between them. Damn, how he loved the silky grip of her pussy around his cock.

John rubbed his erection in his fist as he looked at her and she reached for him. He shook his head, spread her thighs wide and went down on her.

She tasted so sweet. No wine could match the flavor of her juices. She moaned and writhed as he licked her and sucked her clit. He pounded his fingers in and out of her pussy as he relentlessly pushed her toward the edge.

"John, please," she begged.

He loved it when she begged.

"This is your punishment for that snowball fight." He looked at her as she squirmed from the loss of contact between his mouth and her pussy. "No coming until I say. Understand?"

She had a pained expression but nodded and he started devouring her again. She sobbed, squirmed and cried, but he didn't let up until *he* couldn't take it anymore.

He plunged his cock into her pussy in one hard motion, causing her to cry out. She grasped his ass, digging her nails deep in his flesh as he thrust hard. Her cries became louder and longer and perspiration gleamed on her forehead from fighting against her orgasm so hard.

His own climax built inside him, a hard concentration in his groin that threatened to shoot through his body and out the top of his head.

When there was no stopping his own orgasm, he barely got out the words, “Come, sweetheart,” before he exploded inside her. She cried out at the same time he did and he felt the hard contractions of her pussy around his cock as he throbbed inside her. He thought he was going to pass out from the intensity of his orgasm.

Moments later he was cuddling her by the firelight, never wanting to let her go.

Chapter Six

ജ

Elsie shook her head as John hobbled into his living room on his crutches. "You look so cute," she said with a grin. "And to think *I* was the one worried about breaking my leg."

He gave her an evil look and she sniggered again.

When he was settled on the couch with his broken leg resting on a chair, she curled up beside him and laid her head on his shoulder. He felt so warm and solid and smelled of the outdoors and his comfortable masculine scent that she'd come to love.

He'd broken his leg their last day in Aspen when he'd decided he wanted to ski down one of the more treacherous slopes. That's what he got for being a he-man.

Elsie sobered a little. She'd been so scared for him when she saw him tumble down the slope. It was like a piece of her had crashed against that mountainside.

They'd had to stay an extra day so that he could get his leg set in a cast that went up to his thigh. They'd changed their plans and had driven back—since he couldn't fly with a newly broken leg—and had arrived in Tucson just an hour or so ago.

John stroked her hair, which she'd left down just for him despite the fact that it was curly and unruly as hell.

"It's Valentine's Day," he murmured, his warm breath feathering against her ear and causing her to shiver.

"Oh yeah." In all the "excitement" she'd forgotten. "Sorry. I didn't get you anything."

He turned his face so that they were close enough for him to brush his lips over hers. "There's one thing you could give me."

Mischief was in his eyes and he brought her hand down to rub his erection.

"I'll just bet."

"It's in my jeans pocket," he said, a definite spark to his gaze.

"Uh-huh." To tease him a little more she slipped her finger into the pocket closest to her and ran her fingers along his cock through the thin material of the inside of the pocket.

"The other side," he said, sounding like he was clenching his jaw from the torture she was inflicting on him.

To humor him, and to have a little more fun, she reached across him—and immediately felt a bulge that had nothing to do with his erection.

A warm flush stole over her skin and she paused.

"Go on," he said.

She met his eyes as she dug it out then held the jewelers box that matched the one he'd given her before that had contained the gold choker. Only this one was the size of a ring box.

Her heart pounded. It wasn't what she thought it was. It couldn't be. No. Probably a pair of earrings to match the choker was inside the box. "When did you have time to get me anything?"

"I picked it out before we left," he said quietly. "Open it."

Elsie swallowed and lifted the lid of the box—to see a beautiful square diamond flanked by emeralds.

Her gaze shot to his, her lips parted, but she had no idea what to say. Her mind spun as if she was in a dream world.

"Your Valentine's Day gift to me would be to say yes." John took the box from her hand and drew the diamond from it. He slipped it on her ring finger. "Say you'll marry me, Elsie."

"I—wow." She held her hand to her forehead as she looked at him. "It's only been six weeks, John."

"Long enough for me to know you're the only woman I want in my life." He held both of her hands in his. "Say yes."

Warmth spread through her body and even unfroze her mind and her words. Six weeks had seemed like a lifetime with John. A lifetime she wanted to continue to share with him.

"Don't leave me hanging, sweetheart." He stroked the side of her face. "We can have as long an engagement as you want, but I'm not letting you go."

A smile spread across her face and she threw herself against his chest and wrapped her arms around his neck.

At the same time she almost knocked his broken leg off the chair and he laughed. "I guess that would be a yes?"

She moved her mouth to his and kissed him thoroughly, letting her mouth, her tongue, her lips, tell him everything she wanted him to know.

When she pulled back, she smiled and said it anyway. "Yes." She laughed and hugged him again. "Most definitely yes!" Then she drew away, paused and gave him a mock-serious look. "Under one condition."

John cocked an eyebrow. "And what's that?"

Elsie couldn't help a teasing grin. "From now on you have to let someone else do all of your interviews. The only interviewing you're going to be doing is with *me*."

"Ditto." He rubbed the ring on her finger. "I love you, sweetheart."

She gave a huge sigh of happiness. "I love you too." She straddled him and started unfastening his belt. "Let me give you your other Valentine's Day present…"

TAKING IT PERSONAL

Author's Note

ꙮ

Taking it Personal incorporates only elements of Domination/submission and BDSM. It is not intended to accurately portray a true BDSM or Dom/sub relationship.

Trademarks Acknowledgement

ꙮ

The author acknowledges the trademarked status and trademark owners of the following wordmarks mentioned in this work of fiction:

Corvette: General Motors Corporation

Lycra: E. I. du Pont de Nemours and Company

Mercedes: Daimler Chrysler AG Corporation

Chapter One

ഇ

Drew Bennett guided his sleek black Corvette along the interstate toward the health club where he spent part of his time as a personal trainer. He was a professional trainer for various pro athletes and he was late leaving his appointment with the current lightweight championship boxer who had his own personal gym.

A smile tipped the corner of Drew's lips. Sarah Fairland was going to be pissed that he was late—and that's exactly what he wanted. The uptight executive needed to be thrown off balance before they started today's workout. She'd been giving off sexual vibes for the last few sessions—scorching hot vibes that he'd purposely ignored. She wanted him and damned if he wasn't attracted to her more than any woman he'd been with in a long time.

He rubbed his erection through his gym shorts and pictured Sarah on her knees, her hands bound behind her back as she sucked his cock.

Oh, he was going to give her what she wanted...and far, far more. Sarah Fairland was going to learn a few lessons if she wanted to play with him. Maybe she was used to dominating the business world, but when it came to him, she'd be on her knees begging him to take control. Control that she would hand over freely once he introduced her to his world.

* * * * *

Sarah Fairland checked her reflection in the exclusive health club's bathroom mirror. Regardless of the fact that Drew Bennett was going to put her through the paces today, she'd taken special care with her makeup—not too much and not too little. Just right. Her shoulder-length brown hair was held up in a twist, giving her a look that heightened her cheekbones and complimented her blue eyes.

As a CEO she was driven and known in the business world as a woman with brass ovaries. She had no qualms about doing whatever she had to in order to get what she wanted.

In this case she wanted Drew Bennett.

A fling with her sexy physical trainer was exactly what she needed to release the frustrations of dealing with incompetent people on every level in the business world. She ground her teeth at the thought of her last encounter with a competing firm's president and CEO. The bastard had tried to treat her as if she were a low-ranking peon.

She'd sure as hell put the SOB in his place and took him down a few notches.

Sarah strode out of the bathroom that smelled of lemon disinfectant that didn't hide the reek of sweaty socks. There was absolutely no excuse for that stink. If she ran the club she'd put everyone in their place and make sure the club was in perfect shape in every way.

Sounds of voices and the clanking of weights were loud on the gym floor and the place smelled of testosterone. Damn, there were some good-looking hunks pumping iron, but she had her sights set on only one man today.

Humid air touched her skin exposed by her bright yellow crop-top and low-rider Lycra workout shorts. She looked good and she knew it. Her body was toned, perfectly fit, and she kept it that way by working out four times a week and utilizing a personal trainer.

When she reached Drew's office she was surprised to see he wasn't there. He was always on time for their training appointments. Sarah pursed her lips. She didn't tolerate tardiness. She seated herself in one of the blue plastic chairs in front of his desk, crossed her knees and stilled her foot to keep it from swinging. No matter the situation, she always maintained control.

Her irritation level grew as the minutes passed by on the large, round, black-rimmed clock that reminded her of those clocks that had always been in her classrooms during her school years. As a student she had only been impatient to move on to the next class because she always finished her work ahead of everyone else. Even then she'd been an achiever, a type-A personality.

Six minutes passed before Drew strolled through the doorway. Even though she was irritated as hell, he nearly took her breath away as she looked up at him. Shoulder-length blond hair and brown eyes the color of warm cocoa. He was muscular perfection with his tanned skin, his carved biceps and triceps revealed by his sleeveless T-shirt. His shoulders and chest were powerful beneath that shirt, and she itched to run her hands down his rippled six-pack abs to his trim hips and beyond. The bulge in his gym shorts had told her from the beginning that he was definitely worth her time.

"Hey, Sarah." He pulled open a desk drawer and tossed in a set of car keys. "I've got a new workout I'd like to start you on."

No apology for being tardy and making her wait? No explanation?

"You're late," she said, her words coming out clipped as she stood. It wasn't exactly the way she'd intended to start out her plans to get him into her bed.

An amused expression crossed his features, rather than annoyed like she'd expected. She straightened her five-foot ten-inch frame, but the man was still a good five inches taller than her.

"Let's get started." He grabbed a clipboard off his desk and waited for her to exit the room ahead of him. A gentlemanly gesture that was not unusual for him. Surprising in today's world and certainly not necessary.

They walked side by side to the private workout room utilized for personal trainers and their clients. Again Drew held the door open for her and she stepped inside before the door eased closed behind them. Only a small, vertical, rectangular window in the door took away from complete privacy and the door had no lock. Unfortunate.

As always, Drew started her out with warm-up exercises. They both stood on mats in front of the mirrored wall.

"I have a few new exercises I'd like you to try." Was she mistaken or was his voice warmer, deeper?

She stretched from side-to-side then righted herself. "I'm ready for anything."

"Are you?" His hands brushed over her bare waist as he moved her in front of the mirror.

Sarah sucked in her breath at the unexpected intimate contact. Her nipples peaked against her cropped top and they were large and obvious in the mirror. The hint of a smile curved the corner of Drew's lips as she watched his gorgeous features. He could easily have passed for a Greek god.

The romanticized thought almost made her shake her head.

For the first time since he had become her personal trainer a few weeks ago, Drew positioned her with his hands instead of just telling her what to do.

"That's it," he said as his fingertips brushed her hips.

The sensuous movement caused moisture to dampen her thong. Her eyes met his in the mirror and he gave her a slow, sexy smile.

He *knew*.

He knew exactly how much she wanted him. The past few weeks she had let off a few vibes, but he hadn't acknowledged them. Today, though—today he was touching her in ways that aroused her. Small, intimate movements, but they turned her on more than she'd been in a long time.

After she finished stretching on the mats, Drew took her hand and helped her to her feet. He looked at her body from head to toe in a way that made her nipples tighten more and her pussy to grow even wetter.

"You're in perfect shape, Sarah." The way he said her name sent tingles through her belly.

Ridiculous. She was no sexual novice. But everything he said and did was making her horny as hell.

She couldn't help the little gasp that escaped her when he ran his knuckles from beneath her breasts to her abs. "Perfect," he said again. "Like I told you, I'm going to change up your routine today."

"What are we doing different?" Sarah found herself almost trembling from the sexual currents running between her and Drew. She raised her chin, sucked in her breath and fought to get her hormones under control. She did *not* let a man affect her like this. Even if she did want to fuck him.

"We're going to work on your upper *and* lower body, rather than concentrating on one area." He gave her an intense look before turning away and leading her to the bench press.

The way he said "upper and lower body" made her think he meant more than just a normal workout.

Well, that was what she wanted, wasn't it?

When she was on her back beneath the barbell, Drew caressed her breasts with his gaze. She took a deep breath and tried to calm herself to control the now rapid beating of her heart. Instead of walking behind her to spot her, he straddled her waist so that his groin was close enough to touch. And through his tight gym shorts, it was obvious he was as aroused as she was.

She wanted to run her fingers along the length of his cock but resisted—barely. Instead she raised her arms up and grasped the bar, pushed up to get the barbell off its rest and began her presses. Damned if her arms didn't shake a little, making it more difficult. When she had reached the count of fifteen, she raised the bar up and Drew helped her put it back on its rest.

After three sets, she finished bench pressing. Drew took her hand and helped her to a sitting position. Just the way he held her fingers, a little too long, sent thrills throughout her body.

Rather than helping her to her feet, he sat on the bench facing her, brought his hand up and ran his fingers along her triceps, causing her to shiver. "Did you feel it here?" he asked as he slowly stroked. He looked at her breasts. "You should feel it in your triceps, chest and shoulders."

Sarah's face was hot, not only from lying down and bench pressing but from the way he was touching her, now trailing his fingers from her triceps to her shoulder and back while meeting her gaze.

She had to take control of this situation and she had to take it fast.

Doing her best to sound unaffected, she said, "What kind of workout are we having here, Drew?"

"I like the way you say my name." He skimmed his fingers from her shoulder down to her breastbone, dangerously close to her breasts. "What kind of workout do you want, Sarah?"

"I think this is something we should discuss in your office." She made her tone strong, firm. Oh yeah, she wanted to take this someplace private, *now*.

"No." He shook his head. "We're going to continue your workout right here." Before she could respond, he trailed his fingers all the way to one of her nipples and squeezed.

She gasped and widened her eyes in shock at his brazen move. "Drew—"

Further words failed her as he raised his free hand and pinched her other nipple then twisted them both, hard.

Sarah gave a surprised cry and brought her hands up to cover his. Instead of trying to force his hands from her breasts, she moaned and pressed his palms tighter against her globes and she tipped back her head.

"Touch me." His voice was a command that had her snapping her attention back to him. "Grab my cock with that pretty little hand of yours."

Heat flooded her and she glared at him. "No one tells me—"

Drew took her hand off his and had it on his firm erection before she could finish her sentence. He returned his hand to her nipple and twisted them both hard again and she held back a cry of surprise and pain.

A wild sensation tore through her, as if she'd been shocked, followed by a chill.

After a stunned second, anger rose like a heat wave.

Well, two *can play the squeeze-and-tease game.*

Her gaze locked with his and she squeezed his erection, running her fingers along the length of it. *Good God, he's big.* She brought her fingers all the way down to his balls and cupped them firmly, her eyes still meeting his. It would be so easy to squeeze them and bring him to his knees.

He didn't look in the least bit concerned. Instead, his eyes grew smokier, his gaze more intense. She could picture him laying her back on the bench and fucking her, that big cock driving in and out...

Sarah thought she was melting, as if he was casting some kind of spell on her. He moved one of his hands to cup her pussy and her hold on his balls faltered. The material between her thighs was moist and grew wetter as he rubbed his fingers up and down the stretchy material covering her folds.

Almost without thought, she began stroking the length of his cock faster and faster. His fingers matched her rhythm, and she felt herself actually climbing closer to orgasm by him touching her through her clothing.

He slid his other hand up to the back of her head, cupped it and took her mouth in such a hard kiss he stole her breath.

He smelled of the outdoors and testosterone—a combination that added to the lust building within her. And his taste, sweet like he'd just drank a soda pop, yet all male.

Vaguely she was aware that she had totally lost control over the situation. Drew was mastering her, dominating her. It set her body on fire. She'd never felt this way. Ever.

And she wanted more.

His mouth commanded hers. His tongue thrust inside her mouth, exploring, claiming. She cried out as he bit her lip hard—she'd never felt anything so erotic. He sucked her tongue into his mouth as he continued to rub his fingers against her clit through her shorts.

Dizzy. She was dizzy from his kiss. Out of control and flying—soaring higher and higher. Her body hummed and her body raced toward her climax—

Drew stopped.

He pulled away from their kiss and took his hand from her pussy. He still cupped the back of her head and studied her with his intense brown eyes.

"Why—" She blinked and shook her head to try to shake some sense back into herself. "Why the hell did you stop?"

His expression was dark, smoldering. "You have to wait for your orgasm. Until you've earned it."

"Until I—*what*?" She tried to jerk away from where his hand cupped the back of her head but he gripped the twist in her hair. When she attempted to draw back, the movement yanked her hair at her skull and she ended up with tears pricking the back of her eyes from the pain. "Let go of me, you sonofabitch," she hissed in her best ice-witch voice.

Drew's look only became darker, as if he was displeased with her. Somehow, disappointing him made her feel contrite and she had the insane desire to do something that would please him.

What the fuck *is the matter with me?*

"Sarah," he said in a flat, almost angry tone, "if you want to play, we play my way."

She blinked. He'd taken her by surprise again. "Play?" What did he mean by *play*?

Without even looking to see if anyone was near the small window in the door, Drew jerked her workout top up and over her breasts. The top had a built-in bra, so when he raised it, he completely bared her. She had no time to react before his hot mouth was licking and sucking one of her nipples. He kept her head cupped in one hand while bringing his other back to her pussy, which he began rubbing in earnest.

She gasped at the feel of his mouth on her nipple and his hand on her pussy. When he moved his mouth to her other nub, her now bare, wet nipple felt cool in the room, but she was on fire inside. She grasped her hands in his hair as he suckled. "God, Drew—"

"Don't climax unless I allow it, Sarah." He rubbed her clit harder and licked her nipple in between words. "Do you understand?"

"I—" She started to respond, but he brought his mouth to hers in another hard kiss. Her nipples, wet from his mouth, were smashed against his chest as he kept his grip on her hair twist and rubbed her clit.

Dizzy. Christ, she was dizzy again. And flying. Why did she feel like she was soaring?

Who the hell cares? Go with it, Sarah.

She was actually whimpering. Her. *Whimpering*. A dominating, commanding, controlling sonofabitch was taking her to heights she'd never been to. Making her want things she'd never wanted before.

But who the hell was he to say when she was allowed to come? What did he think he would do if she climaxed without his so-called permission?

Another whimper rose up within her that she couldn't hold back as he kissed her literally senseless. Her bare nipples rasped against his T-shirt and he was rubbing her clit harder, faster, rougher and she knew she was about to lose it. Her thighs began to vibrate and her moans grew louder as she prepared to come.

She was at the edge. Ready to tip over.

He stopped.

Again.

The bastard *stopped*.

Her breathing was heavy as he pulled his hand away from her pussy and broke their kiss. Heat flushed every part of her and she wanted to punch him. She was so on edge, so close to coming that she wanted to scream.

"Do you want me to fuck you, Sarah?" He gripped her hair twist tighter. "Do you want my cock inside you?"

She should have said no. All of this was wrong. *She* was supposed to be in control. She was *always* in control. No man could ever dominate her—it was something she *never* allowed.

But what came out of her mouth was, "*Yes*. I want you to fuck me."

Drew gave her a long, hard look. "When you've earned the right."

Chapter Two

ꝏ

Drew almost smiled at the look of outrage on Sarah's features. She'd been having a hard time forming complete sentences since he'd taken control of her and now was no exception.

Her face flushed and she reached up to jerk down her cropped top. He grabbed both of her wrists in one of his hands, forcing her to stop. He still had a hold on her pinned-up hair, keeping her from moving her head. To his amusement and arousal, even her breasts grew pink when she was angry.

She struggled against his hold. "I could scream."

"You could." He shrugged one shoulder. "But you don't want to."

"You arrogant sonof—"

To shut her up again, he jerked her head toward him and kissed her. She fought against him at first and then she as good as melted, becoming pliable, soft, but kissing him back with her own intensity. She made the cutest little mewling sounds when he kissed her, and she tasted of mint and feminine fire.

This time when Drew broke the kiss and looked into her eyes, he saw her surrender and knew he'd won—this round.

She licked her lips, as if tasting his kiss.

"Do you want me to fuck you, Sarah?" He kept his hold on her wrists, preparing her for the kind of play he intended to continue past this moment.

She hesitated but then raised her chin, spirit flashing in her eyes. "Yes."

"Good girl." First things first. Still holding her hair and her wrists, he pulled her up to a standing position so that they were both straddling the bench. "Come here," he ordered her as he backed them away from the bench and were standing in an open space.

He pushed down on her head and pulled her wrists in the same direction, forcing her to kneel in front of him. Then he held her wrists over her head, forcing her naked breasts to jut out.

"If you want to fuck," he said, "the first thing you're going to do is take my cock into that sassy mouth of yours."

She looked at him with incredulity and tried to stand, but he kept his hand fully on her head, forcing her to stay down. "Drew..." she said in what sounded like a warning tone.

Drew grasped her hair and tugged her head back so that she was looking directly at him. "If you want me to fuck you, then you do as I command. That's how this works, Sarah."

She opened her mouth. Closed it. Opened it again. "Someone might walk in on us."

"We have the room reserved for an hour." He smiled, knowing he had her now. "It's all ours."

"But the door doesn't lock." She glanced up at the big clock on the wall. "And we only have another thirty minutes."

"Doesn't the thought give you a thrill?" His voice was low, husky with his need for her. She didn't even seem to realize he'd let go of her head. "The fear of getting caught?"

By her hardened nipples and the look of lust on her features, he knew he was right. She couldn't deny she wanted what he was offering. He wasn't forcing her to do anything that she ultimately didn't desire—if she insisted she'd have nothing to do with him, he would stop their play in a heartbeat. But she'd admitted she wanted him to fuck her. And she was going to have to earn it.

Now that his hand was free because he'd let go of her hair, he pulled down the front of his gym shorts and exposed his cock, right in front of Sarah's face.

"You're so big..." She tried tugging her hands from his hold on her wrists, but he didn't allow her to. He kept her arms high over her head. Being his captive was all part of what he had planned for her.

By the breathless tone of her voice, there was no doubt she was his. "Let me fuck your mouth, Sarah."

She hesitated then parted her lips. Drew barely restrained a groan as he felt the heat of her mouth slide over the head of his erection. It about blew his mind when she applied deep suction and moved her tongue from side to side. He began moving his hips, being careful to not go too deep, but deep enough that he thought his balls were going to explode.

Sarah made soft little moaning sounds as she began going down on him in earnest. *Shit.* If he let her at it much longer, he wasn't going to last. He focused on holding back his own pleasure, knowing that it would be all that much sweeter when he did come inside her.

When the need to come was beyond painful, he forced her to stop.

As she looked up at him, her chest rose and fell with her heightened breathing and her face was still flushed light pink, a fine sheen of perspiration on her skin. The tough corporate executive wanted him bad enough that she was turning control over to him.

"Fuck me now, Drew." She tried to stand, but he put his hand on her head to keep her down.

"You don't give the commands here, Sarah." He caught her hair again and held the tight knot at the back of her head. "For once in your life, you're not the boss. To get that through your pretty head, I'm going to have to punish you."

"*What*?" To begin with, Sarah couldn't believe she was allowing this man to keep her on her knees and insist on her sucking his cock before he'd take her. But now he was talking about some kind of punishment, like he was into some kind of freaking BDSM?

"Oh no." She tried to shake her head. "You're into bondage and shit, aren't you?"

"You're catching on." He gave what looked like a tolerant smile. "You've been fighting me every step of the way, and you tried to tell me what to do. I'm going to turn you over my lap and give you the spanking of your life."

Despite the fact that they were on a whole new level she hadn't expected, and never dreamed she'd be on the receiving end of it, her body raged, ready to obey whatever he asked of her. She had to come so bad that she wanted to scream with the power of her frustration.

"I'm not into pain." It was pissing her off that he wouldn't let her stand, but at the same time turning her on staring at that big cock that she wanted inside her so bad.

Drew's eyes were dark, threatening but not. "By the time I'm ready to fuck you, you'll be into pain, Sarah. Overcome with it. Wrapped and stroked in it until you feel so much, so good, so perfect, you'll come the moment I tell you to."

Sarah shivered at the sensual promise in his voice. In the next moment he was drawing her to her feet, her wrists still over her head. The fact that her breasts were bared and his cock was out of his shorts had the effect of making her knees weak. This whole situation was almost surreal. She felt outside of herself, in a delicious, abandoned sort of way.

He sat on the bench they'd vacated earlier and had her over his lap, her wrists pinned behind her back so fast her head spun. She hadn't even caught her breath before he jerked down her shorts, exposing her bare flesh, and his hand landed hard on her ass.

"*Ow!* You sonofabitch!" She struggled but he spanked her again, and she let out another shout.

"Not another sound or you'll get double the punishment." He rubbed his palm over her burning ass and a strange sort of pleasure went straight to her pussy. "It's going to be so good when I fuck you, Sarah, you won't be able to see straight."

"Or sit," she mumbled, and then wondered what the hell she was thinking. She was going to go through with this?

Oh hell. They'd gone this far, and she was so close to having that thick cock inside of her. Right now it was pressing against her belly as she lay across his lap and she was so damn wet she was slick between her thighs.

She gritted her teeth and held back another shout as his hand landed on her ass again and again. Gone was the corporate CEO who ate powerful men for breakfast. In her place was a woman dying to do anything to get fucked—and for some dumb-ass reason, wanting to please the dominating, controlling man who was now spanking her.

When he finished, her ass was stinging so bad tears moistened her eyes. She never cried, but a combination of pain and sexual frustration made her come real close to letting those tears fall.

He rubbed her ass then placed kisses on each of her tender globes before helping her to her feet.

Sarah was breathless and filled with anticipation. Her spandex shorts were down around her thighs, her shirt above her breasts, and Drew's cock was hard and ready.

"Bend over and put your hands on the bench," he commanded as he released her wrists.

At this point she wasn't about to argue about anything. It was hard to admit to herself, but the way he had taken control from the beginning was totally turning her on.

She placed her palms on the bench and he pushed her shorts down to her knees. She looked to her right and saw their reflections in the big wall mirror and her pussy instantly ached even more. Just seeing herself mostly naked, her ass pink, and Drew's erection ready to enter her made her lightheaded. She watched as he pulled a packet out of his pocket and in moments had a condom out and his cock sheathed.

"Don't come without my permission, Sarah," he warned. "Do you understand?"

"Yes, yes, yes." She wiggled her ass. "Please, Drew."

Their eyes met in the reflection and he smiled, a carnal, hungry smile, right before he thrust his cock into her pussy.

Sarah couldn't hold back the scream that tore from her lips. She almost came the moment he penetrated her, stretched her, filled her. Her core clenched down on his cock and she had to take deep breaths as he stayed still, his groin tight against her burning ass.

All the waiting, the teasing, the spanking—everything made her so on edge she didn't know if she was going to be able to stop an orgasm the minute he started moving in her. Did she even want to hold back? Who was he to tell her—

He slapped her ass and she cried out. "Don't even think about coming, Sarah. You'll be punished if you do."

Yeah, right. When and how?

Drew gripped her hips and started to pump in and out of her body, slowly at first, then harder and faster. He pounded against her and she closed her eyes, lost in the sensations.

He slapped her ass again and she gasped as her eyes flew open. "Watch us in the mirror, babe."

Sarah parted her lips as she looked at their reflections and saw his cock moving in and out of her pussy. He was so long, so thick, so big and it was incredible seeing him fuck her.

She needed to climax so badly that she thought she'd pass out from the power of it. That dizzying sensation he caused within her came back with a vengeance, and she could barely focus on the images of the two of them. Her chest hurt from breathing so hard and she'd broken out into a full-blown sweat, as if she'd just had a hard workout.

Well, if that wasn't what this had turned out to be.

The peak was so close she had to fight to keep from toppling over it. Why was she fighting it? Because Drew told her to. Why did she care what Drew thought?

He drove her hard. "What if someone walks in on us now, Sarah?"

The moment he said that, she lost it. The thought of being seen totally threw her over the edge. She screamed and her whole body shook. Her vision swam, her knees buckled and her arms didn't want to hold her up anymore where she'd had her palms braced on the bench. Drew kept her from falling by grasping her hips as he continued to fuck her. He gripped her hard enough to keep her from dropping, but at the same time he was making her even weaker from the power of the spasms racking her body with every one of his thrusts.

Her orgasm wouldn't stop. It was shaking her, making her almost blind by the pleasure and pain of it. Everything blended until she was one ball of sensation. Vaguely she heard Drew's shout and felt the pulse of his cock in her core. He slammed into her a few more times and she cried out with every thrust.

Finally he stopped and held his groin tight to her hips. Through her blurry vision she saw his reflection—he was baring his teeth like a tiger claiming its territory. And she was his territory.

Ridiculous, she thought as her entire body slumped.

Drew helped lower her gradually to her knees and she braced her head on her folded arms on the bench as she tried to return to her senses. She felt him pull up her thong, then her shorts so that she was no longer bared from the waist down. He did the same with her cropped top, bringing it down over her breasts so that she was now fully covered.

Sarah couldn't stop shaking and her pussy continued to spasm. She didn't know what just happened to her, but she wanted the license plate number of the truck that just hit her.

Or more likely the phone number of the man who'd just turned her world upside down and inside out.

When she managed the strength to raise her head, she looked over her shoulder to see Drew had his shorts up and he was tossing something into the garbage can by the door. Probably the condom.

He returned to her and caught her under the arms, bringing her to her feet with the power and grace of the tiger she'd seen in him when he climaxed. She barely managed to stand on her own two feet and had finally regained her vision so that everything wasn't so blurry anymore.

The smell of sex and sweat was heavy in the room and she was so hot. Sweltering. She needed a nice cold shower to bring herself back to reality and to douse the flames that continued to run through her body.

Sarah looked up at Drew as he put his arm around her shoulders to steady her as they walked through the door. A man stood just outside the door when they opened it and she saw Drew slip him what looked like a twenty.

Sarah's mind tried to process that little piece of information as they reached his office. She looked up at him and he had his usual expression.

"Time's up for today, Ms. Fairland."

Chapter Three

ꟃ

"Time's up, my ass!" Sarah paced the length of her office and clenched her hands into fists so hard her nails dug into her palms. Her office was fairly new and the smells of new carpeting and wood added to the headache building at her temples. "Sonofabitch."

Yesterday, after his statement, Drew had left her standing in the doorway and strode around his desk to sit in his chair. He had opened his date book and studied it.

She had stared at him, incredulous. Her body had still hummed from their "workout" and she had to grip the doorframe to stand straight.

He'd glanced up, his expression the same as if they'd had a normal workout. "Tuesday next week?" he asked without the slightest hint in his voice about what had just happened.

"Fuck you," she'd said with venom under her breath.

"You just did," he'd replied, not even fracturing his calm expression. "I've got you down on the calendar for your regular workout."

Sarah stopped pacing and clenched her teeth as hard as she was clenching her hands as she stared at her desk. That glass paperweight of a bird in flight would look real good buried in the wall across the room.

Last night, unable to believe any of what had happened—or his response—she'd slammed Drew's office door shut, stormed off to the locker room and grabbed her things. She'd gone straight home instead of taking her usual shower at the club. Due to the way he'd dismissed her, she'd gone from boneless to so stiff she could hardly walk. When she reached her home she'd filled a glass with chardonnay and took a long, hot bubble bath to try to control the anger and tension in her body.

What really pissed her off, though, was that despite her fury at Drew she kept reliving every moment, every touch, the way he felt inside her, the way he *dominated* her.

Sarah shook her head at the thought. *Absolutely fucking unbelievable.* She held her hand to her forehead and rubbed her temples. The best sex she'd had in her life regulated to appointments?

She snorted and hiccupped, which almost led to maniacal laughter. As she thought about it, she wasn't sure what had happened, but somehow she didn't regret it. Who could regret once-in-a-lifetime sex like that?

After last night, today had been an interesting day. As pissed as she'd been, she'd barreled through every appointment she'd had, controlling each meeting with her usual directness and I-don't-put-up-with-shit demeanor. She had taken care of some difficulties by firing an attorney and ensured a general manager was now up shit creek when she'd exposed his incompetence to his employer.

A knock at the door to her office had Sarah jerking her head up and composing her features into her business mask. "Yes," she said firmly.

The door handle clicked and her assistant, Tammy, pushed the door open. "Ms. Fairland, this came for you." The petite blonde walked in carrying a long white box that looked like it might have come from a florist. She set the box on Sarah's desk.

"Is there anything you need right now?" Tammy asked, her gaze meeting Sarah's. The thing Sarah liked about Tammy was that she never acted intimidated around her. Tammy was extremely competent and held her ground well.

But today Sarah waved Tammy away, barely paying attention to her assistant. "Not right now."

As soon as Tammy closed the door behind her, Sarah picked up the box, raised it and almost pitched it across the room. No doubt morning-after-regret-the-way-I-acted flowers. Well, fuck him.

She gripped the box, ready to heave it, and looked down at the lid. Just a simple white lid with nothing on it.

Out of sheer, morbid curiosity she opened the box—

Inside, nestled in red tissue paper, was a black flogger with suede straps.

A flogger?

She raised it and felt the weight of the leather handle and trailed the soft straps over her fingers before looking at the box again.

A small white card lay in place of the flogger she'd just picked up. It pissed her off that her fingers trembled a little as she opened it. The card listed an address then below it was written in bold male handwriting:

Tonight, 7:00 p.m.

If you dare.

She blinked and read the card again. If she dared?

Her jaw tightened. Oh, she'd show up all right.

She'd put Drew Bennett right in his place.

* * * * *

Sarah parked her Mercedes in front of the home that had the address Drew had given. The card hadn't been signed but she had no doubt in her mind that it had been from him.

When she cut the lights, darkness stole over her, the only light coming from a single streetlight at the end of the cul-de-sac, and from the lights along the walkway to his front door. His home was on the northwest side of Tucson and from the outside looked gorgeous with its high arched entryway and bay windows to either side.

Despite herself, a strange fluttering sensation in her belly caused her nerves to be on edge. She didn't like the feeling one bit. It made her feel out of control, out of her element.

She'd kept on the power suit she'd worn to work to give her added confidence, a lipstick-red fitted jacket with a matching slim-fitting skirt that reached just above her knees. Her red heels were a modest two inches but made her long legs look even sleeker.

After taking a deep, calming breath, Sarah put on her best boardroom face and exited the car holding the white florist box containing the flogger under one of her arms. She didn't bother bringing in her purse since she wasn't staying. She would let Drew have it up one side and down the other and rip him a new one. *Bastard.*

Out of habit, she locked her car after closing the door behind her. Keys in one hand and box under her other arm, she strode up the walkway to the home. Her gaze took in the manicured desert landscaping and the spotlights that illuminated the walkway as well as illuminated the big saguaro and other cacti in his front yard. His home was on a good-sized lot, not too close to his neighbors.

When she reached his front door, she ground her teeth and punched the doorbell hard enough that she jammed her finger. She didn't have to wait long before the door opened and Drew stood in the doorway.

A sexy smile tilted the corner of his mouth and his shoulder-length hair hung in soft waves to his shoulders. But what got her was the fact that he was bare from the waist up. Oh God, he was even more gorgeous than when wearing clothes. Every muscle was so clearly defined. He was barefoot, wore only faded jeans, and had a definite bulge beneath the worn cotton material.

Her mouth watered.

She had to force anger into her expression and push away thoughts of him fucking her at the health club. The images, the memories, were enough to make her knees weak.

Sarah thrust the box against his chest, hitting him hard with it. "I think this belongs to you."

"Oh no, baby. It's yours." His grin only became sexier and he didn't take the box. Instead, he grabbed her arm and jerked her into the foyer. Her heels made her stumble with the movement, and she found herself up against him with the box crunched between their chests. He grabbed the box from her hand and tossed it aside. She heard a dull thump on the tiled foyer. She tried to jerk away and opened her mouth to verbally let him have it.

But he caught her by her head with one of his big hands and her ass with his other, and crushed her up against him before taking her mouth in a fierce, dominating kiss.

Sarah fought against him, banging her fists on his hard bare chest, only making him laugh against her mouth before biting her lip and causing her to cry out. He thrust his tongue inside her and she tasted him along with the hint of a beer he must have been drinking. His scent seeped into her senses. Outdoor breezes and some kind of musky cologne.

It was embarrassing to admit, but it didn't take long before all fight left her as she fell under the magic spell of his kiss. He held her ass tight with one hand, pressing her to him, and ground his erection into her belly, making her pussy ache to have him inside her. He felt warm and surrounded her with barely leashed power.

Her nipples grew to hard, painful peaks, her breasts heavy, and the wetness between her thighs at an all-time high. Still kissing her, he brought her into the house and slammed the door behind them, probably using his foot, because he never took his hands off her. No, he took complete control and didn't let up one fraction.

That damned dizzying sensation took over again and she felt as if she was his to play with, his to command. Vaguely she heard the loud clatter of her car keys on the tile of the foyer as they slipped from her fingers. It was like she didn't have command over her own body or her mind as she wrapped her arms around his neck and held on for dear life.

His kiss was so masterful, passionate, and she simply melted under his assault. She tangled her fingers in his long hair, the strands so soft while his kiss was so hard. Those annoying whimpering sounds rose up within her but she couldn't hold them in.

He stepped back, bringing her with him, until her heels sank into thick carpet. She was too busy kissing him to have any idea what the place she was now in looked like. She could have been in front of fifty people for all she knew. All that mattered was his kiss.

Drew sank down, bringing them both to their knees. She had the sensation of falling, then her back was on the floor, his mouth still ravaging hers, and his knee between her thighs.

A groan rose up in him, almost like a growl as he shoved her skirt to her waist and she felt cool air above her thigh-high stockings and touching her damp thong. Drew's hand quickly warmed her pussy as he rubbed her through the material.

Not this. No, he wasn't going to bring her to the edge and then leave her hanging again.

She squirmed, trying to get away from his touch, but he slipped his hand beneath the thong and slid his fingers into her wet folds. She cried out against his mouth and he thrust two fingers into her channel and started slamming his knuckles against her pussy.

Sarah gripped her hands tighter in his hair but he broke their kiss and moved his lips along her jawline to her earlobe then ran his tongue over the edge of the delicate shell of her ear.

"Grab my cock, Sarah," he commanded, his breath whispering over her ear and causing her to shiver.

The urge to obey came too easily. She moaned and released his hair to move her hand between their bodies. She was more than willing to touch him. His cock felt so damn hard beneath his jeans and she wanted him inside her so badly she squirmed beneath him with need. It pleased her when he groaned as she squeezed his erection.

"You're so beautiful." He moved his hand from the back of her head, brought it to the lapel of her fitted jacket and began to unbutton her top one by one. "I love the way your nipples tighten and grow larger in my mouth. I love the way your pussy looks when you're bent over."

She shivered from his erotic words and from his fingers touching her bare skin as he took care of the buttons. He moved his mouth from her ear to her throat and released all the buttons while continuing to thrust his fingers in and out of her pussy with his other hand.

Sarah felt like she was on another world, like all of this was happening to someone else. It almost felt surreal. But it was happening to her and being honest with herself, she *loved* it. Only because it was Drew. No one else could touch her, control her, dominate her like him.

He pinched the front clasp of her bra with his fingers and it fell open, revealing her breasts. "Perfect," he murmured before suckling one of them. She arched her back, whimpered, and rubbed her hand harder and harder up and down his erection, imagining him plunging in and out of her like he had at the health club.

The images of the two of them, and how he'd made her watch him fuck her by looking at their reflection in the mirror, brought her closer to orgasm. She writhed against Drew's hand as she pictured that moment and remembered the feel of his cock deep inside her.

Her body vibrated against his hand. "I'm going to come," she cried.

He slowed his strokes and their gazes met. "You already have one punishment coming for climaxing yesterday without my permission. Do you want another?"

Punishment. There was that word again.

Sarah could barely think. The woman she was outside his front door was not the same woman who writhed beneath this man now. No, this woman was different. She wanted to please him, was willing to do whatever he asked of her.

What's wrong with me? went through her mind, followed by, *Who cares? I need him. I need* this.

Her body was going crazy as he moved his finger from inside her core to stroke her slick folds and her clit, bringing her closer to an orgasm she didn't think she could stop. He was biting her nipples now, hard enough to make her cry out and arch her back.

"Fuck me, Drew." She slipped her hand from his cock to the button of his jeans at the same time she gripped his biceps with her other hand. All that rock-hard muscle, and that rock-hard erection turned her on beyond belief.

He brought his fingers out of her thong and knelt between her thighs, forcing them wider with his palms. His gaze took her in and she could imagine how she looked. Flushed with arousal, her breasts completely bared, her skirt up around her waist exposing her thong and her sheer thigh-high nylons.

He slowly stroked the insides of her thighs from the sensitive place beside her pussy, all the way to her knees and back.

"Please." A part of her couldn't believe she was begging. Right now she'd do anything to have him inside her.

"I told you that when we play, we play *my* way." Drew's expression grew stern, shocking her out of her dazed stupor. "Is that understood?" he asked.

The need for him was so bad that Sarah hesitated only a moment before she nodded. Yesterday evening the spanking had actually been pretty hot and had made her orgasm even more spectacular.

He bent one of her knees, held her ankle in his hand and slipped her shoe off before tossing it aside. "You're a powerful woman, Sarah. We both know that." He brought her other knee up and got rid of that shoe as well. "But when it comes to sex, *I'm* the one in control." She held her breath as he peeled off one of her stockings. "You do what I say, and if you disobey me, you will be punished."

The pounding in her ears and the beat of her heart told her how much his words excited her at the same time they pissed her off. But the excitement outweighed the anger, even though her mind told her she was crazy.

"Do you understand what I'm saying, Sarah?" He pulled down her other stocking, easing it down her leg and over her foot then tossed it aside. "In the business world you're in control. When it comes to sex, I am in control."

Her mouth and throat were too dry to get a word out.

"Answer," he commanded. "Do you understand that I am the Master when it comes to sex?"

She swallowed. This was the truth of it, where she would cross that line she never dreamed she would pass over. "Yes," she managed to get out.

"Yes, Master." He gripped her thong on either side and started to pull it down. He moved out of the way and she arched her hips a bit so that he could take it completely off her. "You will refer to me as Master every time you speak to me."

Sarah's mouth opened and her eyes widened. *Master?*

He leaned forward and braced his hands to either side of her arms as he looked down at her. "I won't tolerate any kind of disobedience, Sarah. And that includes not addressing me properly."

"Yes, Master," she said but immediately thought, *who is this woman and what has she done with the real Sarah Fairland?*

Drew gifted her with a sinfully sexy smile as he unzipped the side zipper of her skirt. "Good girl." He tugged her skirt down over her hips and knees until he had it all the way off and she was naked from the waist down. "Now pay attention to the ground rules."

Chapter Four

ꙮ

Ground rules?

Drew took Sarah's hand and helped her sit up. Her mind spun a little as he pushed off her fitted jacket and bra. She was completely naked save for a pair of half-carat diamond studs at her ears.

"As I've already said, you'll refer to me as Master at all times." He reached behind her head and pulled the pin holding her hair up so that her brown hair fell to her shoulders. "You'll do anything I ask of you without question. You'll let me do anything I want to do to your body without argument. If you break any rules or fail to follow my instructions, you'll be punished." Her heart beat faster with every one of his words. This was all so unreal. "Now you need to choose a safe word."

Confusion about everything whirled within her. She wrinkled her brow. "A what?"

Drew gave a heavy sigh. "Master. That's your last warning."

Shit. I can't believe I'm doing this! "I don't know what you mean, er, Master."

"A safe word is an out for you." He leaned close and sifted his fingers through her hair, fluffing it. "If you want to end our play, then you say your safe word. Everything ends and you go home. Now choose a word."

Sarah felt so out of her element that she had a difficult time thinking, much less choosing some kind of safe word. She took a deep breath. "Wall Street," she said, then added, "Master," as an afterthought.

His lips twitched as if he wanted to smile. Instead, he swept his hand over the top of the long white box they'd dropped, knocking off the lid, and pulled out the black leather flogger. He took her by her hand and brought her quickly to her feet. Her legs felt shaky as she looked at the flogger and stood.

He slapped the straps of suede on his palm as his gaze traveled over her from head to toes and back. His voice was low, husky. "You have the sexiest body."

Sarah's cheeks warmed. She knew she looked good—she worked hard to maintain her fit body. But somehow it was different the way Drew looked at her and the way he said it.

"Thank you…ah, Master." Damn, that Master thing was not coming very easy at all.

He slipped his fingers through hers and she felt a little electrical jolt when he led her from the room they were in. It was the first time she'd had a chance to look around, and she took everything in with a sweep of her gaze. A well-built home with an expansive great room and kitchen with hallways leading in either direction. Oak furniture and everything done in navy blues, with a taupe-colored carpet. It was obviously a lived-in home with his things casually strewn over the couches, chairs and coffee table, such as clothing, newspapers and books. It wasn't what she'd call messy—just lived in.

Drew took the left hallway that had at least twelve-foot ceilings like the great room and kitchen. Strangely, he strode ahead of her with her tagging behind, holding onto his hand and barely able to keep up with his long strides. He'd always been so gentlemanly at the club, but now he was apparently playing a completely different role. He was the Master and she was subservient to him.

Her stomach twisted at the thought. Over and over she wondered what she was doing.

Subservient. Her?

Yet he'd made it clear he understood that she was a high-powered businesswoman and expected nothing less of her. But he'd also made it clear that when it came to sex, he was the one in control.

She padded down the carpeted hallway after him, completely naked while he was dressed only in jeans. She watched his tight ass and wanted to see it, touch it. When they'd been in the health club, all she'd gotten a good look at was his cock. And was it ever good to look at. Not to mention taste.

They reached a room that was brightly lit and when he brought her up beside him, at first she thought it was a workout room—until she really took a look at it. Yeah, there was a bench and free weights, dumbbells, an exercise bike and other workout machines.

But what caught her attention and took her breath were the things that were definitely *not* your average workout machines.

There was some kind of "furniture" with two A-frames separated by a bar that was about five feet in length. It had chains and restraints hanging from it, and the frames were taller than she was. Some kind of leather and chain sling hung from one corner and there were a variety of tables and benches. The thing that struck her the hardest was seeing the great X-shaped cross up against one wall. It was wooden with restraints at all four ends of it.

Mouth open, she looked up at Drew and he gestured with the flogger toward the cross. "Time for your punishment."

She stared at the cross. "I don't *think* so."

"Sarah," Drew said in a barely tolerant tone. "You have two choices. Accept your punishment and continue. Or say your safe word and leave."

Crap. One thing she never did was back down from a challenge. And God, after their kiss and the way he'd touched her, she was so fucking horny, she could hardly stand it.

She raised her chin. Paused. Then said, "Okay."

"Okay…what?" Drew asked, his voice even firmer. "You've already earned a second punishment for having to be reminded again."

Two? Her gaze snapped to his and she met his smoky brown eyes. "Okay, *Master*."

He pointed the flogger at the X again. "Face forward on the St. Andrew's cross."

So that's what it was.

Her belly fluttered. "Yes, Master." She slowly walked up to the cross feeling like she was approaching her doom. She pressed one of her cheeks flat against the X as she moved herself against it.

Drew came up behind her and she felt his body heat along with the scrape of his jeans across her ass, which was still a little sore from being spanked yesterday. His grasp was firm as he raised first one of her hands, then the next, anchoring her wrists with leather cuffs. He restrained her high enough that she stood on her tiptoes. She gasped when he took one of her ankles and clasped a leather cuff around it. If her wrists weren't so firmly bound, she would have fallen.

When he fastened her other ankle to the cross, so many sensations bombarded her at once. Her breasts and her mound were pressed tight against the smooth wood, her naked body splayed wide and her pussy so wet she could smell her musk. The fact that Drew was staring at her from behind was an erotic sensation all on its own. And being up off the floor and held only by the straps gave her the sensation of flying. Always with him she felt like she was flying. He was a high all unto himself.

When he trailed the suede straps down her spine, it caused her to shiver and she caught her breath. Immediately her body tensed. He was going to strike her with that flogger, and she didn't know just how much it would hurt, considering how sore her ass still was.

"How does this feel?" he asked as he brushed the flogger across her shoulders then went down her spine to her ass.

She had to take a deep breath to be able to speak. "Good, Master. It feels good." She couldn't see him from where he was standing, but she imagined his smile. He had such a sexy, irresistible smile.

Drew brushed each of her thighs slowly, then her calves and ankles with the soft leather, finishing at her feet. She was grateful she wasn't ticklish as he trailed the flogger up and down the arch of each of her feet.

She started to relax into the caress of the suede against her flesh, her eyelids lowering. It soothed her at the same time it made her more aroused. This she could get used to.

The flogger snapped against one of her ass cheeks and she cried out. Her eyes went wide. He struck her again, on the other cheek this time, and tears instantly beat at the backs of her eyes.

Fuck, that hurt. Maybe she should shout her safe word and get the hell out of this place.

But damned if she'd give up.

If you dare...the note had said.

He flogged her thighs, her calves, her ass again and even her back. She cried out with every strike. What was bizarre was how good the flogging started to feel. That Goddamned dizzy feeling swept over her again and she felt lightheaded and way turned on.

And when he pussy whipped her, she thought she'd lose it for sure.

No coming without permission.

Fuck that.

Been there, done that, Fairland.

She was already being punished for coming without permission. She didn't need another punishment to top it off. What she needed was a good fuck.

Drew had probably flogged her only ten times, but it felt like it would never end…and that it would end too soon. The conflicting feelings were driving her crazy, confusing her.

Abruptly he stopped and she sank against the cross, her body limp and hanging from her restraints. He came up behind her, pushed her hair aside and kissed her nape. "How did that feel, Sarah?"

"It hurt like hell, Master," she muttered.

He gave a soft laugh. "What about the pleasure?" He caressed her back with the soft suede straps, the smell of leather and his musky scent filling her with warmth exceeded only by the warmth of the straps marks across her back, ass and thighs. As he moved the flogger lightly over her skin she did feel extreme pleasure straight through to her bones, enough that she whimpered again.

Whimpered for more.

Drew smiled as he drank in Sarah's light perfume. It was a clean, citrus-y scent that went with her driven, business persona. But to him, it was delicate, arousing. As were the pink stripes lining her back down to her thighs. He knew she was so sensitive already that she could come on command.

Damn, but she looked so good strapped to his cross, her naked body marked as his. She had a perfect, toned body, and he loved to look at her rounded, smooth ass and long, sexy legs. He liked to see her legs spread wide, exposing her pussy and her soft, pink flesh. Her silky brown hair brushed her shoulders and her features looked somewhat fragile with her hair down, unlike her professional upswept look.

His erection strained against the tough denim of his jeans, the material practically strangling his cock. With one hand he continued caressing the flogger over Sarah's back and used his other hand to unbutton his fly in an attempt to give his cock some relief.

Didn't help one damn bit.

He was intent on giving her pleasure. He played the tough Master, but what he wanted to do was teach Sarah what pleasure was all about. Giving up control in the bedroom would enhance her life, make her more powerful in the business world by having the freedom of letting herself go sexually when away from the job.

From the first time she'd breezed into his office and told him exactly what she wanted in no uncertain terms when it came to her personal training, she'd intrigued him. It was obvious she was a ball-busting bitch to the world. But he could tell that beneath that tough veneer was a softer side of her crying out for attention. The fact that she'd been attracted to him from the start made him want to teach her what it was like to give up control.

"Mmmmm…you smell so good," he murmured as he nuzzled her nape again. He reached down with his free hand and slipped his fingers into her slick folds. Another one of those adorable whimpers rose up in her and he smiled. "Would you like me to fuck you now?"

"Yes, Master." Need filled her quick response. "I want to feel you inside of me."

Drew dropped the flogger and brought both of his hands to the button of his jeans. She was strapped at the perfect height for fucking.

When his cock was free, he sheathed it with one of the condoms he had stuffed into his jeans. He nudged her pussy with the head of his erection, and she gave a low moan and a tremor wracked her body. The slickness of her pussy moistened his cock and he remembered what it felt like to be inside her when he'd taken her at the health club. His groin ached and he couldn't hold back any longer.

He gripped her hips and rammed his cock straight into her core. Sarah shouted and tilted her head back. Goddamn she felt good wrapped around his cock, her channel so tight, hot and wet.

Those little sounds rose up in her throat as he started to slowly thrust in and then eased back out. Slowly in, easing back out. "You like that, baby?"

"Yes, Master." Her voice cracked. "Please fuck me harder. Faster."

"That's not the way we're playing this game, Sarah." He continued his slow pace and she pressed her ass back against his groin, taking him deeper. "I know you're close, but you know better than to come without permission."

"Y-yes, Master." Her breathing was harsh. She squirmed, her channel clamping down on his cock and *he* almost lost it.

He ground his teeth and forced himself to continue his slow, erotic torture—that was torturing her as much as it was him. But this was all about control and pleasure. He licked the skin at the curve of her neck and brought his hands up to cup her breasts. A cry of pleasure and pain tore from her lips as he pinched her nipples hard and twisted them.

Sarah felt like her entire body was one sensitive nerve. Every push and pull of Drew's cock inside her made her ache and brought her so close to coming. He was so thick, so filling, so deep. But too damn slow.

It was a challenge to her now—withholding her orgasm for as long as she had to. She'd never failed at anything. Yesterday she'd had a different take on the whole "coming without permission" thing. Pretty much a "screw you" mentality. Now she was determined to show him—and herself—that she could do it. She could control her body.

If she could just get her body to listen to her.

He completely withdrew and she made that stupid little whimpering sound she couldn't stop. God, how she wanted him back inside of her.

She watched from her side view as he disposed of his condom in a garbage can and to her disappointment zipped his jeans back over his raging erection. Though she had to smile because it seemed to pain him to do so.

Drew returned and crouched behind her. "It's time for your next punishment."

Wasn't being fucked and left hanging enough of a punishment?

He unbuckled first one ankle, then the other. She was able to reach the carpeting with her tiptoes. He paused to massage each of her ankles, relieving the slight ache from the leather cuffs.

When he moved up her back to reach for one of her wrist restraints, his denim-clad crotch brushed against her extra-sensitive skin. She closed her eyes at the sensation that sent tingles of pleasure throughout her.

She gripped the cross with her now free hand as he moved to her other wrist and carefully let her down. Her legs were shaky and he held her for a moment, letting her regain her strength. He kissed the length of her shoulder, his lips soft against her skin as she rested her back against his warm, bare chest.

"You all right, baby?" he asked as he took her by her upper arms and steadied her so that she was standing fully on her feet.

She really wanted to say no, she wasn't okay, so that he'd continue to hold her, but she went with the truth. "Yes, Master."

"Good." He took her by the hand.

As he led her, her legs felt like jelly and her body on fire and screaming for an orgasm. He led her to the corner where there was some kind of flesh-colored ball that reminded her of one of those giant rubber balls at the gym that she used for various types of exercises, including sit-ups and cardiovascular exercises. They looked almost like those hop balls that children bounced up and down on. She'd had one as a kid. The balls at the gym didn't have handles, of course.

They reached the ball, and Drew released her hand to pull it from the corner. Her eyes widened. It had a huge dildo on it! And it had a handle right in front of the rubber cock.

Her gaze shot to his and he gestured toward the ball. "Climb on top and bury the dildo in your pussy. You're going to ride that, baby." He slapped her on the butt, causing her to cry out from the pain of her sore ass.

With a wary gaze, she walked up to the ball, Drew following her. He held it still, the rubber cock sticking straight up. Her heart pounded as she positioned the dildo beneath her and started to slide down the shaft.

"Jesus Christ," she muttered, feeling as if she was sliding down a telephone pole. "I think it's too big, Master."

"Keep going down on it before I 'help'," he said, his arms folded across his chest.

She shot a look at him and saw his firm expression. Oh sure, he'd help. He'd ram her down on it and it would be up and into her pussy before she had a chance to adjust to it.

Damn the thing was so thick and long that her eyes watered as she took it in inch by inch. She held onto the handle to steady herself. She was wet and slick enough that she was taking it inside her, just not too quickly.

"Hurry, Sarah." His tone was disapproving.

"Yes, Master," she said through gritted teeth.

Finally, she had the entire thing inside her body and she almost slumped in relief. Instead, she maintained her poise but didn't move as she tried to get used to the feel of the dildo in her core. The damn thing pushed so deep inside her that she was afraid to move.

"Bounce."

Her jaw dropped and her gaze met his. "Do what? Master?"

His arms were still folded across his chest and his look was stern. "Hold on to the handle and bounce the ball up and down so that it's fucking you."

"Uh..." She gripped the handle hard enough her knuckles ached.

"*Now,* Sarah."

His tone was so forceful she almost snapped "*Fuck you,*" but reined her temper in.

She swallowed, pushed with her feet, bounced and cried out. "It hurts, Master."

"Don't stop."

Fuck you, fuck you, fuck you.

Sarah ground her teeth and started bouncing up and down. The pain made her eyes water a little more, but as she became used to the dildo fucking her, it started to feel good. *Real good.* Her breathing elevated and perspiration swept her skin as she flushed from head to toes. Her ass burned as it rubbed against the ball, her breasts bounced and her hair brushed her shoulders with every movement.

The feelings wound up inside her until they were almost too incredible for her to take. The rubber cock felt like it was touching her belly where the fluttering sensation was intensifying. Her breasts felt so heavy, her nipples aching so much, and her whole body was on fire.

She'd been concentrating so hard on bouncing up and down on the ball, that she hadn't been paying any attention to Drew.

When she took her focus off the fucking ball, she looked up at Drew and came to a complete stop. He was naked, stroking his cock from balls to tip as he watched her.

Chapter Five

ℵ

Sarah looked so hot on that fucking ball that Drew wanted to slam her to the floor and take her now. He strode the few feet needed to reach her, grabbed her by her upper arms and raised her off the ball. It toppled as she gave a little cry and he had her on the exercise mat in seconds, his hips between her thighs, his cock pressed against her belly.

She gasped as she looked up at him. He felt savage and primal as he ground his erection against her belly and took her mouth with all the need that had been building up in him since he sent that flogger to her earlier today. He'd anticipated this, wanted this and he could barely restrain himself from plunging his cock into her pussy.

He mastered her mouth, his tongue taking control. She whimpered as he sucked her tongue into his mouth then bit her lip hard before licking the spot he had bitten. Wild, barbaric urges stormed him and he had to leash them tightly before he ravaged her. He wanted to sink his teeth into her neck, bite her nipples, then flip her over and take her from behind like an animal dominating his female.

The intense feelings of ownership were almost overwhelming. He'd only known this woman for a few weeks, but already he felt as if she was his, and he wasn't letting her go.

His kiss was so fierce that she struggled against him. He broke the kiss, giving her a chance to breathe before taking her mouth again. He had braced his hands to either side of her chest and as he kissed her he thrust his cock against the softness of her belly.

Goddamn, but he was losing it in every sense of the word. He'd never had a woman affect him this way before, ever. His muscles strained as he fought to keep himself from pounding into her. There were things he needed to do to her before he took that step.

Abruptly he jerked himself away. Sarah's eyes were wide, her face was flushed, her lips red and swollen, and her eyes dark. Her chest rose and fell with every harsh breath she took.

His own breathing was so heavy his chest ached with the power of it. He tore his gaze from hers and tried to focus on the restraints at each corner of the pad. He'd laid her down on an exercise mat, but a very special one that had adjustable locking restraints at each corner.

"Wh-what are you doing, Master?" She sounded like she could barely speak.

"Are you questioning me, Sarah?" His own voice shook with his restraint, which pissed him off, and he gave a low growl.

She moved her head from side to side. "No, Master."

Sarah Fairland actually looked delicate, innocent and incapable of being the powerful businesswoman she truly was. She'd given up complete and total control to him, and probably didn't even realize how far she had crossed over.

She was *his*, and that was all there was to it. It might take her time, but in time she would realize it.

He restrained her ankles in thick iron manacles, spreading her as wide as the mat was. In short order had her wrists locked in place as well. Yeah, this was definitely the way he liked her. Spread out for his pleasure.

Drew straddled her chest and leaned forward, bracing his palms on the floor above Sarah's head, so that his cock touched her lips. Her gorgeous blue eyes locked with his as she took him inside the warm silk of her mouth.

He ground his teeth against the need to come and have her swallow his semen. The pain of holding back his orgasm tensed every muscle in his body, causing them to ache. He was a professional trainer, in perfect shape, but right now he felt almost weak, his arms trembling as he fucked her mouth.

The climax he would experience hovered, waiting for him to unleash it. But he had the power to restrain himself until the right moment.

Sarah made soft moans as he moved his erection in and out of her mouth. The way she swirled her tongue over the head of his cock and sucked him made him clench his teeth tighter and he had to force greater control over himself.

When he'd taken all that he could, he pulled his wet cock out of her mouth. He trailed it down her cheek, along the center of her chest and to her belly as he moved down her splayed body.

He once again took her mouth in a punishing kiss. He pushed his mouth from her lips to her neck, sucking and licking a path to the hollow of her throat. He concentrated his exploration of her in that location and she arched her back, telling him without words that she wanted him to suck her breasts.

The primal savagery rose up in him again and he moved his mouth to the place where the curve of her neck met her shoulder, and bit.

Sarah cried out, loud. He bit and sucked the skin, leaving a mark like an animal might. It was beyond a simple hickey that a teenage boy might give. It was his brand, as were the pink stripes across her backside.

He crawled down her body, pausing to suckle and bite her nipples. With every mark he made with his teeth, Sarah moaned, whimpered and cried out.

Fire licked at his veins as he worked his way down her body, kissing a trail leading to the spot he wanted to be at the most right at this moment. He had to taste her. Sarah's musk was strong the closer he got to her pussy. He reached her mound and nuzzled the trimmed brown hair. He used his fingers to part her folds, buried his face against her pussy and delved into the sweet cream between her thighs.

The way Drew was licking, sucking, biting Sarah's clit was mind-blowing. Dizziness overcame her again and she thought she was going to pass out from too many extreme sensations. He slid his palms beneath her ass and devoured her with such intensity she was going to lose it. His evening stubble scraped the insides of her thighs and the lips of her pussy, and his shoulder-length blond hair was like silk against her skin.

She knew it wouldn't do any good, yet still she tugged against her restraints, fighting against them at the same time she fought against climaxing. "Drew, Drew, Drew," she sobbed. "Please, Master, I've got to come. I've *got* to."

"No." He spoke between licks of her clit. "You'll wait until I'm ready to let you climax. When I fuck you."

"Then fuck me now!" She almost screamed the words, then added, "*Master*."

"When I'm ready." The rough way he said it made her realize that her begging was only going to make him drag the sexual torture out longer.

Not that she wasn't enjoying every single thing he was doing to her. But a person could only take so much and she was so close to the edge that it was getting harder and harder not to fall over it. Yet again that sensation of flying took hold of her and she tried to ground herself to keep from losing it.

While licking her pussy, he slid one of his hands from beneath her ass and started finger-fucking her with two fingers.

Oh God, oh God, oh God!

He pounded her pussy, his knuckles hitting her soft flesh hard enough to hurt yet making it feel so unbelievably good at the same time. Too good.

She felt him take his other hand and lubricate his finger in her juices. Before she could even grasp what he was going to do next, he took one of those fingers, shoved it past the tight ring of her anus and started butt-fucking her with his finger.

She almost came up off the mat, manacles and all.

Sarah screamed and thrashed against the assault of his mouth and hands. She'd never thought that taking anything in the ass would feel good or be erotic, but it was beyond erotic. In her wildest, wildest dreams, she would never have believed she'd be lying here, restrained, her backside sore from being flogged, her ass still stinging from yesterday's spanking, her nipples aching from Drew having twisted them so hard, and the sensual attack on her clit, her core, her ass. Not to mention she could still feel the sensation of the dildo from the fucking ball all the way to her bellybutton.

It's too much! God, it's too much!

The power of her need to come caused tears to flow down the sides of her face and cries and moans to rise up from her lips. She didn't dare beg Drew anymore. He'd only make her wait longer.

Drew raised his head and let loose a growl that she felt straight to her core. His eyes practically glowed. He looked so untamed, like he was barely able to hold back a hunger and fire that wanted to consume them both.

He got to his knees, withdrawing his fingers from her pussy and ass and raising himself up on his knees, never taking his eyes from hers. Yeah, he definitely looked like he wanted to eat her.

Letting up on her pussy and ass should have given her some relief, but she couldn't come down at all. She could barely breathe and heat flushed up and down her body. The way he was looking at her, he might as well have continued his erotic assault.

With only a moment's pause, but still too slow, he jerked a condom package from beside the mat, tore it open and had his cock sheathed.

Thank you, thank you!

He gave another growl and leaned over her to pop the spring on the manacle on one wrist, then the other, before releasing the ones on her ankles. She caught her breath as he knelt between her legs and hooked his arms under her knees.

Drew thrust his cock into her so hard and fast it took her by complete surprise. She screamed so loud her throat hurt and she almost climaxed. Her pussy spasmed softly, gripping his cock and threatening to roll into a full-blown orgasm.

With the way he was holding them, her knees pressed against her chest as his mouth met hers and he kissed her harsh and fierce. She felt like he was a warrior of old, conquering her, claiming her for his own. And she wanted him to. At that minute he could take her, have her, keep her. She was lost to him. Or maybe it was that he'd found her. Whatever it was, she was his.

Heat boiled over her as if she was in an oven. Sweat trickled down her forehead to the side of her face, joining with her tears of need. Her hair was damp with sweat.

Drew rose up as he pounded into her so hard and fierce he was bruising her. His long hair hung from his face in wet ropes and droplets of sweat plopped onto her breasts. Smells of testosterone, sweat and sex surrounded her, filled her.

It almost came out of her mouth. She almost begged as her body perched on the edge. She ground her teeth and held onto him, digging her manicured nails into his ass to press him tighter to her even as he put her ankles up around his neck.

Just when she thought she was going to pass out from need, Drew shouted, "Now, Sarah. Now!"

Sarah screamed. Louder and longer than she had before and her throat hurt even more. But she barely felt it as the most powerful climax of her life took over. He continued to pound in her as sensation after sensation exploded in and out of her body. Nothing on earth could explain what was happening to her. Now she was really flying, spinning.

Through blurry vision she saw Drew, his jaw tense and a triumphant look in his eyes as he continued to fuck her.

She writhed and fought against him, needing the powerful contractions in her pussy to stop. But she didn't dare beg him.

Suddenly, Drew shouted and threw his head back. His cock pulsed inside her, throbbing, throbbing, throbbing as her core clenched and unclenched around him. He slowed his strokes but kept going until finally he slipped her ankles from around his neck and eased her fully onto the floor.

He collapsed partially on her, his weight pinning her to the mat. Their sweat-slicked chests pressed against one another and they both were panting, trying to catch their breath.

Drew slipped his cock out of her core and rolled onto his side, holding her sweaty body against his. She thought maybe she heard his heart thundering as loud as hers. He placed a kiss to the top of her damp hair and shuddered against her as if experiencing the last wave of his own orgasm.

When she thought she was going to fall asleep right there in his arms, he groaned and pushed himself up so that he was looking down at her. He gave her a sexy smile and said, "Some things are worth waiting for, don't you think?"

She gave a sated smile of her own. "Most definitely yes, Master Hunk."

His smile turned into a grin. "Master Hunk?"

"Mmm-hmm." She was too lethargic to move. "And you can Master me any time you want."

Drew ran one of his fingers down her damp chest. "I won't let you forget that, you know."

Sarah shook her head. "I still can't believe this. How much I loved everything you did to me."

He gave her an amused look. "Everything?"

She looked up at the ceiling and shook her head again, her damp hair moving beneath her with the movement. "I don't think I've ever felt so…"

"Happy?" he said and she looked at him. "Relaxed? Sated?"

It was her turn to grin. "Yeah, something like that."

His expression was a little more serious when he said, "Don't you feel like a great deal of the world's weight has been lifted from your shoulders?"

"I do." The revelation surprised her, sending tingles through her sensitized skin. "I've never felt so…so…"

"Free?" He continued to trace his finger up and down her chest. "Unencumbered?"

"I guess that's a way to put it." She liked looking up at him. He was so gorgeous, and even more appealing after having had the universe's greatest sex. "Yet more. I feel as if I can take on the world, that nothing can stand in my way."

Drew leaned down and brushed his lips over hers before raising his head again. "That's the beauty of giving up control in some parts of your life. It sets you free."

Chapter Six

ꕤ

Sarah walked out of the board meeting with her normal confidence and satisfaction that she'd done what she set out to accomplish. The sales and marketing employees knew what was expected of them with the new products they were set to launch in a couple of months, and she'd apprised customer support of the rigorous training they were going to be going through. Their work had been shoddy of late, and that was completely unacceptable.

It was amazing. After a month of spending time with Drew, being submissive with him in the bedroom or wherever else they had sex, her confidence level had risen even higher. She maintained the same level of control in the business world as she'd always had, only she was happier than she'd ever been.

When she reached her office, she closed the heavy mahogany door behind her, strode across the plush carpet to her mahogany desk. She sat in her remarkably comfortable executive chair and leaned back for a moment. Her mind continued to churn over what she needed to accomplish today. She had a few clients to contact, another meeting to run with all of her managers, and then the day would come to an end.

Today was Friday, and after work it would be time for her and Drew to "play".

A smile curved the corner of her lips as she pulled one of her drawers open and picked up the black suede flogger. She kept it in her office all the time now, and just touching it made her pussy wet and her nipples ache in anticipation of tonight. She didn't know what they were doing, but she knew whatever it was would be exciting.

Her cell phone rang and she checked the caller ID. *Drew.* Her heart rate picked up and she set the flogger back into the drawer. She pushed the button on her earpiece to answer his call.

"Hi, Master," she murmured. Outside of the bedroom or other sexual situations, she didn't refer to him as Master, but sometimes it really turned her on to call him that while she was at work. It felt naughty and wanton.

"Hey, baby." His low, sexy voice made her tingle even more and she imagined the smoky look in his eyes she'd come to love. She loved everything about him. "What are you doing right now?"

She closed her eyes and imagined him at his desk, his shoulder-length blond hair highlighted by the fluorescent lighting. He would be wearing a sleeveless muscle shirt, his carved biceps flexing as he held the phone to his ear. As usual he would be absolutely delicious-looking, and she would want to eat him all up.

"I'm thinking about you." She ran her tongue over her lower lip. "Imagining sucking that big cock of yours and taking you deep in my mouth."

A low, sensual growl came over the phone. "I'm devouring your sweet taste with my head between your thighs, your hands in my hair, and you're making those adorable whimpering sounds."

Sarah almost whimpered at the images they were creating.

"Touch yourself." His voice was low, husky, and commanding. "Rub your clit."

She gave a little gasp. "Here? Now?"

"You're in your office or you wouldn't be talking about sucking my cock."

Her gaze focused on the big office door. "I should lock the door."

"No, baby." His order was a complete turn-on. "Pull your skirt up to your waist and finger-fuck yourself. Imagine it's me."

She bit her lower lip and shimmied her skirt up to her waist while she continued to watch the door to her office. She gave a soft moan as she parted her thighs and slipped her fingers into her folds. All she was wearing beneath her skirt were her thigh-high stockings because Drew had ordered her not to wear panties or a thong under clothing.

"Yeah," he said. "That's it. I can picture you circling your clit with your finger."

She shivered from need and the danger of being caught. "Are you stroking your cock?"

"I'm standing by my desk, my gym shorts down to my thighs, thinking about you as I run my hand up and down my erection."

The image was enough to heighten Sarah's arousal to the point where she could come on just his order. She groaned aloud. "I want your cock inside me, Drew."

"Thrust two of your fingers into your pussy." He gave a groan of his own. "Feel me, pumping my hips, driving into you hard enough to make you scream."

"Oh God." Sarah squirmed against her hand. "I feel your hips between my thighs. "I'm still sore from the spanking you gave me for being a bad girl."

The sound of his breathing was a little heavier. "Are you wearing your earpiece so both hands are free?"

"Yeah." She pumped her fingers in and out of her pussy, not caring at all if someone walked through that door. They couldn't see her from the waist down, anyway.

"Take your free hand and slide it inside your bra and pinch one of your nipples," he commanded.

"What?" She caught her breath and slowed the movement of her hand in her channel.

"Do what I tell you, Sarah, or I'll punish you as soon as I see you tonight."

The idea of his kind punishment sent a thrill through her belly. But she hated to disappoint him too. She raised her hand, her eyes still on the office door, and slipped her fingers into her fitted jacket and beneath the lacy cup of her bra until she reached her nipple.

"Pinch it. Hard." It was as if he could see her. "I'm stroking my cock harder, picturing you doing what I tell you."

Sarah couldn't help a little whimper as she pinched her nipple and thrust her fingers in and out of her pussy. "This is so hot…Master."

He gave a low sound of approval. "Pull your fingers away from your pussy and taste your juices for me."

Her eyes widened in surprise. He'd never had her do that before.

"Sarah…" he said in a warning tone.

"I am." She felt breathless as she brought her hand from her pussy and put two fingers in her mouth and sucked. Her musk on her hand was strong, and she tasted the same flavor that she did when he kissed her after going down on her. Only this was more intense—and incredibly arousing.

"Mmmm…I love your taste." It sounded as though his breathing had elevated. "Now stroke your clit. Touch yourself until you think you're going to come. And don't stop pinching your nipples." He paused and groaned before adding, "Are you doing what I told you to do?"

"Yes, Master." The thought of being caught added an additional edge to her excitement. Her bra had slipped below her breasts and her nipples were large and obvious through the material of her fitted jacket. Tammy always knocked, but what if this time she didn't?

"Worried about getting caught?" he asked as if reading her mind.

"Yes." She could barely talk with her need to climax. "Can I come now, Master?"

"No," he said and she whimpered again. "Take your hands from your pussy and nipples and straighten up your clothing."

"You want me to stop?" She blinked. "But I need to come *so* bad."

"What have I taught you about delayed gratification?" he said in a demanding tone. "If you argue with me again, Sarah, I'll punish you for that tonight."

"Yes, Master." Her pussy and breasts ached as she rearranged her skirt, pulled her bra back up over her breasts and adjusted her jacket. She'd need to get to the bathroom and wash her musk off her fingers.

Ever the mind reader, Drew said, "I want you to lick your juices from your fingers—and don't wash hands."

She put her palms flat on her desktop. "Drew!"

"That's one punishment, baby. I told you not to argue with me."

"But—"

"Are you asking for another punishment, Sarah?"

"No, Master," she replied, thinking of how she could get through her management meeting and not shake hands or get too close to anyone.

"Now lick your fingers." She obeyed as he continued. "I'll pick you up tonight at seven. Wear something sexy."

"Yes, Master." A thrill ran through her belly. She never knew what to expect when he picked her up. He liked to keep things a surprise and just told her how to dress and when he'd be at her place. It kept her on edge, wondering what he'd do to her next, or have her do.

"Good girl." He lowered his voice and she felt like was brushing his lips over her ear. "I'll see you tonight, baby."

"Bye," she said right before he disconnected.

* * * * *

Sarah's home was large, modern, efficient and she loved it. In her kitchen, all of her appliances were stainless steel, her countertops granite, and her cabinets cherry wood. Large Tuscany tiles had been laid for the flooring and she'd had an interior designer decorate all of her rooms, including her exercise room and guestrooms.

She had to smile at the thought of her exercise room. It certainly was nothing like Drew's, although they'd made good use of it a couple of times. Sometimes they stayed and played at his home, sometimes hers.

Again, Sarah checked her reflection in the hallway mirror. She wore a satin oriental print dress that ended about three inches above her knees and had a mandarin collar. The dress was sea blue, bringing out the blue in her eyes. Inlaid hair chopsticks held back her hair. She wore no nylons and had on heels with the barest of straps. Damned if she didn't look good.

One thing about her was that she had no shortage of self-confidence. She wasn't a woman who relied on others' opinions of her…but it did matter what Drew thought about her. Maybe she was growing to care for him too much.

The door chimes rang and she scooped up her matching oriental print purse off the shelf below the mirror and her heels clicked on the tile as she made her way to the front door. Just as she didn't like to be made to wait, she didn't make others wait for her.

When she opened the door she about melted at the sight of Drew. He wore a black tux that only enhanced his powerful presence. His blond hair was a contrast to the black of the suit, just as his brown eyes were a contrast to his hair.

"Beautiful." He stroked his knuckles across her cheek, so lightly she shivered. "You are always the most beautiful woman I know."

"Thank you." Sarah smiled. "You look great too," she said and he flashed her a to-die-for grin.

She took Drew's hand as he held it up for her. When they went out, he was always the gentleman. It was only when they role-played that she acted like the subservient slave, which she found surprisingly erotic.

Before Drew, she'd thought of what men called gentlemanly as chauvinistic. Now she had a whole different appreciation for men who treated women with that kind of respect.

Yeah, before Drew she'd been pretty damn uptight.

As always, they talked about everything under the sun. Over the past month they'd learned so much from one another. They'd talked about his parents and three brothers, as well as her divorced mother and father. They talked about her work and his clients, even sports and their favorite artists.

Something that had totally surprised her about this hunk of a man was that he was into art and even taking in a performance or symphony now and then. In the past month they'd gone to a couple of spring training games, a ballet, a play, a movie, and went out to eat every Saturday and Sunday. During the week they tended to spend more time at her home because it was closer to her work, where Drew traveled all over the valley working with his clients.

Before she knew it, they arrived at a beautiful custom home in the Catalina foothills. It was a two-story house with great pillars, a commanding entranceway and a paved circular driveway with a huge water fountain in the middle. The house was lit up brightly, crystal chandeliers visible through the great windows as well as a group of well-dressed people. Apparently he'd taken to her a party judging by what she could see in the house and the several cars parked in the driveway.

Drew didn't offer any explanation, just came around her side of the vehicle to assist her in getting out of the low-slung sports car. He liked making her wonder what was going to happen next. It was the teasing part of his personality and perhaps the dominant, too, since he seemed to like to make her wait for everything.

The night smelled of water from the fountain and the scents of the high desert. It was still spring and the breeze was cool against her skin. Drew felt warm and comfortable beside her as he guided her toward the house with his hand at the small of her back

When they reached the house, he simply opened the door and walked in. Apparently it was a small, intimate gathering and there were several people mingling and eating hors d'oeuvres and drinking from champagne flutes.

Before anyone seemed to notice them, Drew escorted her toward an older couple. The man had graying brown hair and wore a sleek black tux like every other man in the room. His keen eyes were a brilliant blue and told her he was sharp, intelligent and not a man to be trifled with.

The woman was elegant in her slim black dress, her blonde hair swept up into a classic French twist. Her brown eyes were the same color of warm cocoa as Drew's and had the same intensity.

"Mom, Dad, this is Sarah Fairland." Drew smiled at her. "Sarah, these are my parents, Barbara and Edward."

Sarah was taken aback by the fact that Drew had brought her to meet his parents, but she smiled. "A pleasure," she said as Edward Bennett took her hand and brushed his lips over her knuckles.

"Such a beautiful young woman," Edward said with a grin as he released her hand and slapped his son on the back.

She was even more surprised when Barbara greeted her like family and kissed her cheek. "It's about time Drew brought you here." When they parted, Barbara gave Sarah a brilliant smile. "He's told us so much about you and we've been looking forward to actually getting a chance to meet you."

Sarah looked up at Drew, surprised that he had talked about her to his parents. He rubbed his hand along her lower back. His touch and his parents' genuine greetings filled Sarah with a comfortable warmth in her chest.

"Today is Mom and Dad's fiftieth anniversary," Drew said as he looked back to his mother and father.

"That's wonderful." Sarah meant it with all her heart. Her own parents had divorced when she was still a child. "Congratulations."

They talked a little more with his parents before they moved on. Too nervous to eat any of the hors d'oeuvres, she declined when Drew offered. He poured them each a glass of champagne in fine crystal champagne flutes before they moved on to mingle with other guests.

"My brother Craig and his fiancée Jessica," Drew said as he introduced them. "Sarah Fairland."

Sarah shook hands with both of them, smiled and chatted, looking completely at ease being in his parents' home and meeting his family. Drew couldn't help a grin as he thought about how his brother and Jessica had met. Craig was a college professor and Jessica had been his sophomore student. She was young but poised, intelligent and mature.

Drew and his three brothers were all into bondage and domination, and had often shared women in the past. Once his brothers became engaged or married, that, of course, had ended. Drew had thought he'd miss the sweet pleasure he and another man could give a woman. He loved to see the looks of ecstasy on their faces from what the men could offer her together. He'd indulged in his own fantasies and had been with more than one woman at a time, but there was something sweet and satisfying about helping a woman experience her deepest, darkest desires.

But once he met Sarah, his feelings changed. Oh yeah, he wanted to give her every pleasure he could, with the exception of sharing her with another man. No way in hell was he going to share her with anyone.

They moved on and he next made introductions to his police officer brother, Dave, and the woman who had been his high-school sweetheart before she dumped him after graduation and left the state. Fifteen years later, Dave pulled Erin over for speeding and they'd fallen in love all over again. They didn't wait for an engagement. Instead they went immediately to Las Vegas to be married and flew to Paris for their honeymoon.

Finally they met up with Drew's third brother, John, and his fiancée Elsie. Drew stifled a grin. Elsie blushed a furious red like she did every time she saw Drew. When John first dated Elsie, John and Drew had spent the night pleasuring her, along with their friend, Aaron Richards. It had been a foursome none of them were likely to ever forget. He honestly didn't think Elsie regretted their night, but she looked awfully cute every time she blushed around himself and Aaron.

But sharing Sarah? Never. As far as he was concerned, she was *his*.

After a couple of hours of getting to know Drew's family, mingling with other guests and enjoying a sit-down catered formal meal, Sarah's head was spinning from too much champagne. Almost like that dizzying sensation she often got from incredible sex with Drew.

When they finished eating, Drew excused them from the other group, saying that they needed to get some fresh air. She was too tipsy to realize he was guiding her upstairs until they were at the top landing. He led her down a hallway, through a beautiful bedroom and out onto a balcony that wrapped around the back of the house. Vines grew in abundance, spilling from the roof above them, onto the porch. More vines had crawled up the house to creep over the railing. Something sweet was carried on the breeze, like honeysuckle and roses.

"Over here, baby." Drew took her by the elbow. "There's something I want to show you."

When they reached one end of the balcony, she caught her breath at the sight of Tucson's city lights spread out across the desert. A carpet of diamonds lay out before them. Because of the Kitt Peak National Observatory being so close, years ago the city had had to change all the streetlights to a soft orange rather than bright white because the lights had been interfering with the observatory's ability to study the skies.

Sarah gripped the edge of the balcony as she stared out into the beautifully clear night. Drew moved behind her, his body warm against hers—until he started to slide her dress up and over her naked ass.

"Drew," she said in a low tone even as she shivered from excitement. "What are you doing?"

He nuzzled her bare nape. "I'm going to fuck you."

"Here?" She could barely keep her voice down. "Someone might catch us!"

"Part of your punishment, baby." He rubbed her ass with his palms. "You'll be worried the whole time that anyone could step out of one of the rooms that lead onto the balcony and see us fucking."

Excitement and fear rolled through her belly and her pussy dampened. "Drew—"

"Are you arguing with me again, Sarah?" His tone was dominating, powerful.

A low whimper escaped her when he reached between her thighs and stroked her pussy.

"You're so wet and turned on, aren't you," he said as a statement, not a question.

"Yes, Master," she replied with another shiver and he gave a sound of satisfaction.

"Widen your stance." He pressed his hands between her thighs as she held onto the balcony railing. He forced her legs to stretch wide and the cool breeze brushed over her naked pussy and ass.

Her heart pounded and blood rushed in her ears. What if they were caught?

She heard the hiss of a zipper, then the sound of a condom package opening. In only a moment, Drew forced her head down by placing his hand at her nape and thrust deep inside of her.

Sarah had to stifle a scream. Her pussy spasmed instantly and she almost climaxed. The tipsy feeling from the champagne added to the experience, making it seem almost surreal. She could hear voices and when she looked down over the railing she saw guests mingling on the patio.

She bit her lip to keep from groaning those small whimpering sounds she couldn't hold back.

"Just think," he murmured as he took her. "Any one of the guests could look up from below and see me fucking you."

His words and the thoughts of being caught either from the porch or the patio made her even more turned on. God, his cock stretched her, filled her, and he hit her so deep inside. He pushed her dress even higher so that he could reach her nipples and she was practically naked.

The pain of him pinching her nipples lingered on and he scraped her ass with his clothing, her sensitive ass still sore from last night's paddling.

It never ceased to amaze her how enormous her orgasms were with him, and this one wasn't going to be an exception. The oncoming storm of it surged through her body and she had to bite the inside of her cheek to keep from crying out. Whimpers still escaped her and she only hoped no one had that good of hearing.

The storm inside her raged and she squirmed beneath his hold on her neck and from her need to climax.

"Now, baby," he whispered. "You can come now."

He clamped his hand over her mouth, holding back a cry that people below surely would have heard. The whoosh of her orgasm reached her head to swirl with the tipsiness she still felt from the champagne.

She wanted to drop to the porch to regain her breath and wait until her legs steadied themselves. But he kept fucking her, driving her on and on until she almost screamed with another orgasm. He still held his hand over her mouth, which in itself was an erotic feeling.

A barely leashed groan came from Drew as she felt his cock pulse in her core. He leaned against her naked backside and she felt him shudder from his release. When he finally pulled out, Sarah tried to catch her breath. He held her for a few moments longer until she thought she could stand then tugged down her dress so that she was completely covered again.

He kissed her nape and she shivered. "I'll be right back," he murmured. "Don't move."

She couldn't have if she tried.

In just a moment, he was back. He caught her in his arms and turned her to face him so that her back was against the stone railing. His slacks were zipped up and his shirt tucked in, and she could only assume that he'd left for those few seconds to rid himself of the condom.

Drew kissed her, his tongue slipping through her lips. This time it was a sensuous kiss, not dominating like usual. She sighed into his mouth and wrapped her arms around his neck.

After the long, passionate kiss, he pulled away and smiled down at her. "Let me see your hand." She raised her right hand and he shook his head. "Your left."

Wondering what in the world he was up to, she obeyed. He took her hand and in the darkness slid something cool over her ring finger. Something that definitely felt like a ring with a large stone on top of it.

A lump rose in her throat as he brought her hand up so that the ring sparkled in the light coming from downstairs. Splinters of light fractured from the diamond and the sapphires surrounding it glittered.

Sarah couldn't speak. She stared at her hand, emotions assailing her. Excitement and fear mingled with…love.

She looked up at Drew and he cupped her face in his hands. "I know what I want," he said, "and I want you. From the moment you came into my office, telling me in no uncertain terms what you wanted, I knew I had to have you."

Sarah was still a little dizzy from the fabulous sex and the champagne, but not so dizzy that she had any doubt in her mind what her answer would be. "Funny," she said. "But that's exactly what I thought about you—that I wanted you. I just didn't know how much until you taught me."

"I won't take anything less than a yes," he said with confidence in his gaze.

"And that's exactly what you'll get from me." She snuggled against his chest. "I love you, Drew, and that's all there is to it."

He kissed the top of her head, surrounding her with his strength. "Considering how hard I've fallen in love with you, it's a damn good thing, Sarah Fairland."

Why an electronic book?

We live in the Information Age—an exciting time in the history of human civilization, in which technology rules supreme and continues to progress in leaps and bounds every minute of every day. For a multitude of reasons, more and more avid literary fans are opting to purchase e-books instead of paper books. The question from those not yet initiated into the world of electronic reading is simply: *Why?*

1. ***Price.*** An electronic title at Ellora's Cave Publishing and Cerridwen Press runs anywhere from 40% to 75% less than the cover price of the exact same title in paperback format. Why? Basic mathematics and cost. It is less expensive to publish an e-book (no paper and printing, no warehousing and shipping) than it is to publish a paperback, so the savings are passed along to the consumer.
2. ***Space.*** Running out of room in your house for your books? That is one worry you will never have with electronic books. For a low one-time cost, you can purchase a handheld device specifically designed for e-reading. Many e-readers have large, convenient screens for viewing. Better yet, hundreds of titles can be stored within your new library—on a single microchip. There are a variety of e-readers from different manufacturers. You can also read e-books on your PC or laptop computer. (Please note that Ellora's Cave does not endorse any specific brands.

You can check our websites at www.ellorascave.com or www.cerridwenpress.com for information we make available to new consumers.)

3. ***Mobility***. Because your new e-library consists of only a microchip within a small, easily transportable e-reader, your entire cache of books can be taken with you wherever you go.
4. ***Personal Viewing Preferences.*** Are the words you are currently reading too small? Too large? Too... ANNOYING? Paperback books cannot be modified according to personal preferences, but e-books can.
5. ***Instant Gratification.*** Is it the middle of the night and all the bookstores near you are closed? Are you tired of waiting days, sometimes weeks, for bookstores to ship the novels you bought? Ellora's Cave Publishing sells instantaneous downloads twenty-four hours a day, seven days a week, every day of the year. Our webstore is never closed. Our e-book delivery system is 100% automated, meaning your order is filled as soon as you pay for it.

Those are a few of the top reasons why electronic books are replacing paperbacks for many avid readers.

As always, Ellora's Cave and Cerridwen Press welcome your questions and comments. We invite you to email us at Comments@ellorascave.com or write to us directly at Ellora's Cave Publishing Inc., 1056 Home Avenue, Akron, OH 44310-3502.

Cerridwen, the Celtic Goddess of wisdom, was the muse who brought inspiration to storytellers and those in the creative arts. Cerridwen Press encompasses the best and most innovative stories in all genres of today's fiction. Visit our site and discover the newest titles by talented authors who still get inspired - much like the ancient storytellers did, once upon a time.

ELLORA'S CAVE
ROMANTICA PUBLISHING